The AMAZING WORLD OF **GUMBALL**™

ADVENTURES IN ELMORE

CARTOON NETWORK

kaboom!™

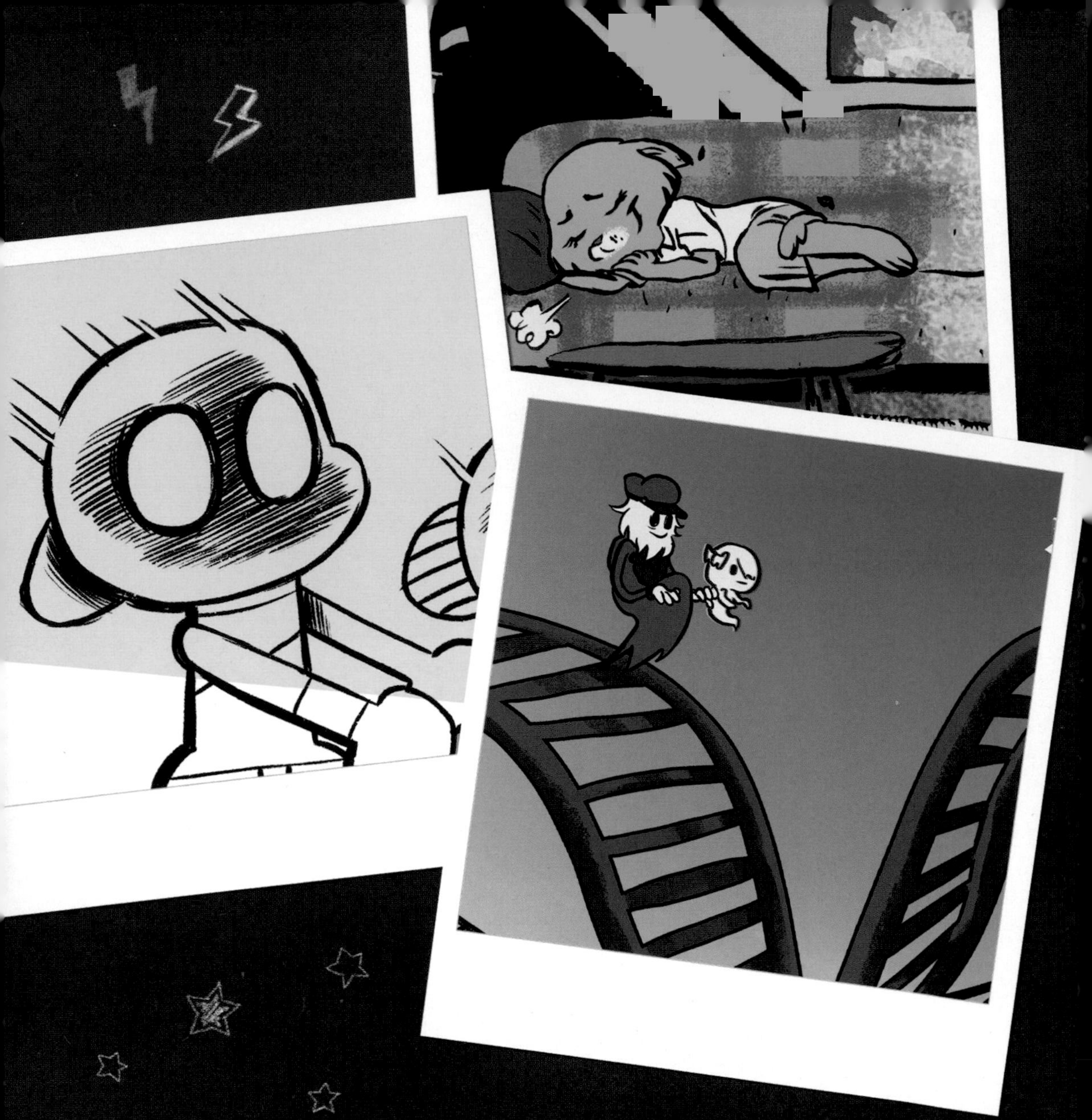

THE AMAZING WORLD OF GUMBALL: ADVENTURES IN ELMORE, MAY 2019. Published by KaBOOM!, a division of Boom Entertainment, Inc. THE AMAZING WORLD OF GUMBALL and all related characters and elements are trademarks of and © 2019 Turner Broadcasting System Europe Limited & Cartoon Network, WarnerMedia. All Rights Reserved. (S19) Originally published in single magazine form as THE AMAZING WORLD OF GUMBALL 2017 GRAB BAG SPECIAL No. 1, and THE AMAZING WORLD OF GUMBALL 2018 GRAB BAG SPECIAL No. 1. © Turner Broadcasting System Europe Limited & Cartoon Network, WarnerMedia. All Rights Reserved. (S18) KaBOOM!™ and the KaBOOM! logo are trademarks of Boom Entertainment, Inc., registered in various countries and categories. All characters, events, and institutions depicted herein are fictional. Any similarity between any of the names, characters, persons, events, and/or institutions in this publication to actual names, characters, and persons, whether living or dead, events, and/or institutions is unintended and purely coincidental. KaBOOM! does not read or accept unsolicited submissions of ideas, stories, or artwork.

BOOM! Studios, 5670 Wilshire Boulevard, Suite 400, Los Angeles, CA 90036-5679. Printed in China. First Printing.

ISBN: 978-1-68415-351-0, eISBN: 978-1-64144-334-0

CN
CARTOON NETWORK

The AMAZING WORLD OF GUMBALL™
ADVENTURES IN ELMORE

created by
Ben BOCQUELET

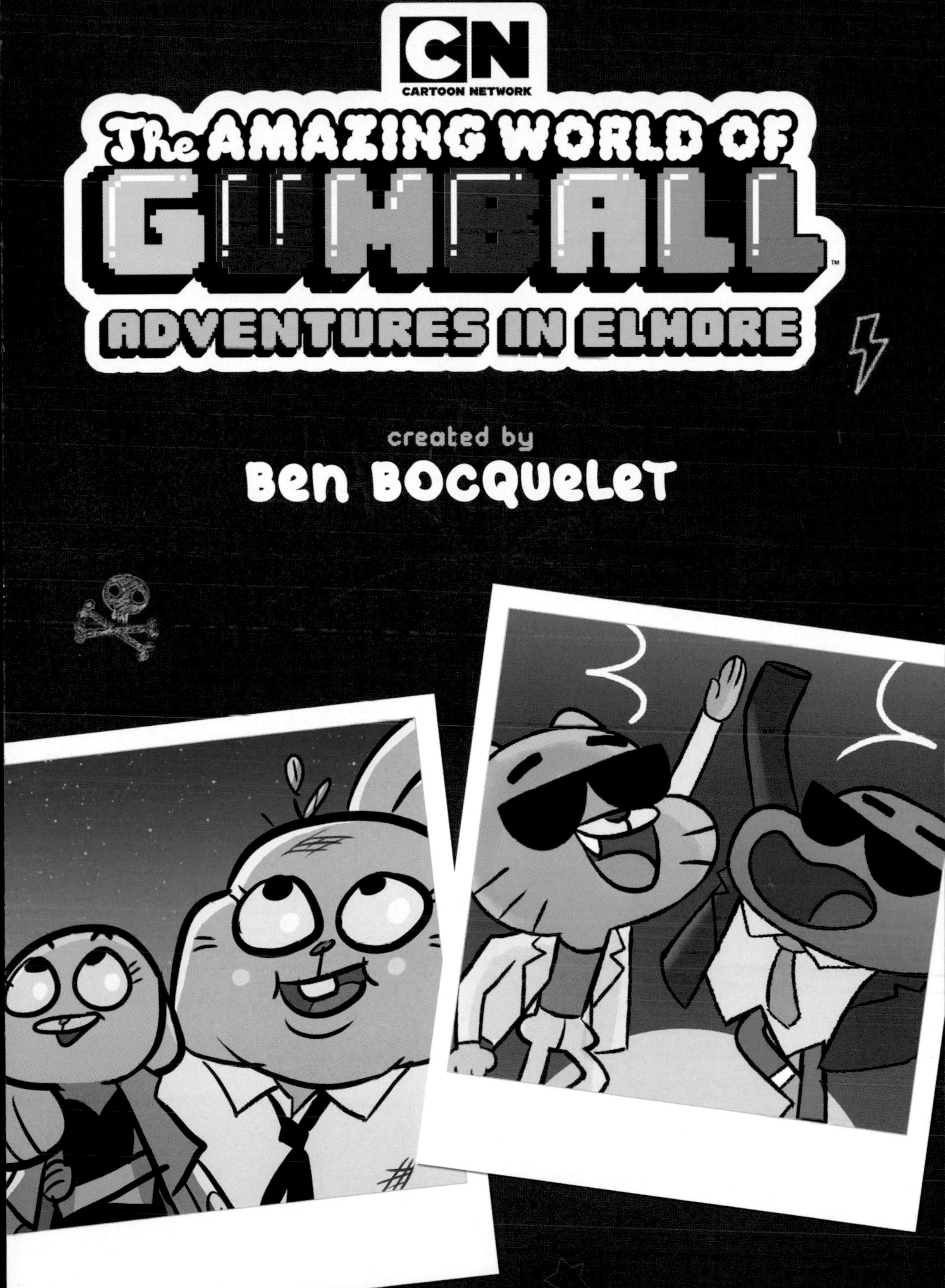

"NIGHT OUT"
script & art by
BRITTANY PEER
letters by
TAYLOR ESPOSITO

"YARD SALE"
script & art by
TERRY BLAS
letters by
WARREN MONTGOMERY

"THE NAP"
script & art by
GUSTAVO BORGES

"BLAST FROM THE PAST"
script by
MAX DAVISON
art by
JORDAN GIBSON
letters by
WARREN MONTGOMERY

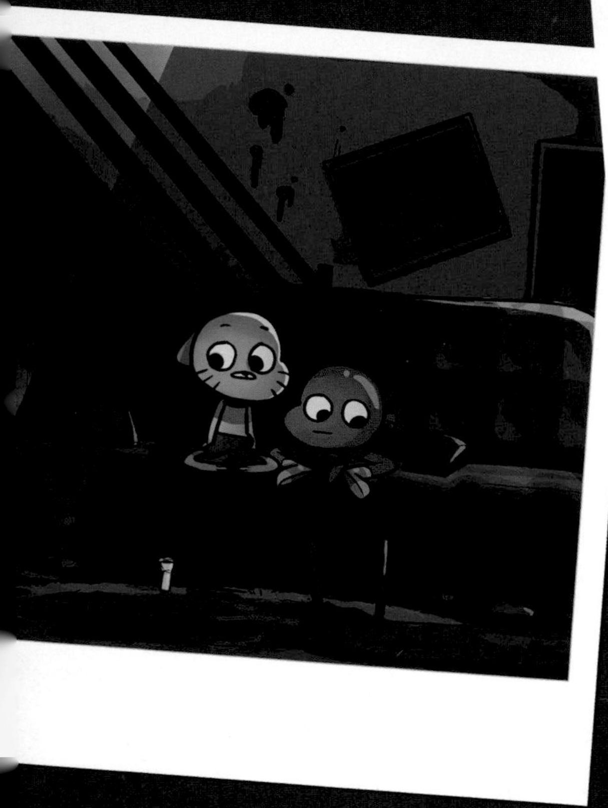

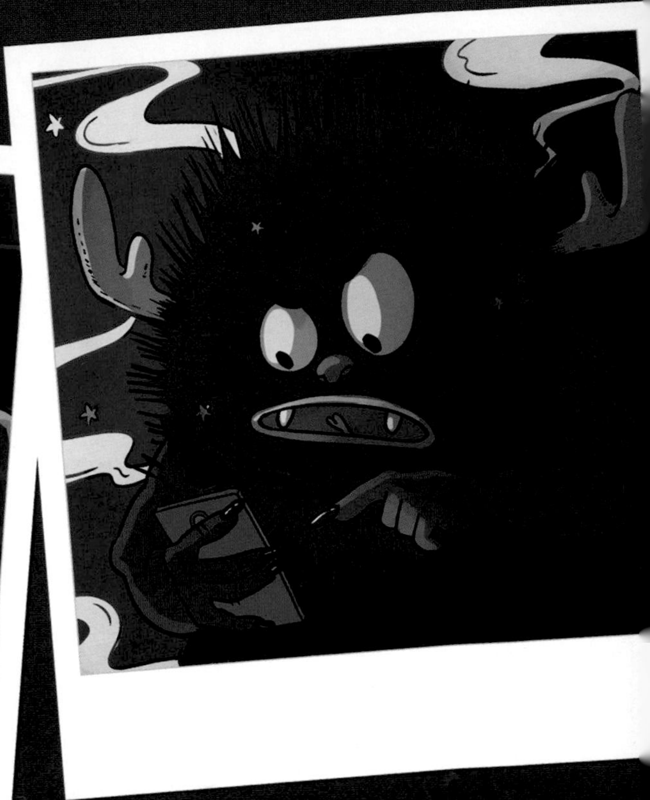

"CARRIE'S BODY"
script by
TED ANDERSON
art by
JEN HICKMAN
letters by
WARREN MONTGOMERY

"SNOW CLOSE, YETTI SO FAR"
script & art by
KATE SHERRON

"THE BIKE"
script & art by
MAC PRYOR

"THE HOST"
script & art by
JULIETA COLAS

"THE HAUNTENING"
script & art by
RACHEL MATILE

"SCIENCE FAIR SHENANIGANS"
script & art by
AMANDA CASTILLO

"FO:MO"
script & art by
XANTHE BOUMA

"BFFS"
script by
LUKE HUMPHRIS
art by
KELLY BASTOW

"GRAND MUMMY'S CURSE"
script & art by
SHIVANA SOOKDEO

"THE TRICK"
script & art by
LORN WATERFIELD

series designers
CHELSEA ROBERTS & GRACE PARK

collection designer
KARA LEOPARD

cover by
NAOMI FRANQUIZ

assistant editor
MICHAEL MOCCIO

editor
MATTHEW LEVINE

with special thanks to **MARISA MARIONAKIS, JANET NO, BECKY M. YANG, CONRAD MONTGOMERY** and the wonderful folks at **CARTOON NETWORK.**

NIGHT OUT

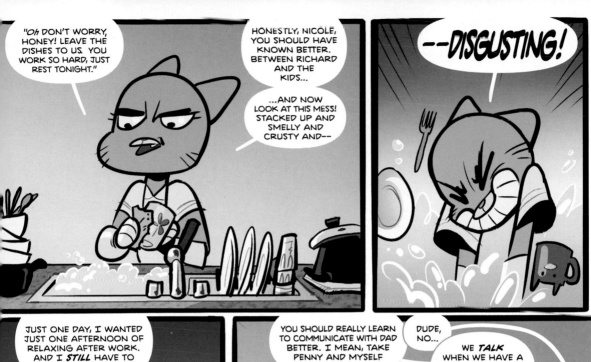

"*Oh* DON'T WORRY, HONEY! LEAVE THE DISHES TO US. YOU WORK SO HARD, JUST REST TONIGHT."

HONESTLY, NICOLE, YOU SHOULD HAVE KNOWN BETTER. BETWEEN RICHARD AND THE KIDS...

...AND NOW LOOK AT THIS MESS! STACKED UP AND SMELLY AND CRUSTY AND--

--DISGUSTING!

JUST ONE DAY, I WANTED JUST ONE AFTERNOON OF RELAXING AFTER WORK. AND I *STILL* HAVE TO COOK DINNER FOR TONIGHT!

WOW, MOM.

YOU SHOULD REALLY LEARN TO COMMUNICATE WITH DAD BETTER. I MEAN, TAKE PENNY AND MYSELF FOR EXAMPLE.

DUDE, NO...

WE *TALK* WHEN WE HAVE A PROBLEM INSTEAD OF IGNORING IT. NOT THAT WE HAVE ANY.

BUT I GUESS WE'RE JUST *SO* IN SYNC BECAUSE WE HANG OUT *ALL THE TIME.* YOU AND DAD DON'T DO *ANYTHING* OUTSIDE OF THE HOUSE.

BY THE WAY, WHEN'S DINNER?

WHENEVER THE PIZZA DELIVERY CAN GET HERE, BECAUSE YOU BOYS ARE ON YOUR OWN.

RICHARD, PUT YOUR PANTS ON! WE'RE GOING OUT FOR DINNER TONIGHT!

AWWW MAN...

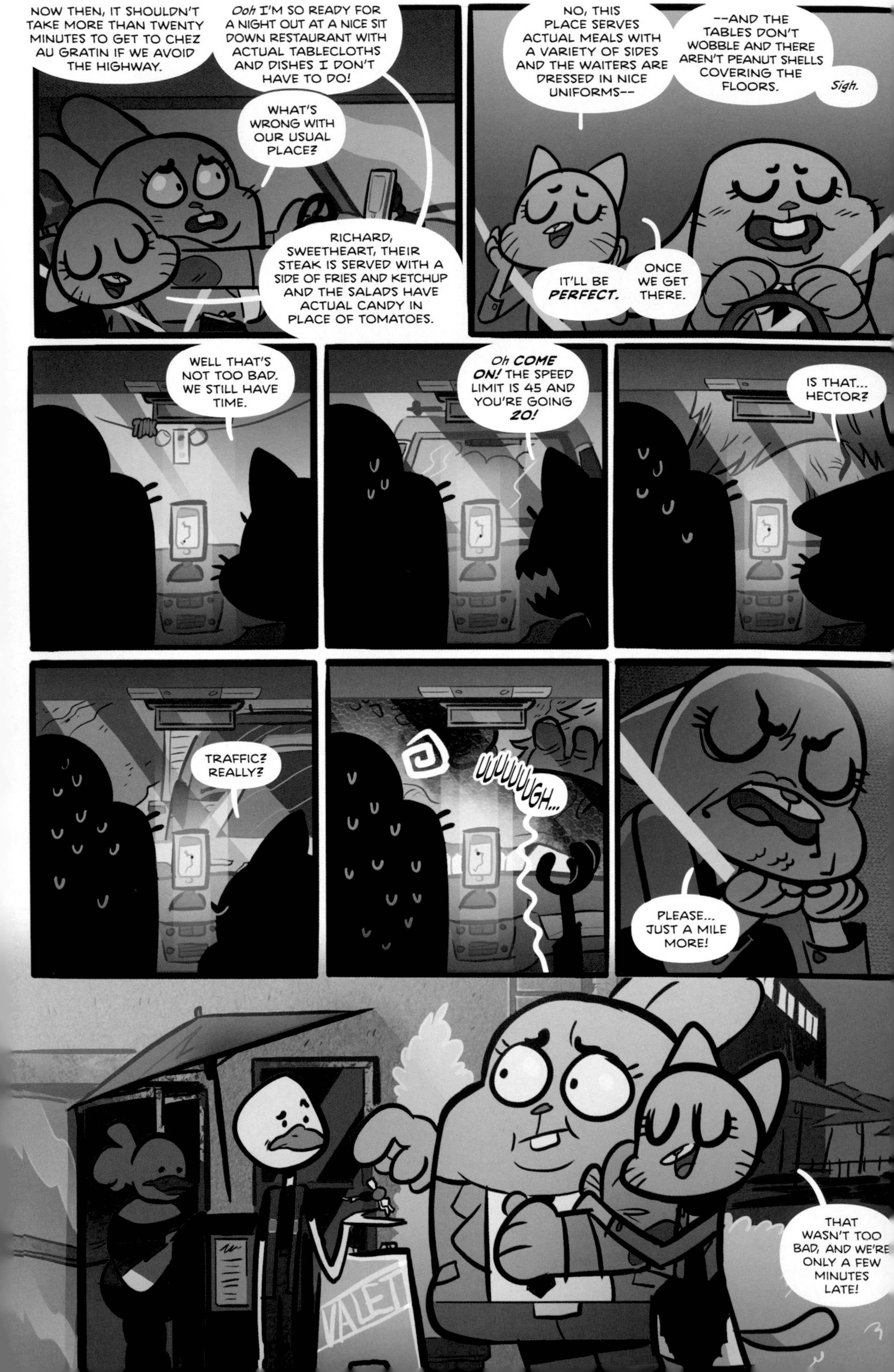
NOW THEN, IT SHOULDN'T TAKE MORE THAN TWENTY MINUTES TO GET TO CHEZ AU GRATIN IF WE AVOID THE HIGHWAY.
Ooh I'M SO READY FOR A NIGHT OUT AT A NICE SIT DOWN RESTAURANT WITH ACTUAL TABLECLOTHS AND DISHES I DON'T HAVE TO DO!
WHAT'S WRONG WITH OUR USUAL PLACE?
RICHARD, SWEETHEART, THEIR STEAK IS SERVED WITH A SIDE OF FRIES AND KETCHUP AND THE SALADS HAVE ACTUAL CANDY IN PLACE OF TOMATOES.
NO, THIS PLACE SERVES ACTUAL MEALS WITH A VARIETY OF SIDES AND THE WAITERS ARE DRESSED IN NICE UNIFORMS--
--AND THE TABLES DON'T WOBBLE AND THERE AREN'T PEANUT SHELLS COVERING THE FLOORS.
Sigh.
ONCE WE GET THERE.
IT'LL BE PERFECT.
WELL THAT'S NOT TOO BAD. WE STILL HAVE TIME.
TINK
Oh COME ON! THE SPEED LIMIT IS 45 AND YOU'RE GOING 20!
IS THAT... HECTOR?
TRAFFIC? REALLY?
UUUUUUGH...
PLEASE... JUST A MILE MORE!
THAT WASN'T TOO BAD, AND WE'RE ONLY A FEW MINUTES LATE!
VALET

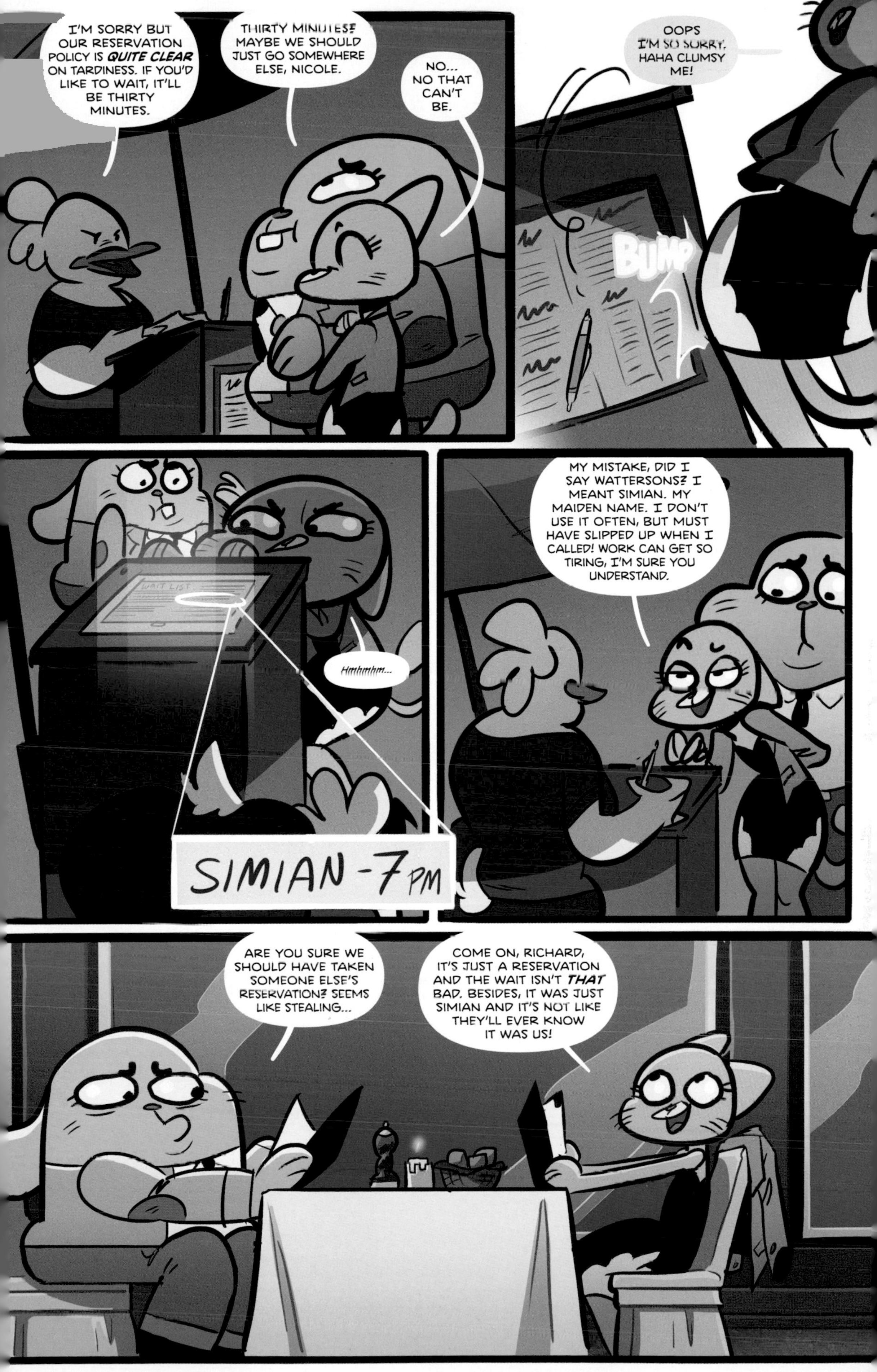
I'M SORRY BUT OUR RESERVATION POLICY IS ***QUITE CLEAR*** ON TARDINESS. IF YOU'D LIKE TO WAIT, IT'LL BE THIRTY MINUTES.
THIRTY MINUTES? MAYBE WE SHOULD JUST GO SOMEWHERE ELSE, NICOLE.
NO... NO THAT CAN'T BE.
OOPS I'M SO SORRY, HAHA CLUMSY ME!
BUMP
WAIT LIST
Hmhmhm...
SIMIAN - 7 PM
MY MISTAKE, DID I SAY WATTERSONS? I MEANT SIMIAN. MY MAIDEN NAME. I DON'T USE IT OFTEN, BUT MUST HAVE SLIPPED UP WHEN I CALLED! WORK CAN GET SO TIRING, I'M SURE YOU UNDERSTAND.
ARE YOU SURE WE SHOULD HAVE TAKEN SOMEONE ELSE'S RESERVATION? SEEMS LIKE STEALING...
COME ON, RICHARD, IT'S JUST A RESERVATION AND THE WAIT ISN'T ***THAT*** BAD. BESIDES, IT WAS JUST SIMIAN AND IT'S NOT LIKE THEY'LL EVER KNOW IT WAS US!

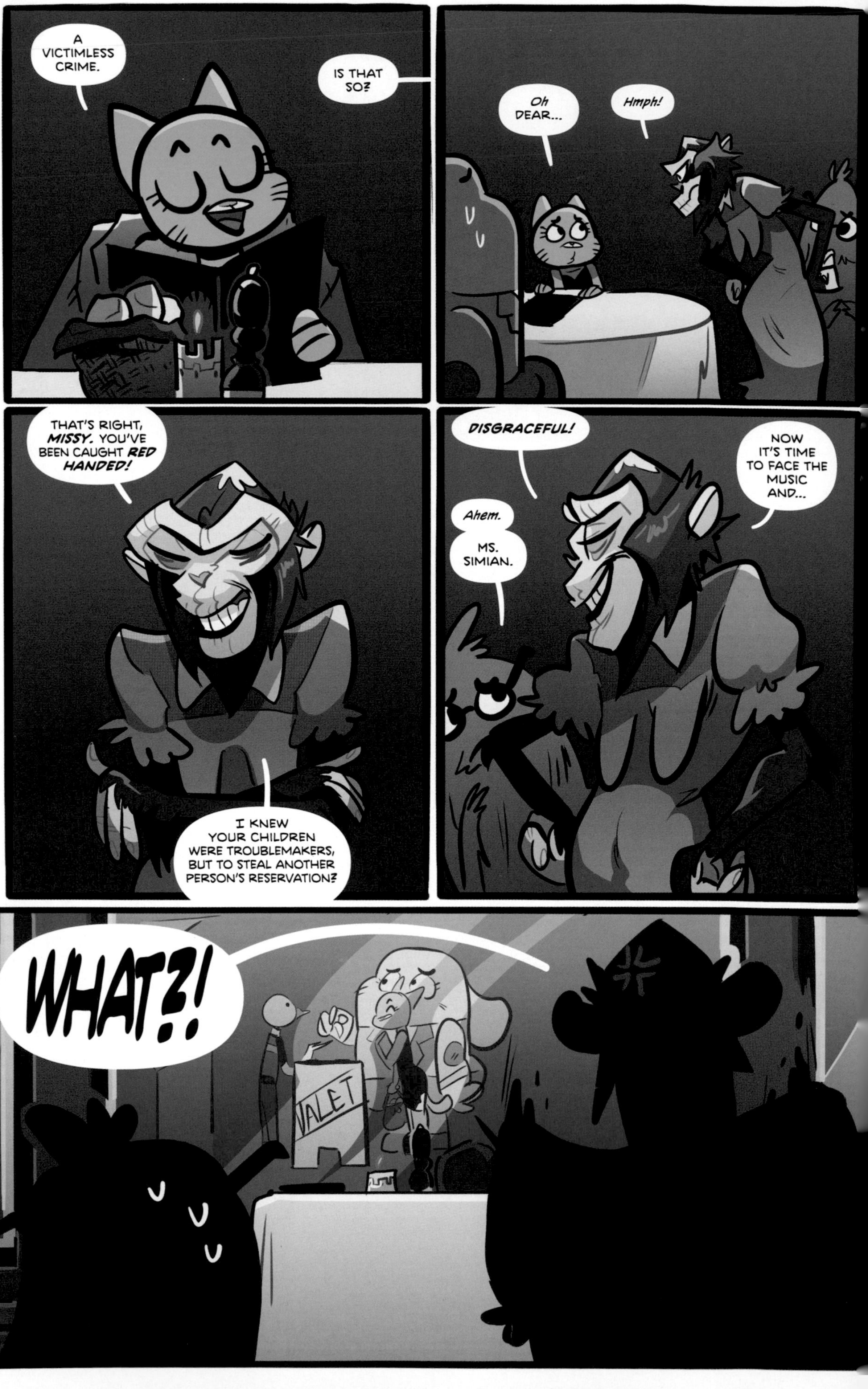
A VICTIMLESS CRIME.
IS THAT SO?
Oh DEAR...
Hmph!
THAT'S RIGHT, MISSY. YOU'VE BEEN CAUGHT RED HANDED!
I KNEW YOUR CHILDREN WERE TROUBLEMAKERS, BUT TO STEAL ANOTHER PERSON'S RESERVATION?
DISGRACEFUL!
NOW IT'S TIME TO FACE THE MUSIC AND...
Ahem.
MS. SIMIAN.
WHAT?!
VALET

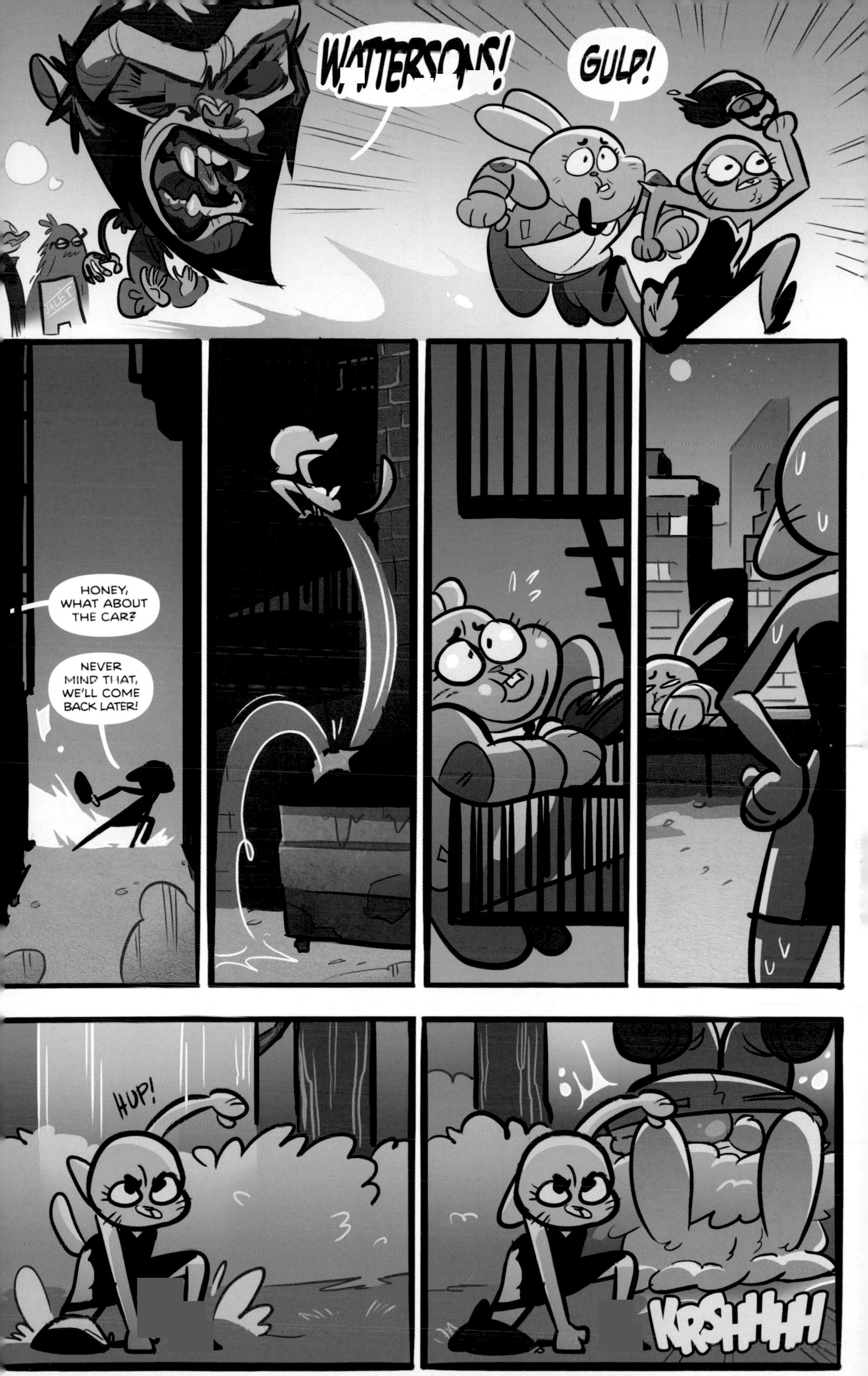
WATTERSONS!
GULP!
VALET
HONEY, WHAT ABOUT THE CAR?
NEVER MIND THAT, WE'LL COME BACK LATER!
HUP!
KRSHHHH

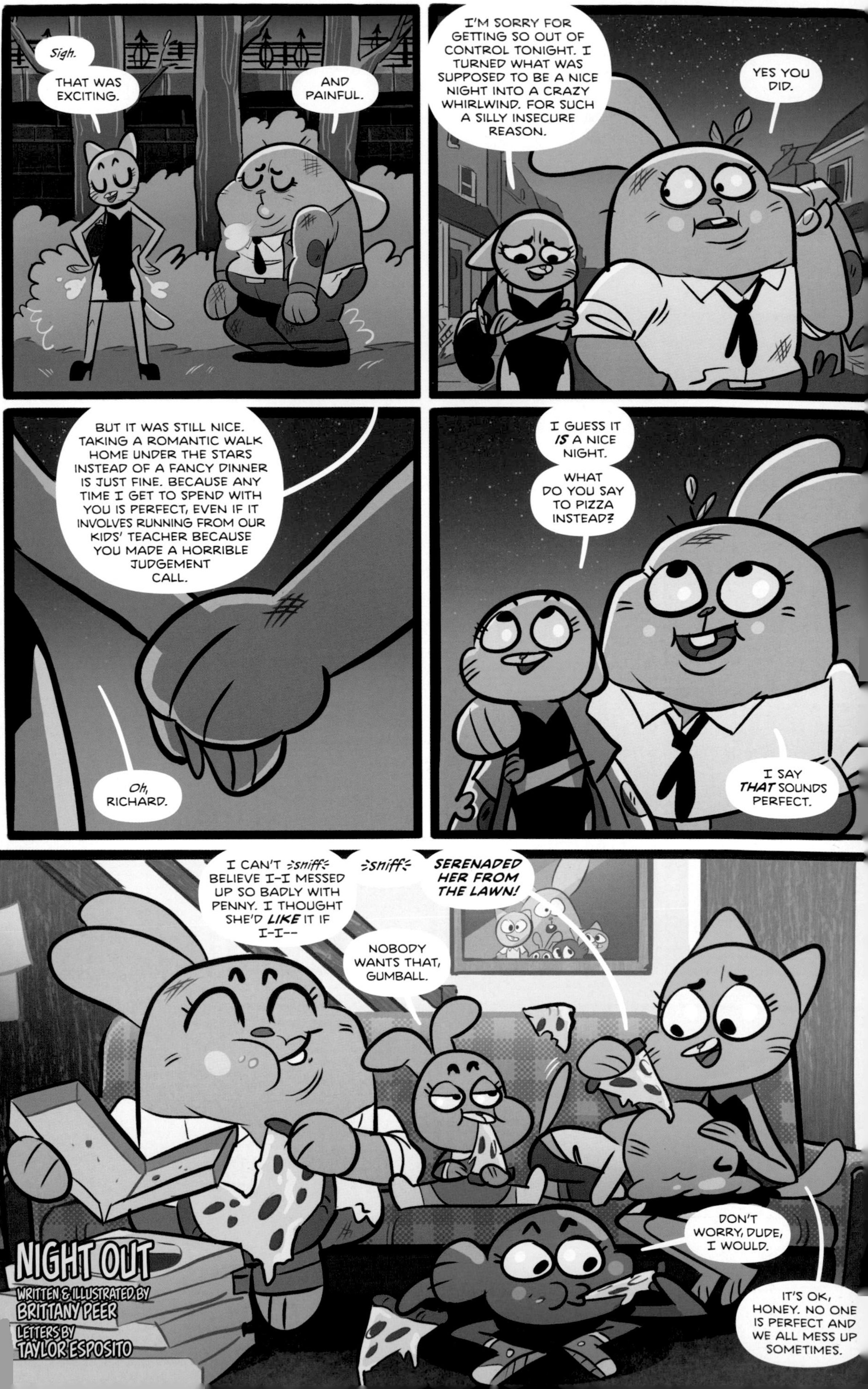

Sigh.
THAT WAS EXCITING.
AND PAINFUL.
I'M SORRY FOR GETTING SO OUT OF CONTROL TONIGHT. I TURNED WHAT WAS SUPPOSED TO BE A NICE NIGHT INTO A CRAZY WHIRLWIND. FOR SUCH A SILLY INSECURE REASON.
YES YOU DID.
BUT IT WAS STILL NICE. TAKING A ROMANTIC WALK HOME UNDER THE STARS INSTEAD OF A FANCY DINNER IS JUST FINE. BECAUSE ANY TIME I GET TO SPEND WITH YOU IS PERFECT, EVEN IF IT INVOLVES RUNNING FROM OUR KIDS' TEACHER BECAUSE YOU MADE A HORRIBLE JUDGEMENT CALL.
Oh, RICHARD.
I GUESS IT *IS* A NICE NIGHT.
WHAT DO YOU SAY TO PIZZA INSTEAD?
I SAY *THAT* SOUNDS PERFECT.
I CAN'T *sniff* BELIEVE I-I MESSED UP SO BADLY WITH PENNY. I THOUGHT SHE'D *LIKE* IT IF I-I--
sniff
SERENADED HER FROM THE LAWN!
NOBODY WANTS THAT, GUMBALL.
DON'T WORRY, DUDE, I WOULD.
IT'S OK, HONEY. NO ONE IS PERFECT AND WE ALL MESS UP SOMETIMES.
NIGHT OUT
WRITTEN & ILLUSTRATED BY BRITTANY PEER
LETTERS BY TAYLOR ESPOSITO

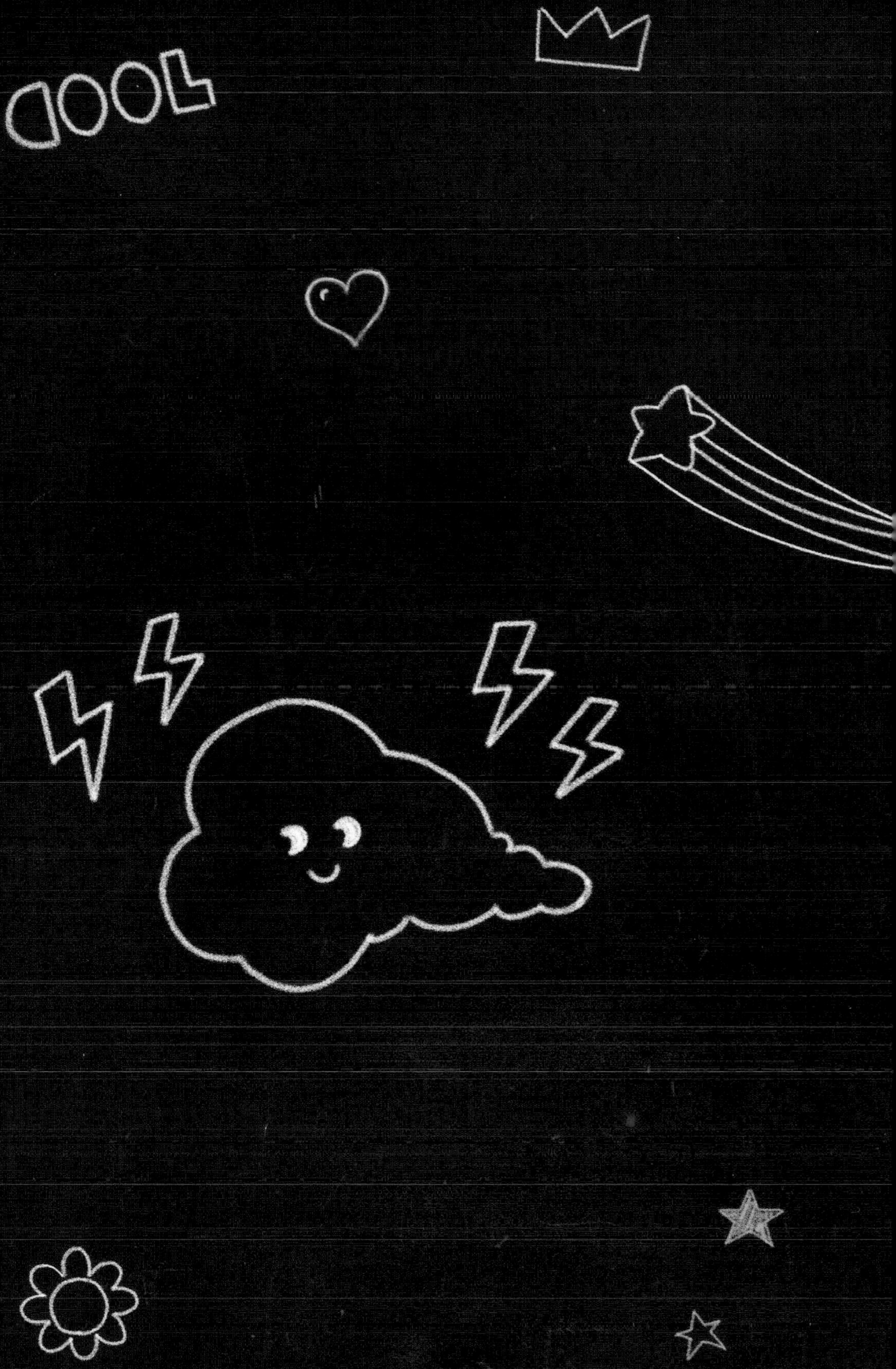
COOL

YARD SALE

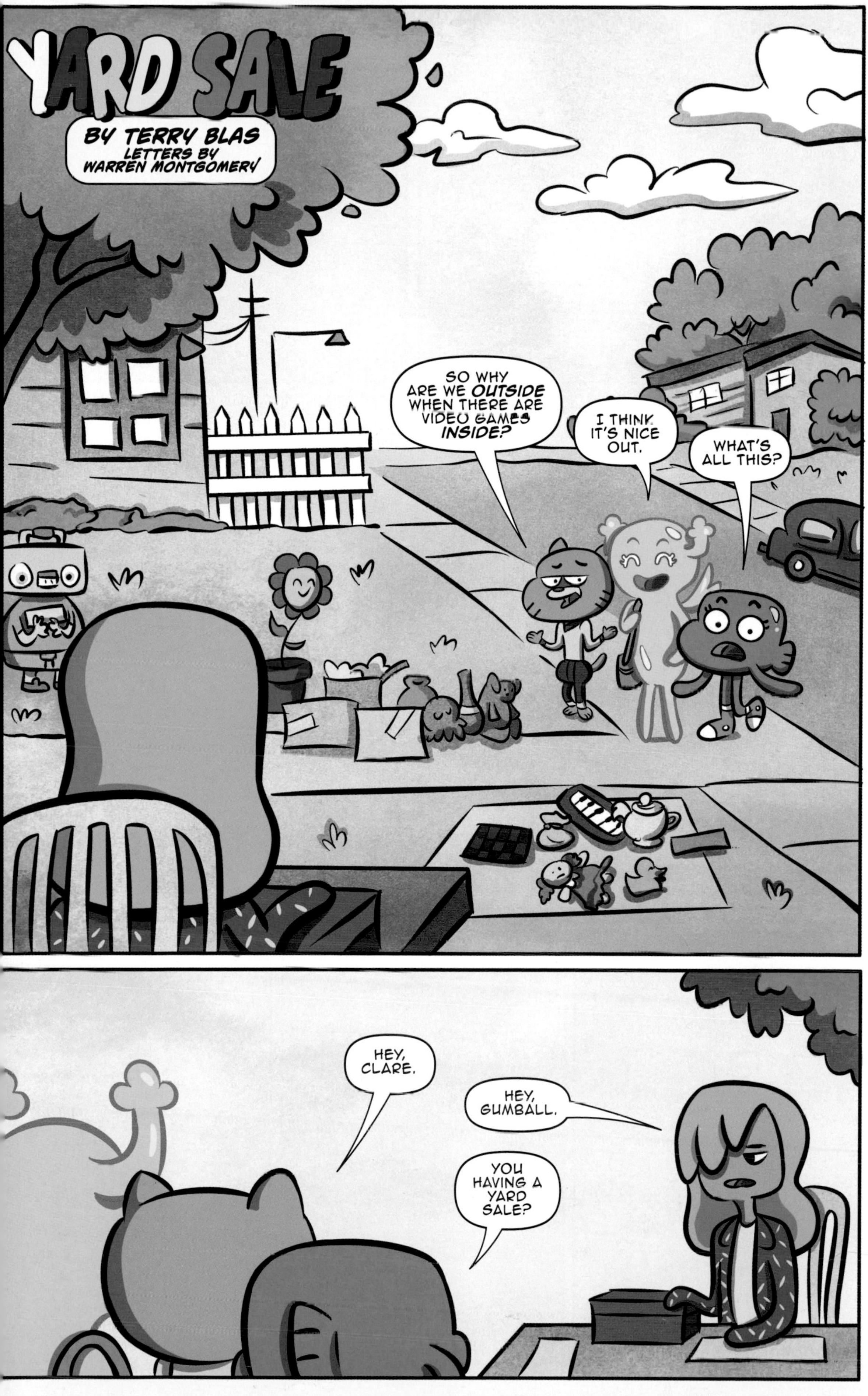
YARD SALE
BY TERRY BLAS
LETTERS BY WARREN MONTGOMERY
SO WHY ARE WE OUTSIDE WHEN THERE ARE VIDEO GAMES INSIDE?
I THINK IT'S NICE OUT.
WHAT'S ALL THIS?
HEY, CLARE.
HEY, GUMBALL.
YOU HAVING A YARD SALE?

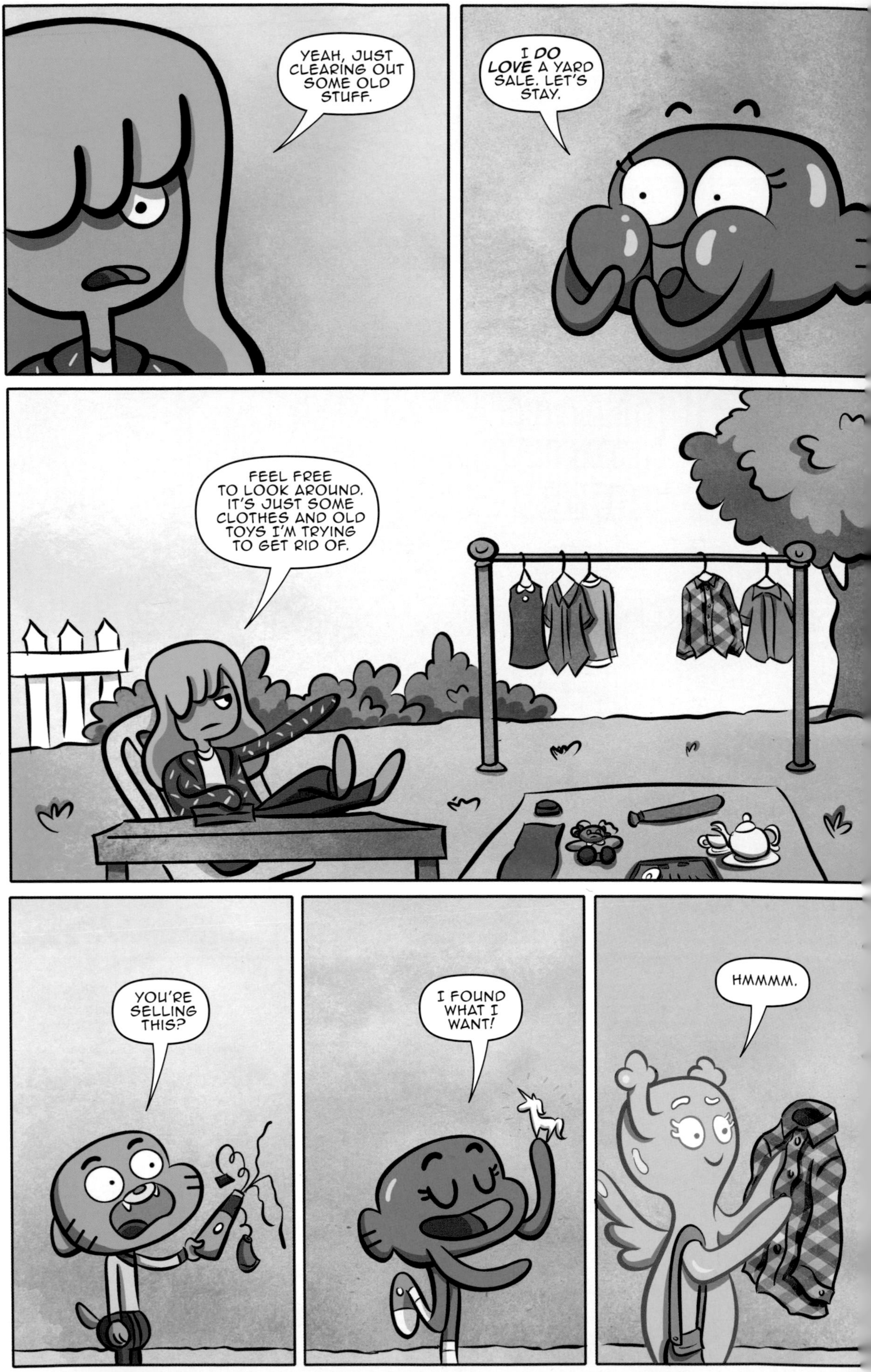
YEAH, JUST CLEARING OUT SOME OLD STUFF.
I DO LOVE A YARD SALE. LET'S STAY.
FEEL FREE TO LOOK AROUND. IT'S JUST SOME CLOTHES AND OLD TOYS I'M TRYING TO GET RID OF.
YOU'RE SELLING THIS?
I FOUND WHAT I WANT!
HMMMM.

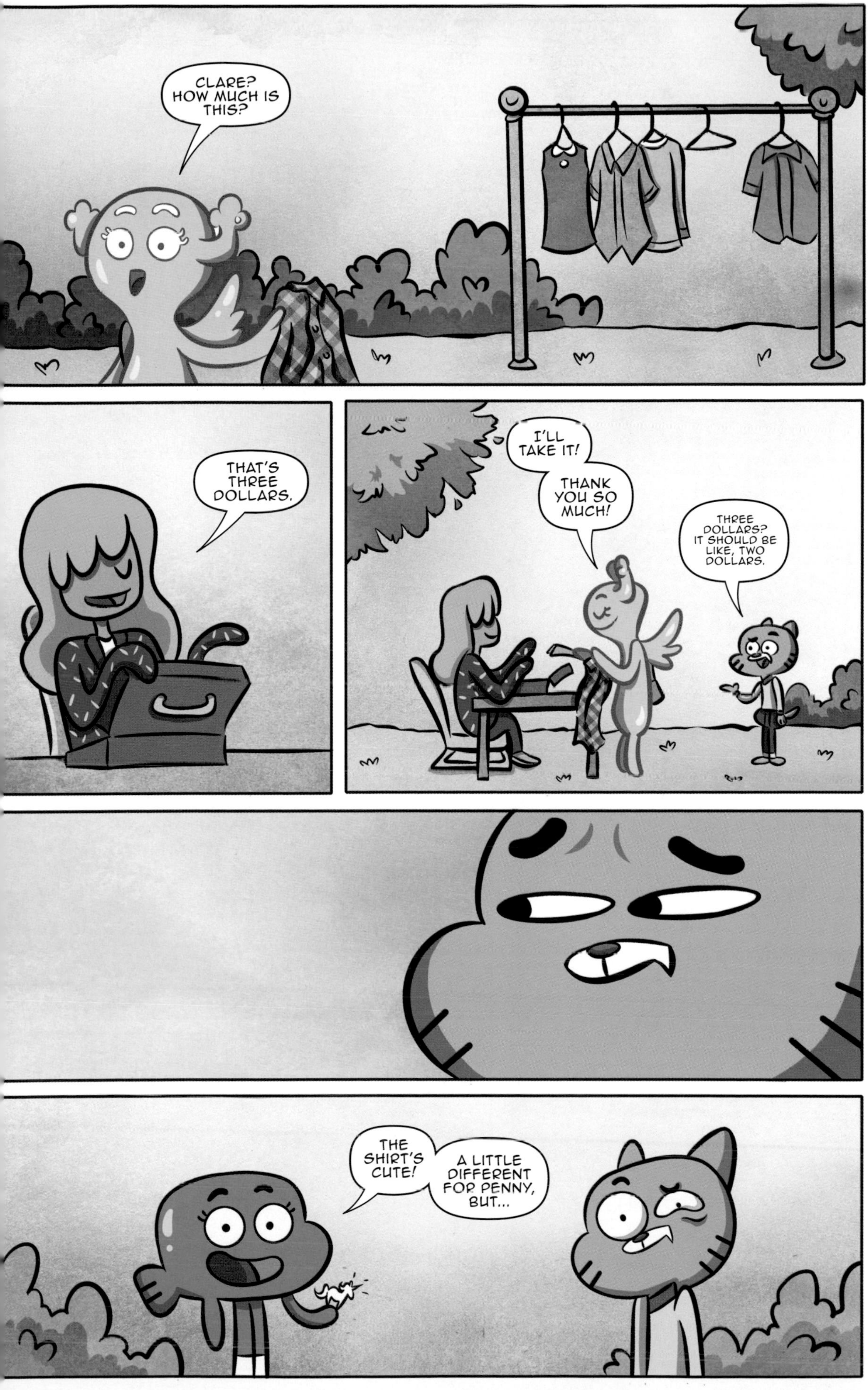
CLARE? HOW MUCH IS THIS?
THAT'S THREE DOLLARS.
I'LL TAKE IT!
THANK YOU SO MUCH!
THREE DOLLARS? IT SHOULD BE LIKE, TWO DOLLARS.
THE SHIRT'S CUTE!
A LITTLE DIFFERENT FOR PENNY, BUT...

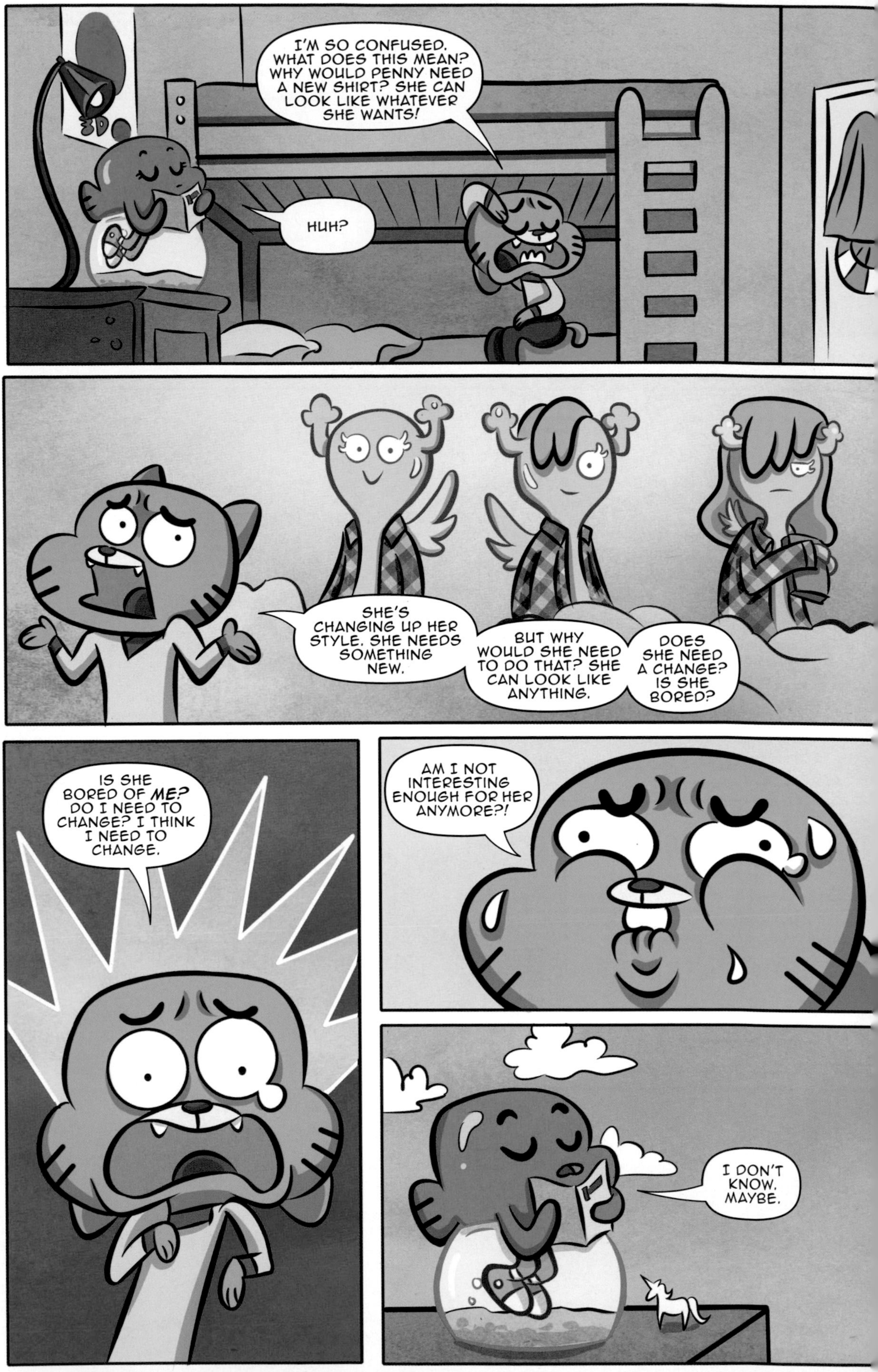
I'M SO CONFUSED. WHAT DOES THIS MEAN? WHY WOULD PENNY NEED A NEW SHIRT? SHE CAN LOOK LIKE WHATEVER SHE WANTS!
HUH?
SHE'S CHANGING UP HER STYLE. SHE NEEDS SOMETHING NEW.
BUT WHY WOULD SHE NEED TO DO THAT? SHE CAN LOOK LIKE ANYTHING.
DOES SHE NEED A CHANGE? IS SHE BORED?
IS SHE BORED OF ME? DO I NEED TO CHANGE? I THINK I NEED TO CHANGE.
AM I NOT INTERESTING ENOUGH FOR HER ANYMORE?!
I DON'T KNOW. MAYBE.

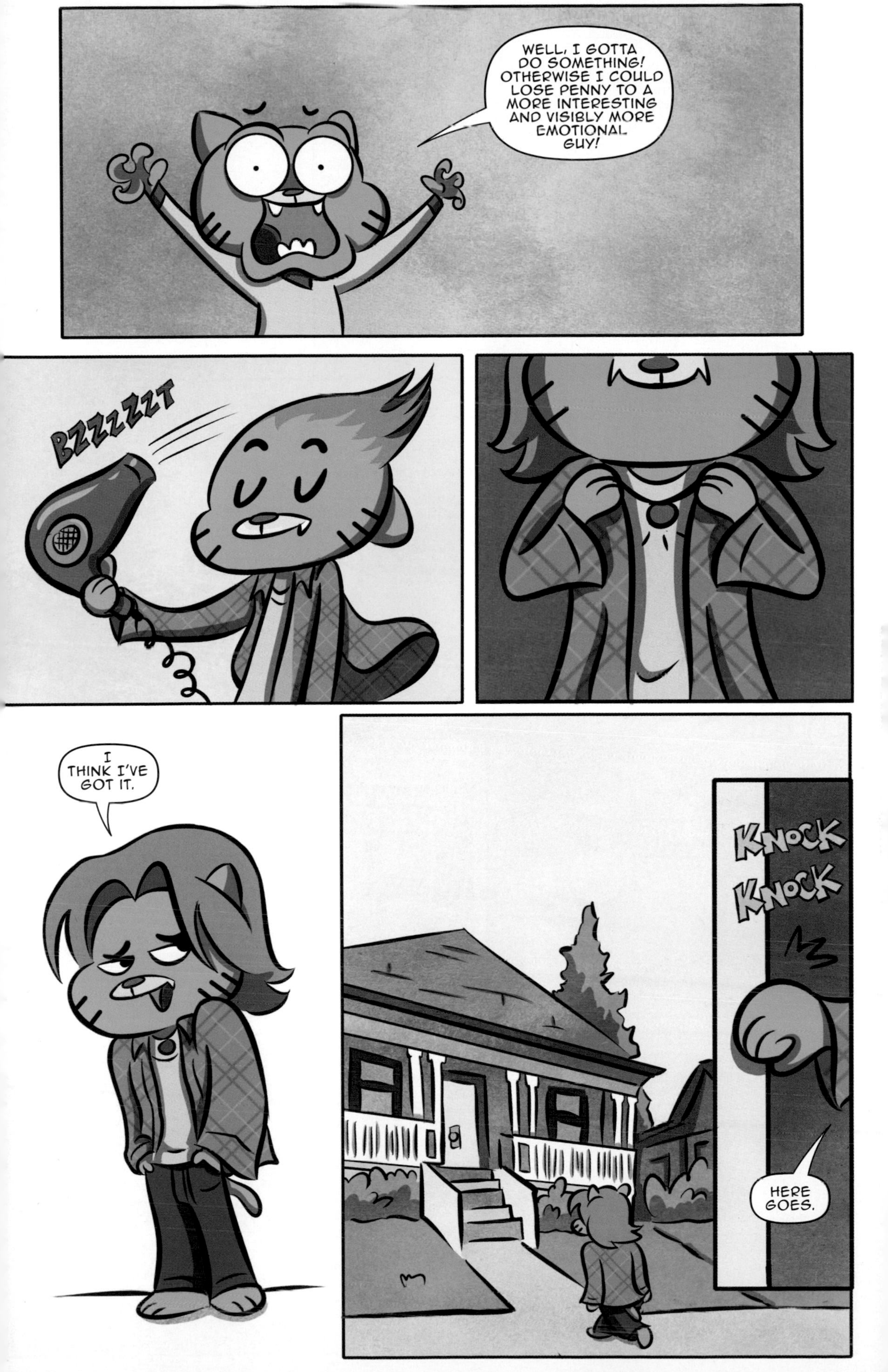
WELL, I GOTTA DO SOMETHING! OTHERWISE I COULD LOSE PENNY TO A MORE INTERESTING AND VISIBLY MORE EMOTIONAL GUY!
BZZZZZT
I THINK I'VE GOT IT.
KNOCK KNOCK
HERE GOES.

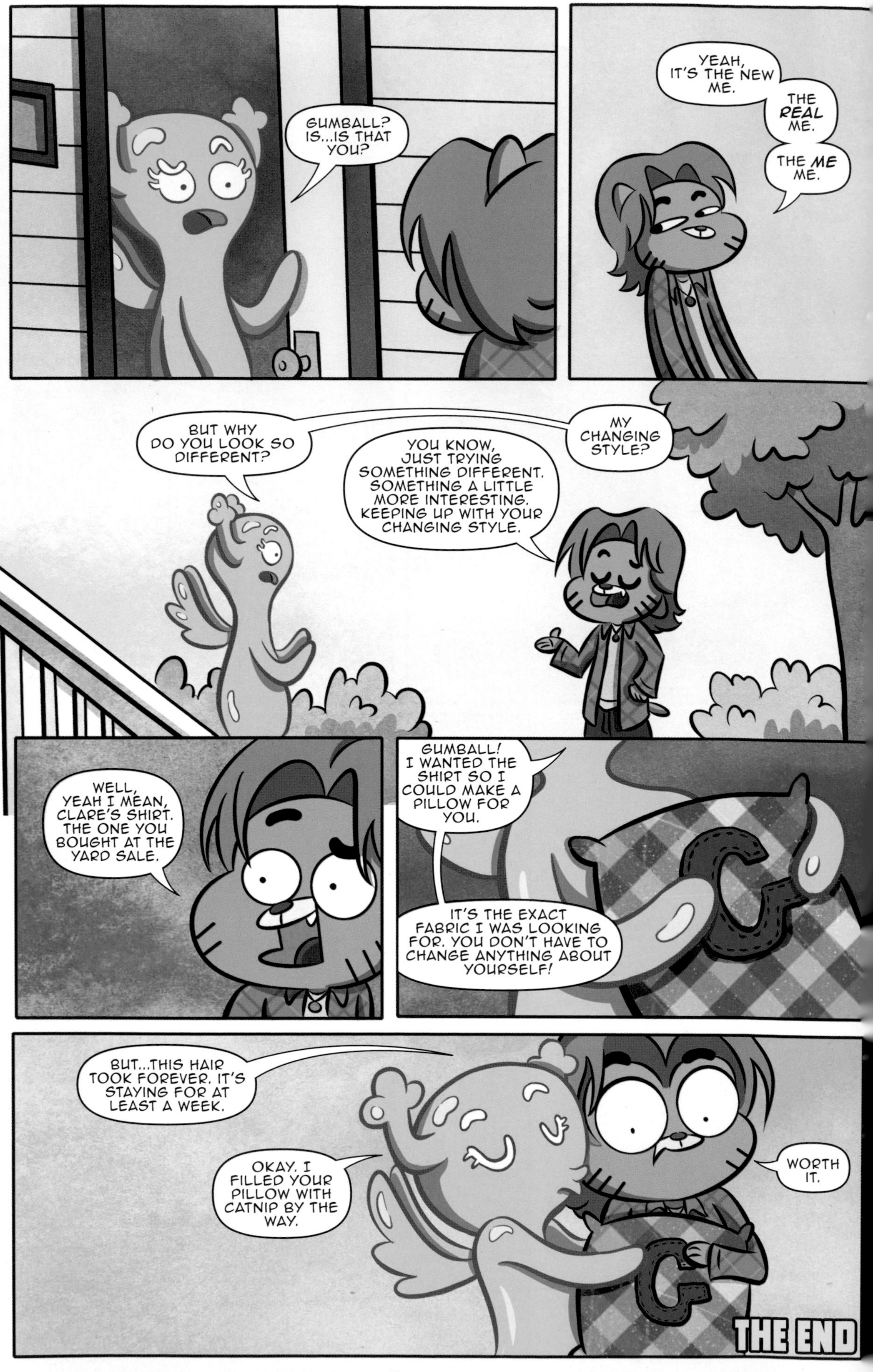
GUMBALL? IS...IS THAT YOU?
YEAH, IT'S THE NEW ME.
THE *REAL* ME.
THE *ME* ME.
BUT WHY DO YOU LOOK SO DIFFERENT?
YOU KNOW, JUST TRYING SOMETHING DIFFERENT. SOMETHING A LITTLE MORE INTERESTING. KEEPING UP WITH YOUR CHANGING STYLE.
MY CHANGING STYLE?
WELL, YEAH I MEAN, CLARE'S SHIRT. THE ONE YOU BOUGHT AT THE YARD SALE.
GUMBALL! I WANTED THE SHIRT SO I COULD MAKE A PILLOW FOR YOU.
IT'S THE EXACT FABRIC I WAS LOOKING FOR. YOU DON'T HAVE TO CHANGE ANYTHING ABOUT YOURSELF!
BUT...THIS HAIR TOOK FOREVER. IT'S STAYING FOR AT LEAST A WEEK.
OKAY. I FILLED YOUR PILLOW WITH CATNIP BY THE WAY.
WORTH IT.
THE END

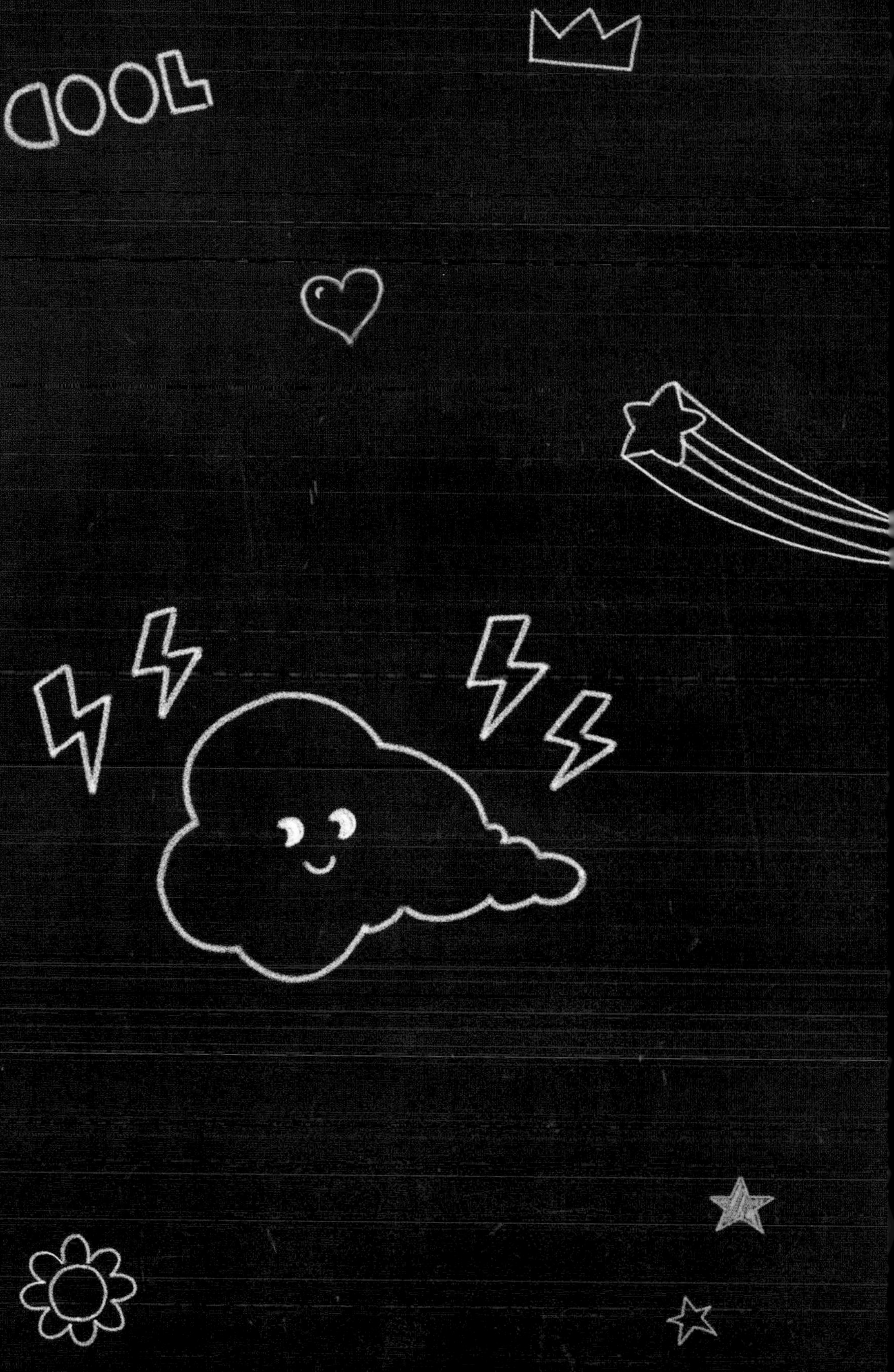
COOL

THE NAP

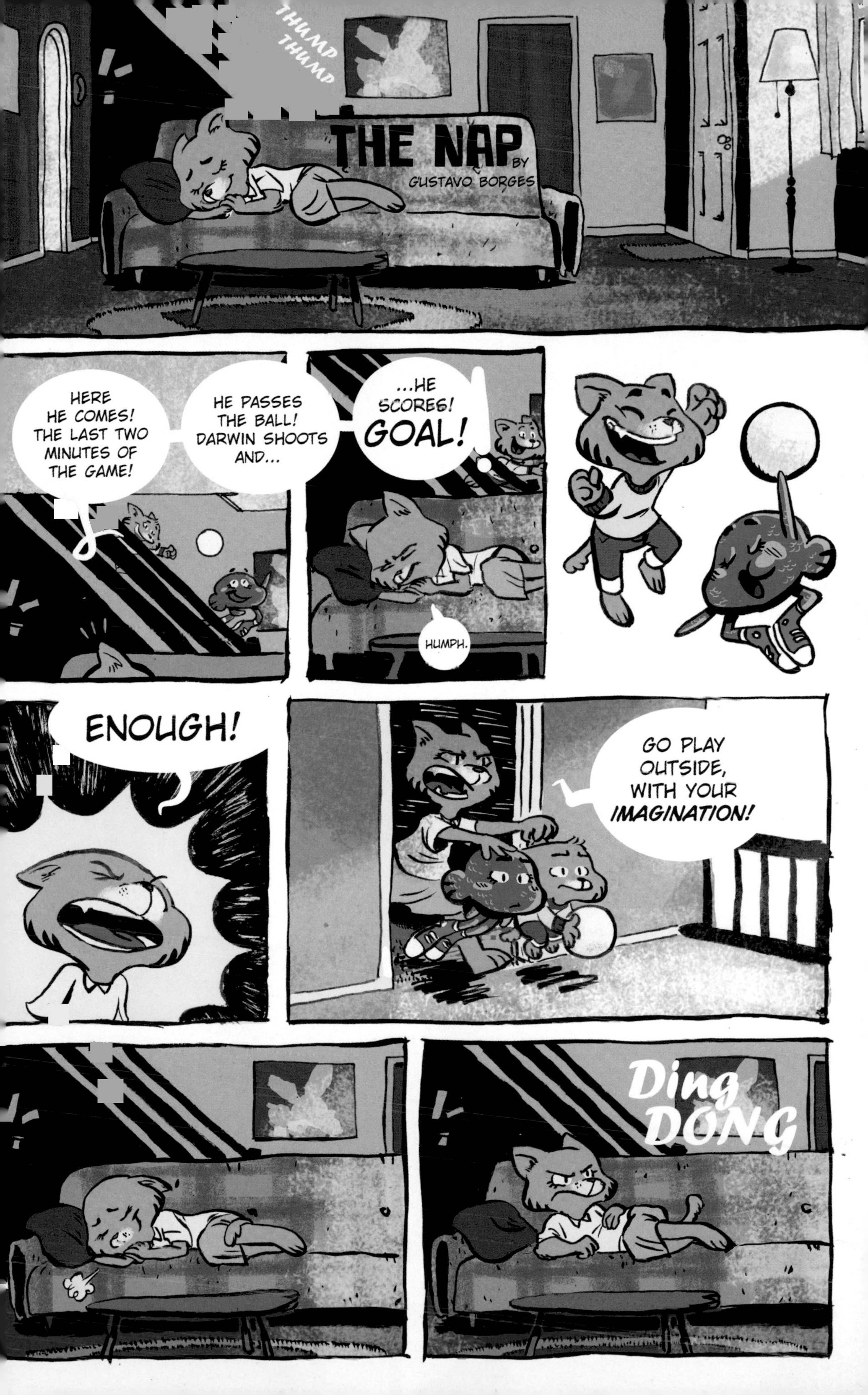
THUMP THUMP
THE NAP
BY GUSTAVO BORGES
HERE HE COMES! THE LAST TWO MINUTES OF THE GAME!
HE PASSES THE BALL! DARWIN SHOOTS AND...
...HE SCORES! GOAL!
HUMPH.
ENOUGH!
GO PLAY OUTSIDE, WITH YOUR IMAGINATION!
Ding DONG

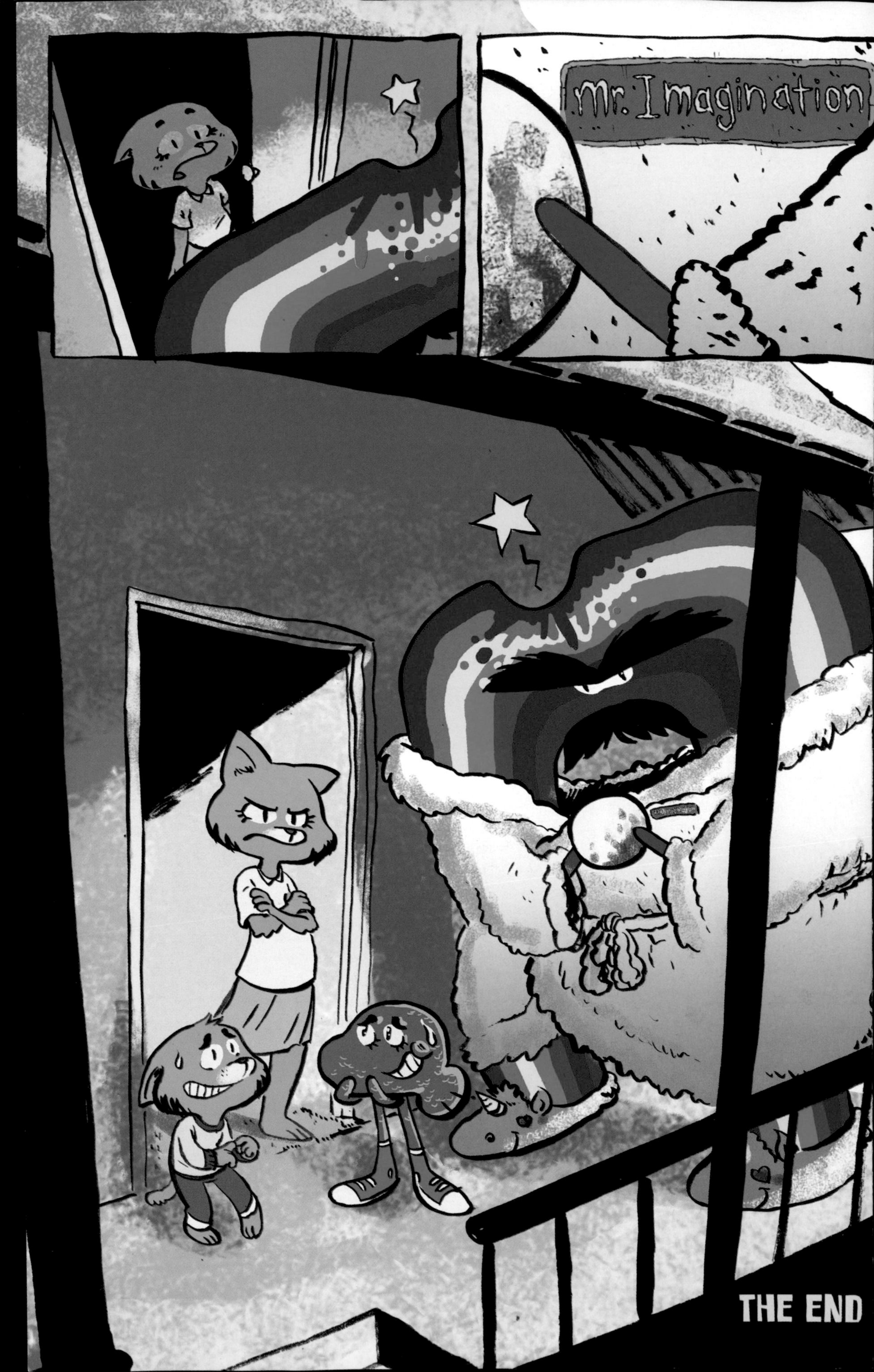

mr. Imagination
THE END

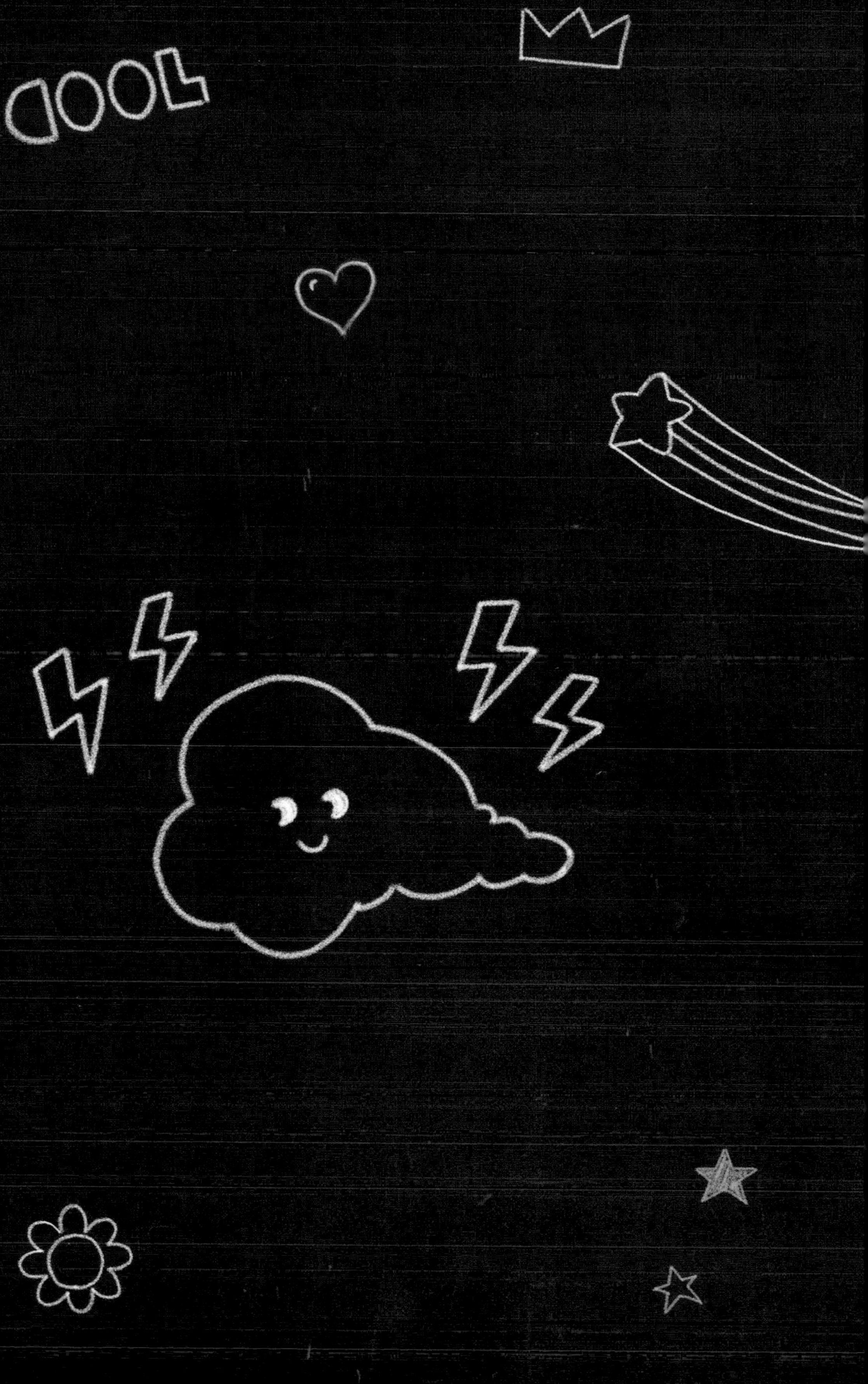
COOL

BLAST FROM THE PAST

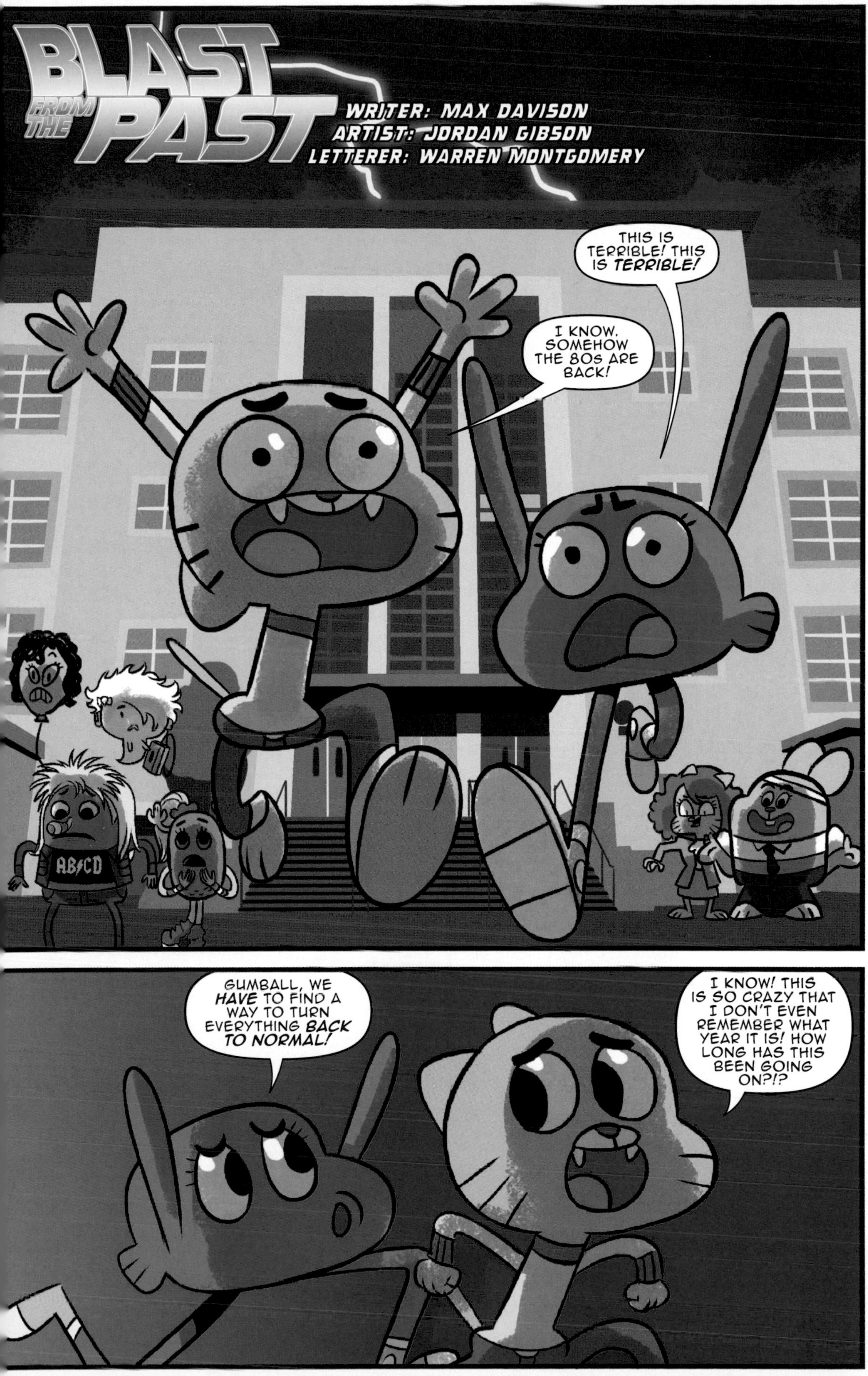
BLAST FROM THE PAST
WRITER: MAX DAVISON
ARTIST: JORDAN GIBSON
LETTERER: WARREN MONTGOMERY
THIS IS TERRIBLE! THIS IS TERRIBLE!
I KNOW. SOMEHOW THE 80S ARE BACK!
AB/CD
GUMBALL, WE HAVE TO FIND A WAY TO TURN EVERYTHING BACK TO NORMAL!
I KNOW! THIS IS SO CRAZY THAT I DON'T EVEN REMEMBER WHAT YEAR IT IS! HOW LONG HAS THIS BEEN GOING ON?!?

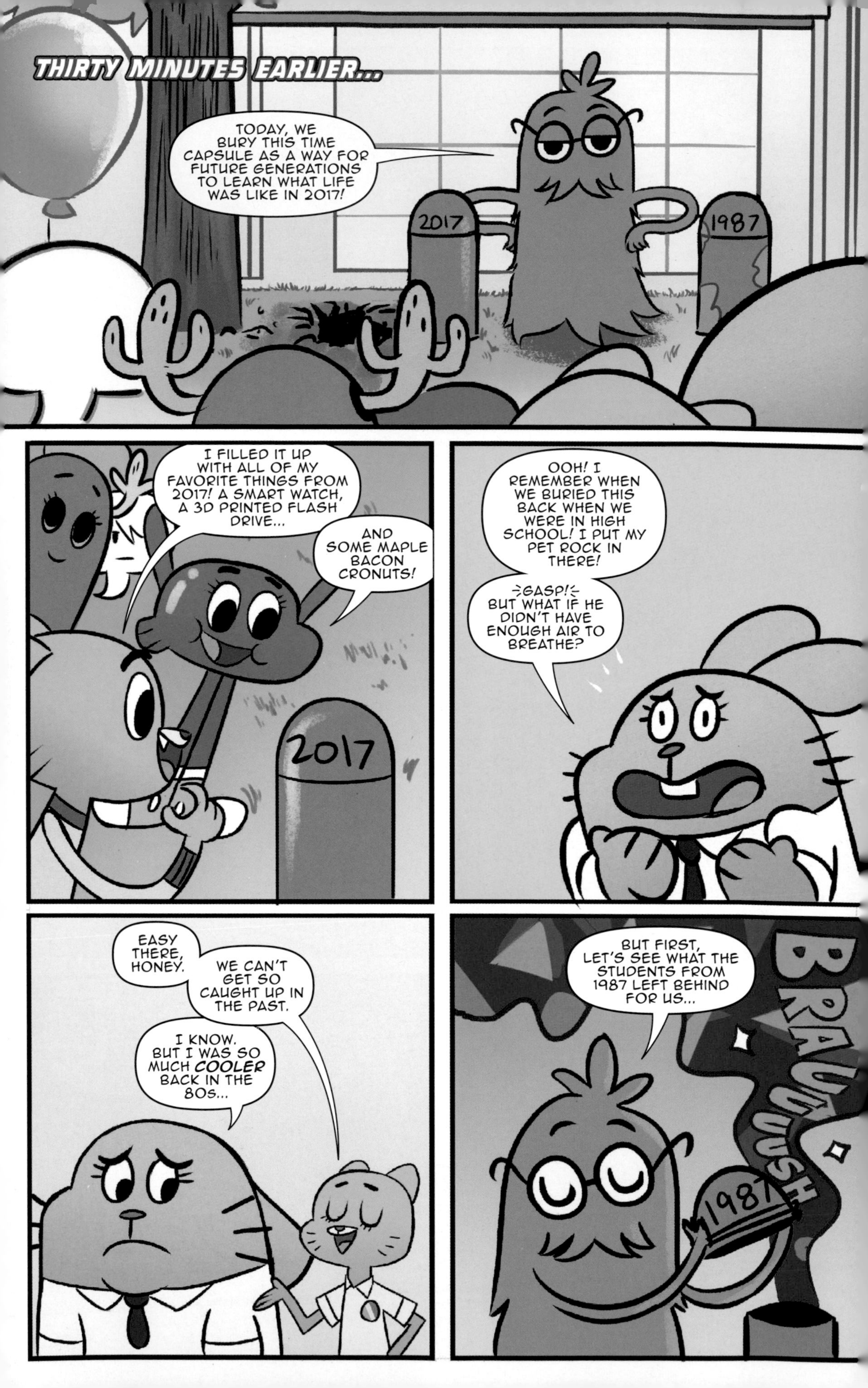
THIRTY MINUTES EARLIER...
TODAY, WE BURY THIS TIME CAPSULE AS A WAY FOR FUTURE GENERATIONS TO LEARN WHAT LIFE WAS LIKE IN 2017!
2017
1987
I FILLED IT UP WITH ALL OF MY FAVORITE THINGS FROM 2017! A SMART WATCH, A 3D PRINTED FLASH DRIVE...
AND SOME MAPLE BACON CRONUTS!
2017
OOH! I REMEMBER WHEN WE BURIED THIS BACK WHEN WE WERE IN HIGH SCHOOL! I PUT MY PET ROCK IN THERE!
GASP! BUT WHAT IF HE DIDN'T HAVE ENOUGH AIR TO BREATHE?
EASY THERE, HONEY.
WE CAN'T GET SO CAUGHT UP IN THE PAST.
I KNOW. BUT I WAS SO MUCH COOLER BACK IN THE 80S...
BUT FIRST, LET'S SEE WHAT THE STUDENTS FROM 1987 LEFT BEHIND FOR US...
BRAUUUSH
1987

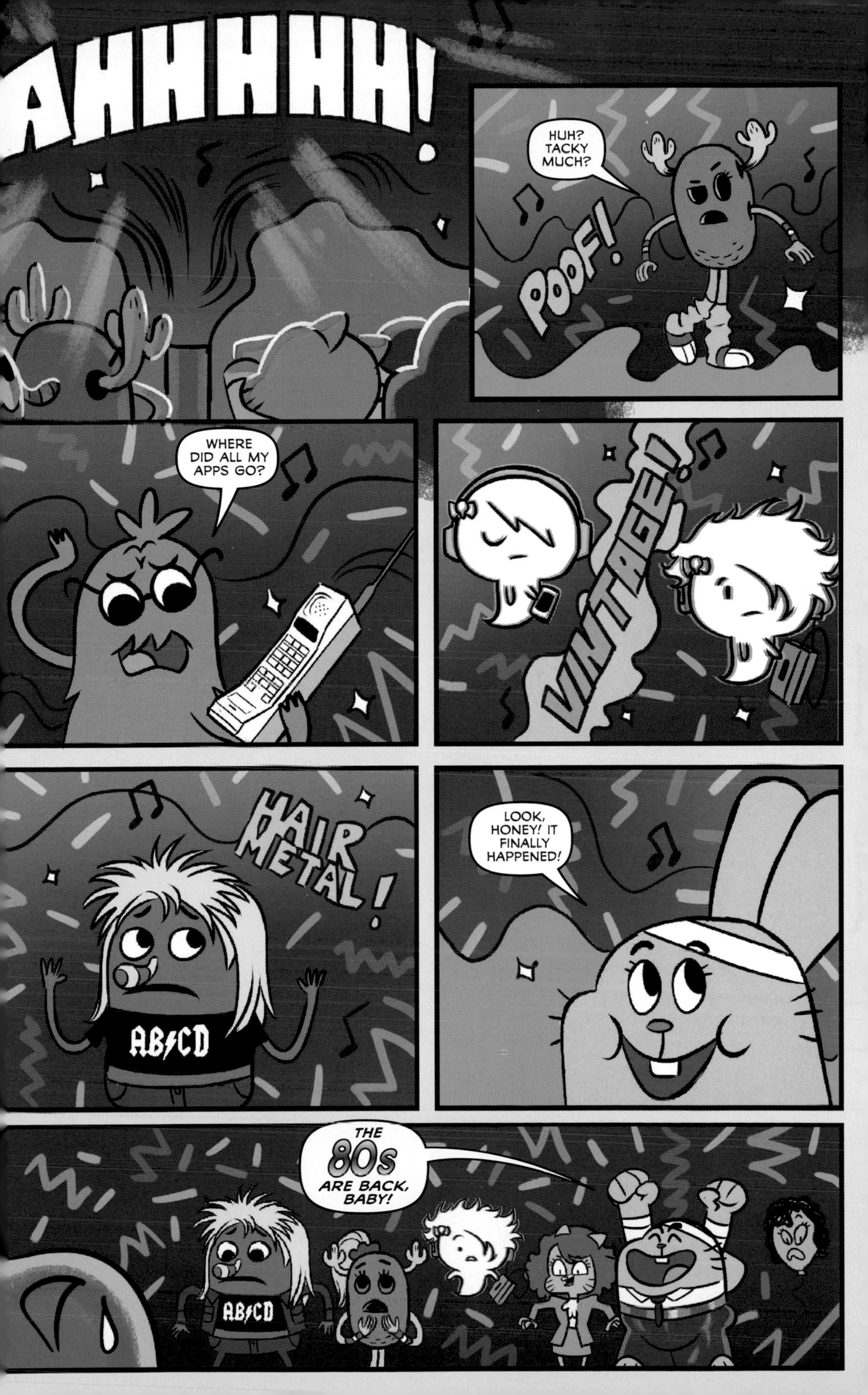
AHHHHH!
HUH? TACKY MUCH?
POOF!
WHERE DID ALL MY APPS GO?
VINTAGE!
HAIR METAL!
AB/CD
LOOK, HONEY! IT FINALLY HAPPENED!
THE 80s ARE BACK, BABY!
AB/CD

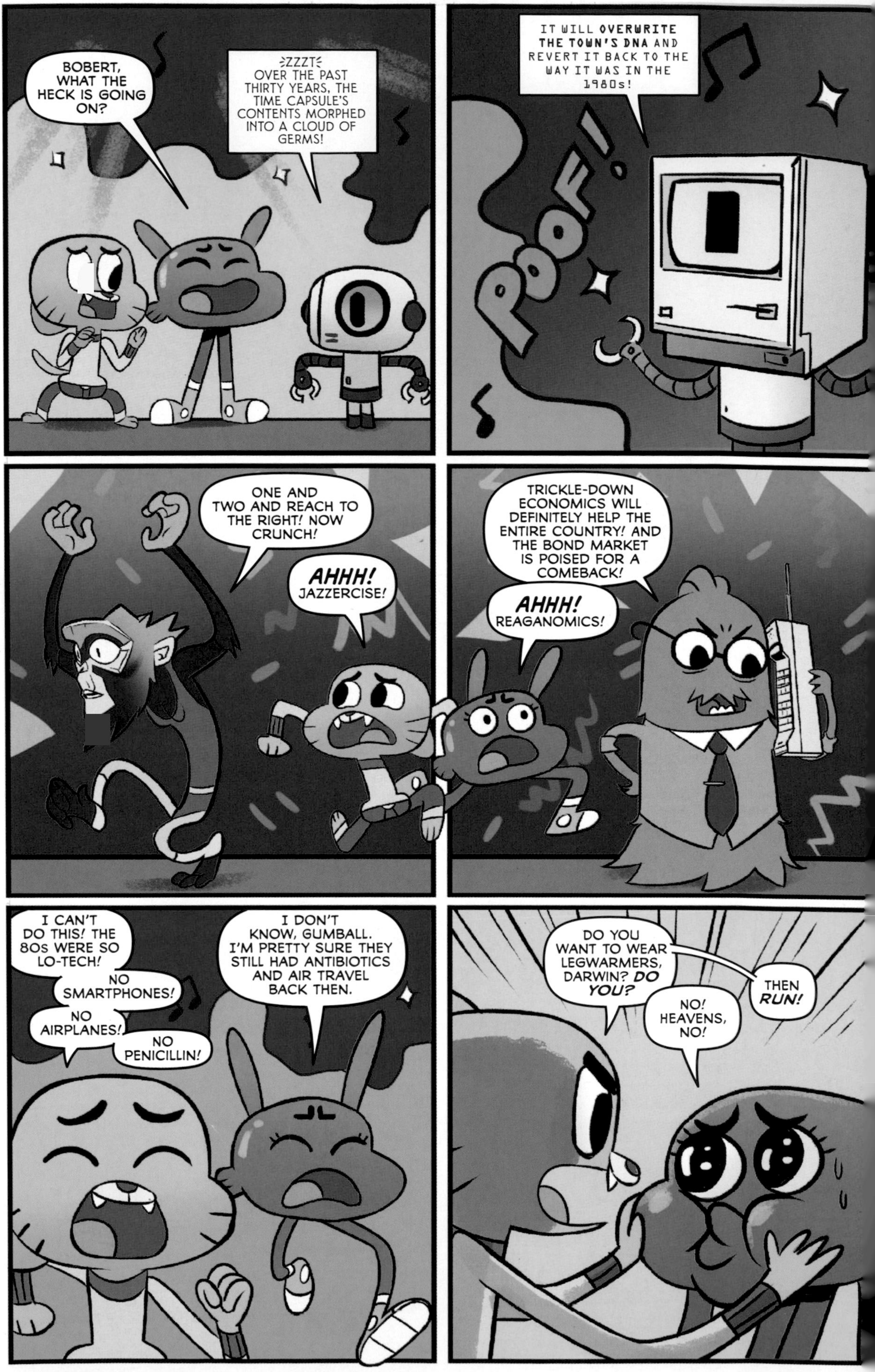

BOBERT, WHAT THE HECK IS GOING ON?
ZZZT OVER THE PAST THIRTY YEARS, THE TIME CAPSULE'S CONTENTS MORPHED INTO A CLOUD OF GERMS!
IT WILL OVERWRITE THE TOWN'S DNA AND REVERT IT BACK TO THE WAY IT WAS IN THE 1980s!
POOF!
ONE AND TWO AND REACH TO THE RIGHT! NOW CRUNCH!
AHHH! JAZZERCISE!
TRICKLE-DOWN ECONOMICS WILL DEFINITELY HELP THE ENTIRE COUNTRY! AND THE BOND MARKET IS POISED FOR A COMEBACK!
AHHH! REAGANOMICS!
I CAN'T DO THIS! THE 80s WERE SO LO-TECH!
NO SMARTPHONES!
NO AIRPLANES!
NO PENICILLIN!
I DON'T KNOW, GUMBALL. I'M PRETTY SURE THEY STILL HAD ANTIBIOTICS AND AIR TRAVEL BACK THEN.
DO YOU WANT TO WEAR LEGWARMERS, DARWIN? DO YOU?
THEN RUN!
NO! HEAVENS, NO!

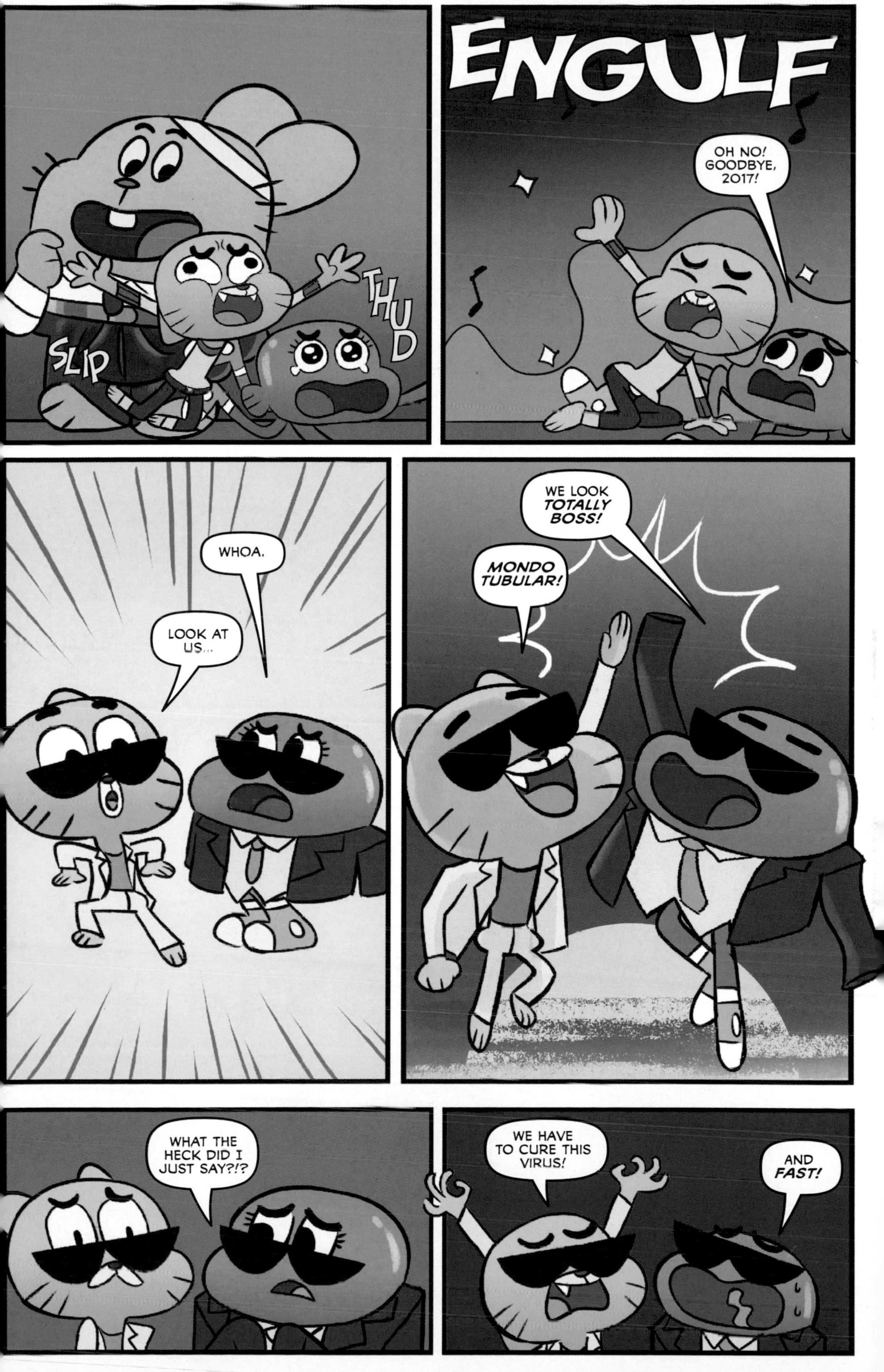
SLIP
THUD
ENGULF
OH NO! GOODBYE, 2017!
WHOA.
LOOK AT US...
WE LOOK TOTALLY BOSS!
MONDO TUBULAR!
WHAT THE HECK DID I JUST SAY?!?
WE HAVE TO CURE THIS VIRUS!
AND FAST!

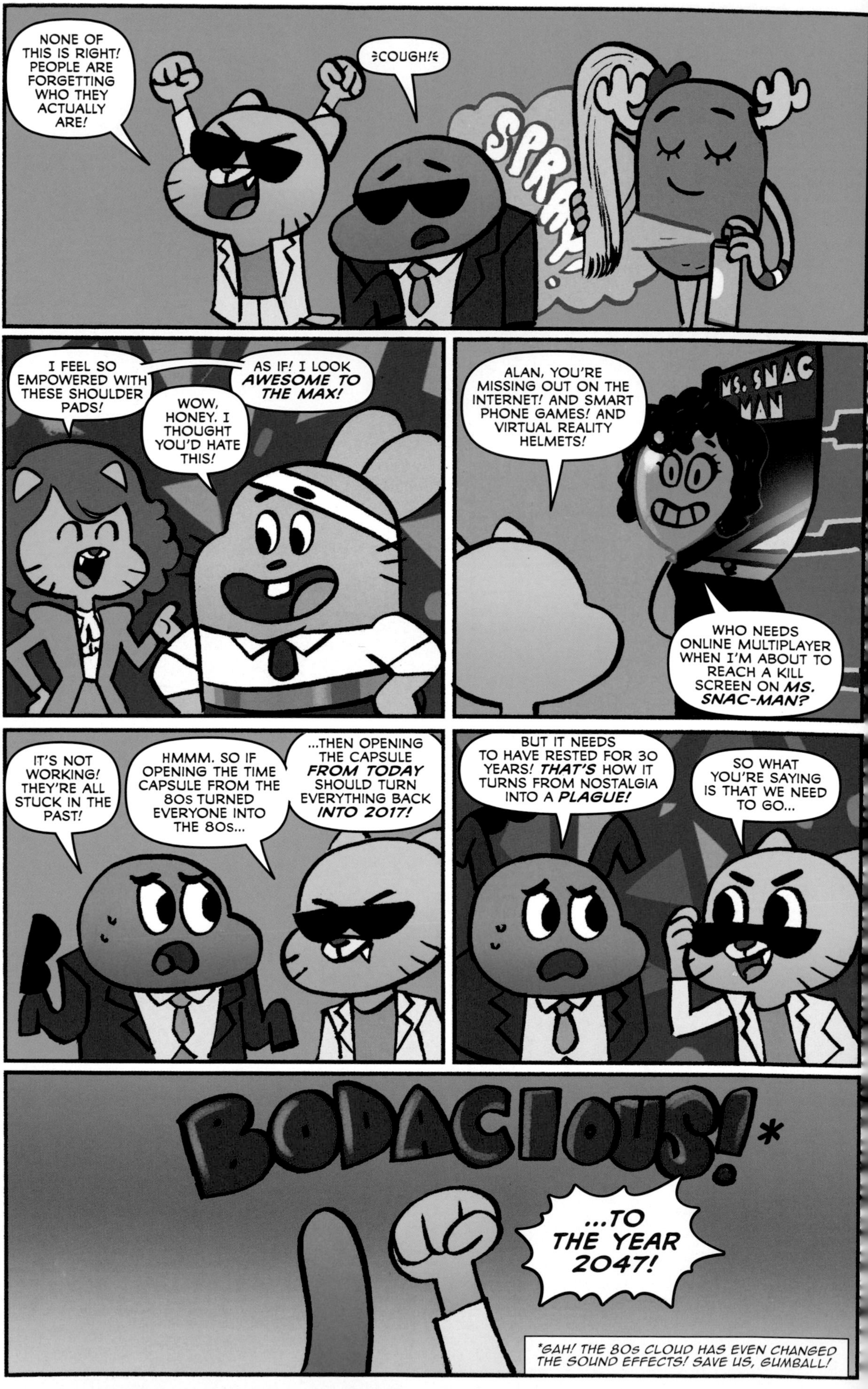
NONE OF THIS IS RIGHT! PEOPLE ARE FORGETTING WHO THEY ACTUALLY ARE!
COUGH!
SPRAY!
I FEEL SO EMPOWERED WITH THESE SHOULDER PADS!
AS IF! I LOOK AWESOME TO THE MAX!
WOW, HONEY. I THOUGHT YOU'D HATE THIS!
ALAN, YOU'RE MISSING OUT ON THE INTERNET! AND SMART PHONE GAMES! AND VIRTUAL REALITY HELMETS!
MS. SNAC MAN
WHO NEEDS ONLINE MULTIPLAYER WHEN I'M ABOUT TO REACH A KILL SCREEN ON MS. SNAC-MAN?
IT'S NOT WORKING! THEY'RE ALL STUCK IN THE PAST!
HMMM. SO IF OPENING THE TIME CAPSULE FROM THE 80s TURNED EVERYONE INTO THE 80s...
...THEN OPENING THE CAPSULE FROM TODAY SHOULD TURN EVERYTHING BACK INTO 2017!
BUT IT NEEDS TO HAVE RESTED FOR 30 YEARS! THAT'S HOW IT TURNS FROM NOSTALGIA INTO A PLAGUE!
SO WHAT YOU'RE SAYING IS THAT WE NEED TO GO...
BODACIOUS!*
...TO THE YEAR 2047!
*GAH! THE 80s CLOUD HAS EVEN CHANGED THE SOUND EFFECTS! SAVE US, GUMBALL!

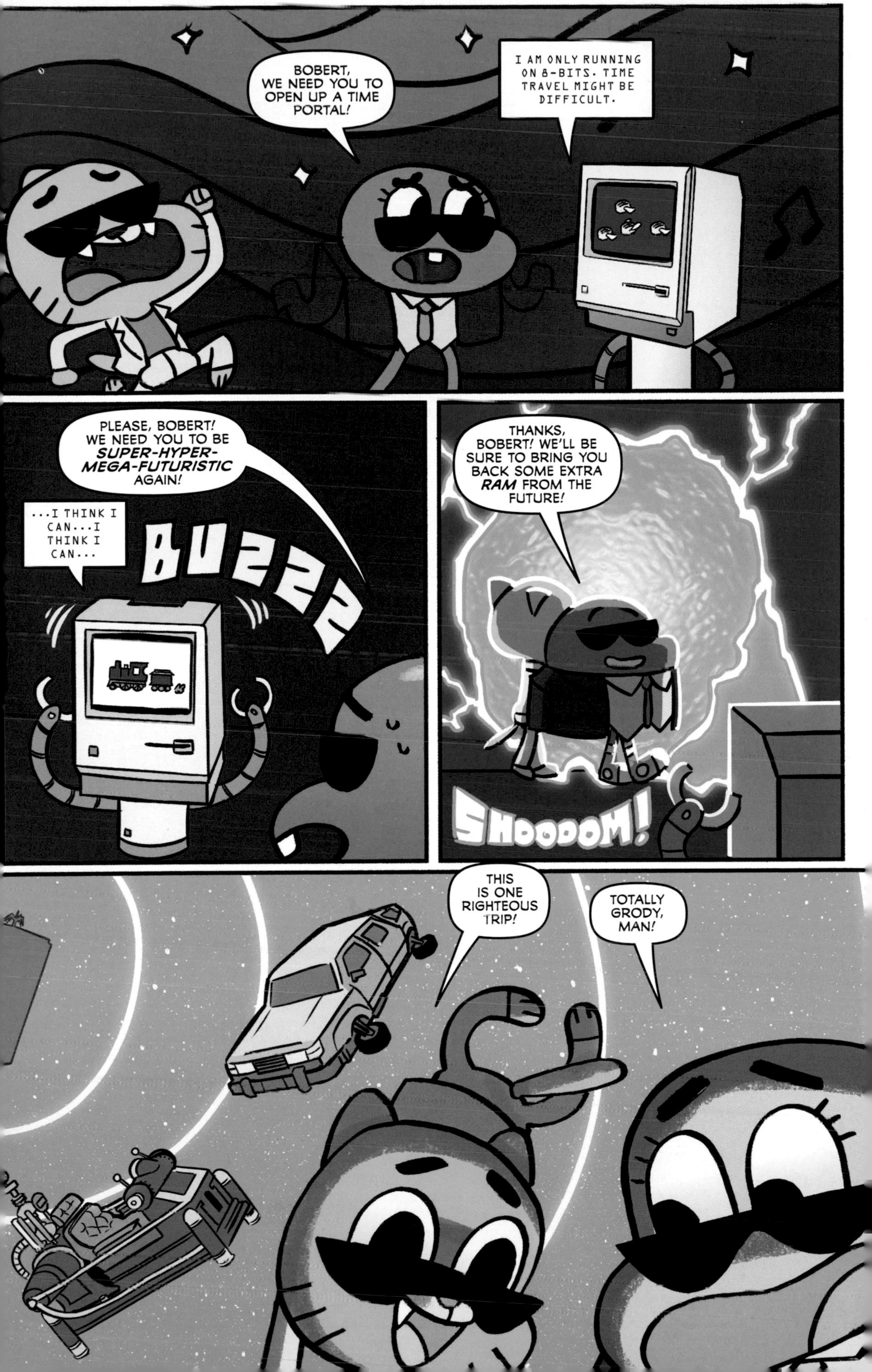
BOBERT, WE NEED YOU TO OPEN UP A TIME PORTAL!
I AM ONLY RUNNING ON 8-BITS. TIME TRAVEL MIGHT BE DIFFICULT.
PLEASE, BOBERT! WE NEED YOU TO BE *SUPER-HYPER-MEGA-FUTURISTIC* AGAIN!
...I THINK I CAN...I THINK I CAN...
BUZZZ
THANKS, BOBERT! WE'LL BE SURE TO BRING YOU BACK SOME EXTRA *RAM* FROM THE FUTURE!
SHOOOOM!
THIS IS ONE RIGHTEOUS TRIP!
TOTALLY GRODY, MAN!

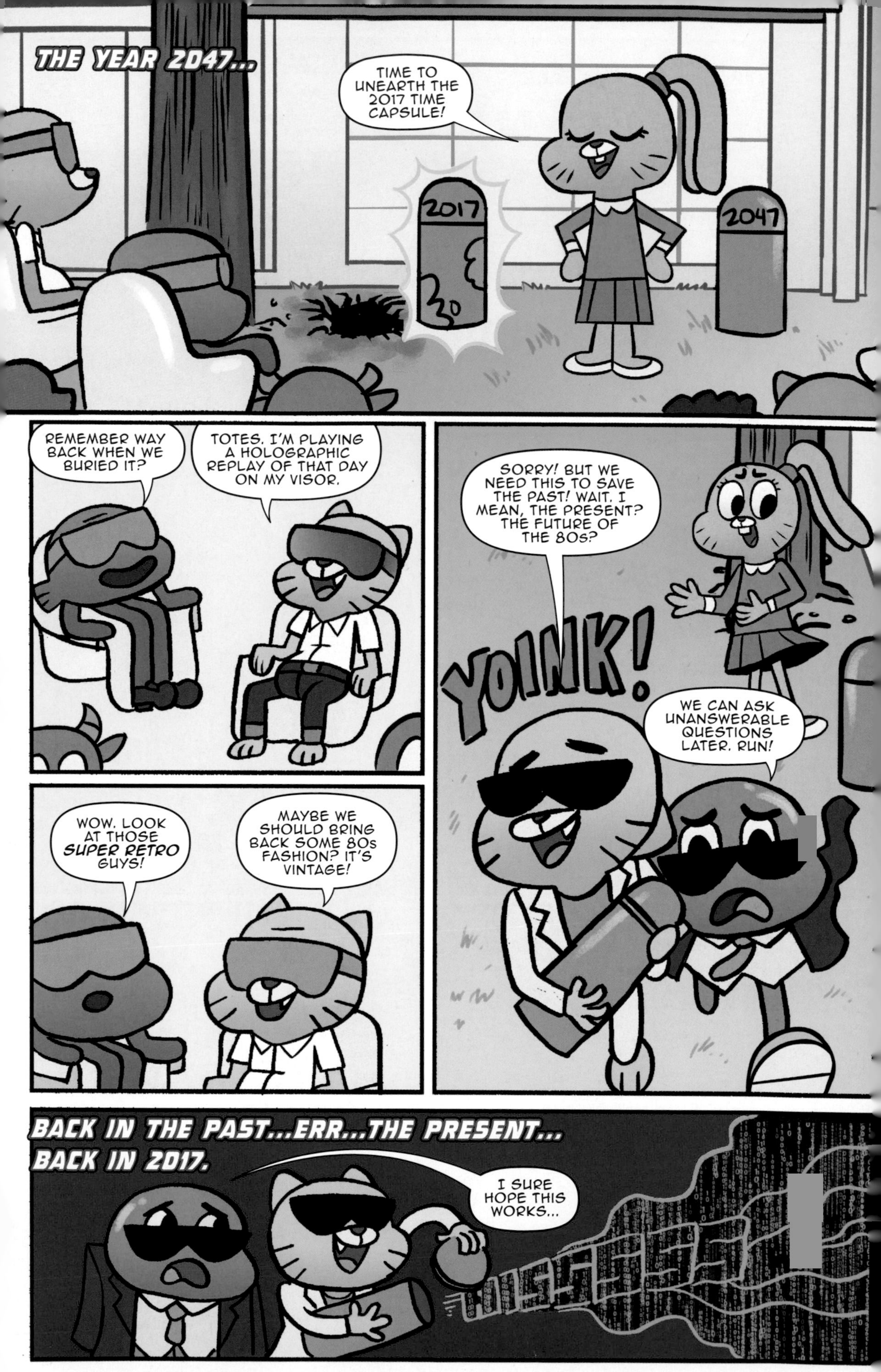
THE YEAR 2047...
TIME TO UNEARTH THE 2017 TIME CAPSULE!
2017
2047
REMEMBER WAY BACK WHEN WE BURIED IT?
TOTES. I'M PLAYING A HOLOGRAPHIC REPLAY OF THAT DAY ON MY VISOR.
WOW. LOOK AT THOSE SUPER RETRO GUYS!
MAYBE WE SHOULD BRING BACK SOME 80s FASHION? IT'S VINTAGE!
SORRY! BUT WE NEED THIS TO SAVE THE PAST! WAIT. I MEAN, THE PRESENT? THE FUTURE OF THE 80s?
YOINK!
WE CAN ASK UNANSWERABLE QUESTIONS LATER. RUN!
BACK IN THE PAST...ERR...THE PRESENT... BACK IN 2017.
I SURE HOPE THIS WORKS...

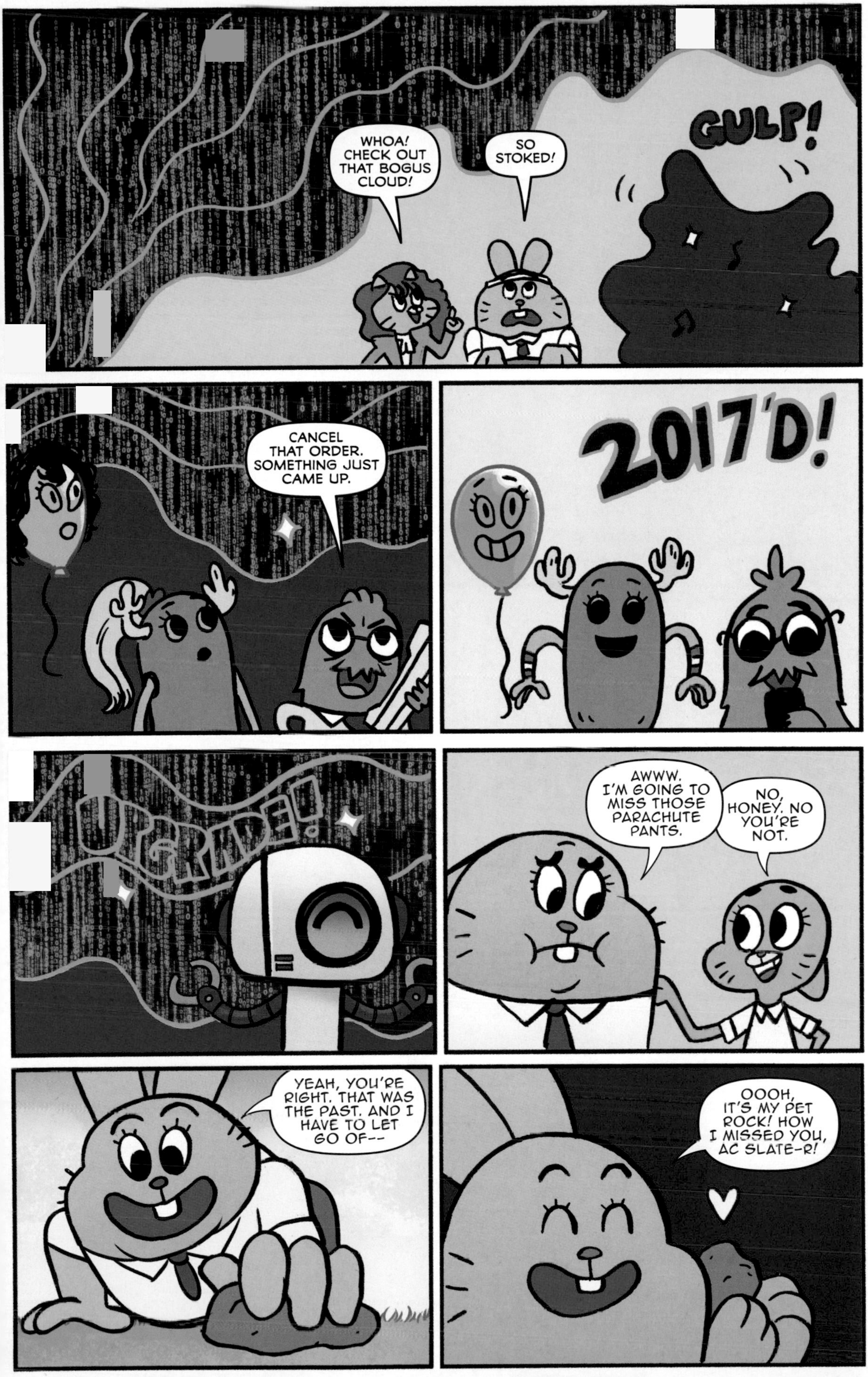
WHOA! CHECK OUT THAT BOGUS CLOUD!
SO STOKED!
GULP!
CANCEL THAT ORDER. SOMETHING JUST CAME UP.
2017'D!
AWWW. I'M GOING TO MISS THOSE PARACHUTE PANTS.
NO, HONEY. NO YOU'RE NOT.
YEAH, YOU'RE RIGHT. THAT WAS THE PAST. AND I HAVE TO LET GO OF--
OOOH, IT'S MY PET ROCK! HOW I MISSED YOU, AC SLATE-R!

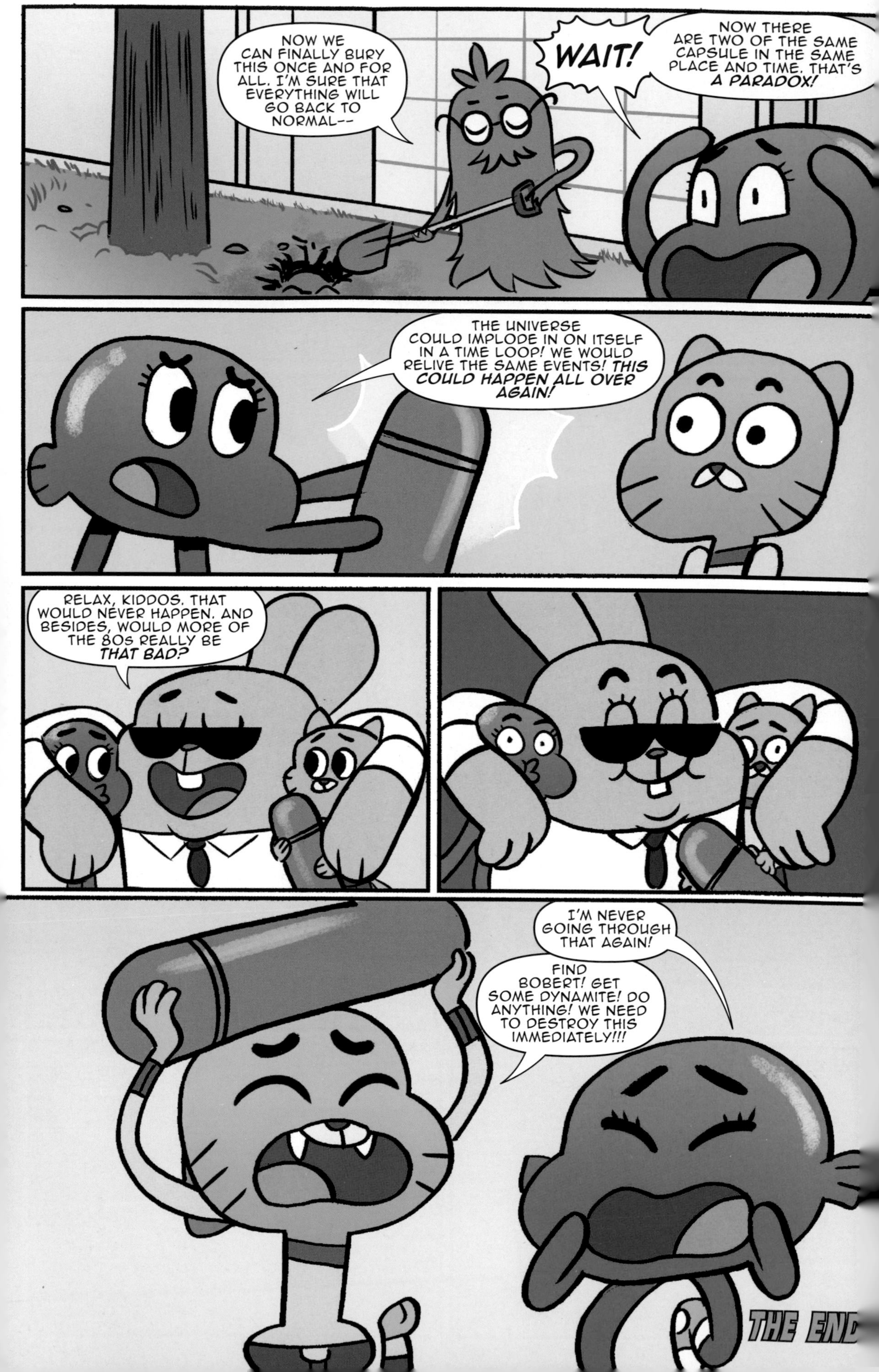

NOW WE CAN FINALLY BURY THIS ONCE AND FOR ALL. I'M SURE THAT EVERYTHING WILL GO BACK TO NORMAL--
WAIT!
NOW THERE ARE TWO OF THE SAME CAPSULE IN THE SAME PLACE AND TIME. THAT'S *A PARADOX!*
THE UNIVERSE COULD IMPLODE IN ON ITSELF IN A TIME LOOP! WE WOULD RELIVE THE SAME EVENTS! *THIS COULD HAPPEN ALL OVER AGAIN!*
RELAX, KIDDOS. THAT WOULD NEVER HAPPEN. AND BESIDES, WOULD MORE OF THE 80s REALLY BE *THAT BAD?*
I'M NEVER GOING THROUGH THAT AGAIN!
FIND BOBERT! GET SOME DYNAMITE! DO ANYTHING! WE NEED TO DESTROY THIS IMMEDIATELY!!!
THE END

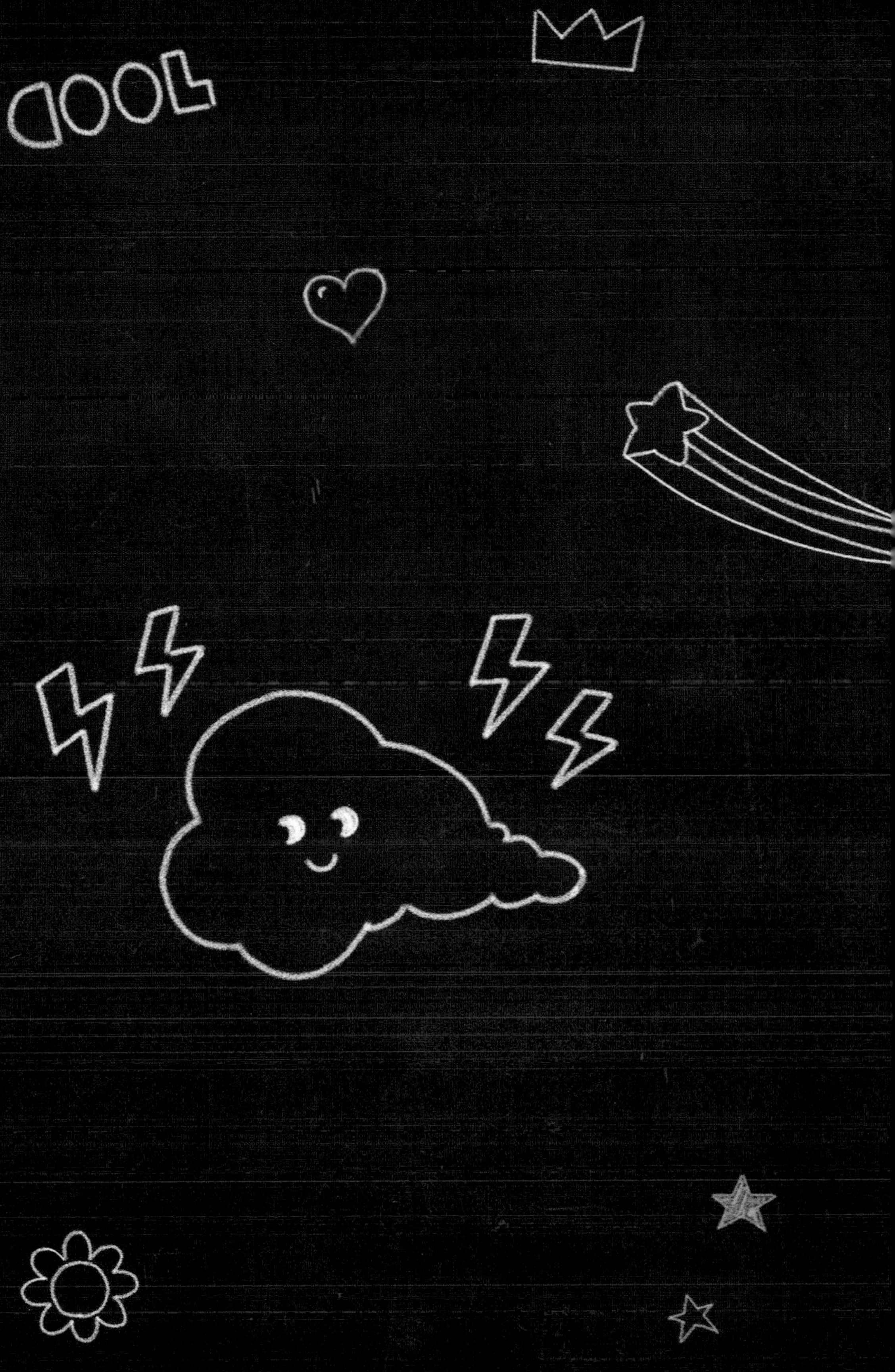
COOL

CARRIE'S BODY

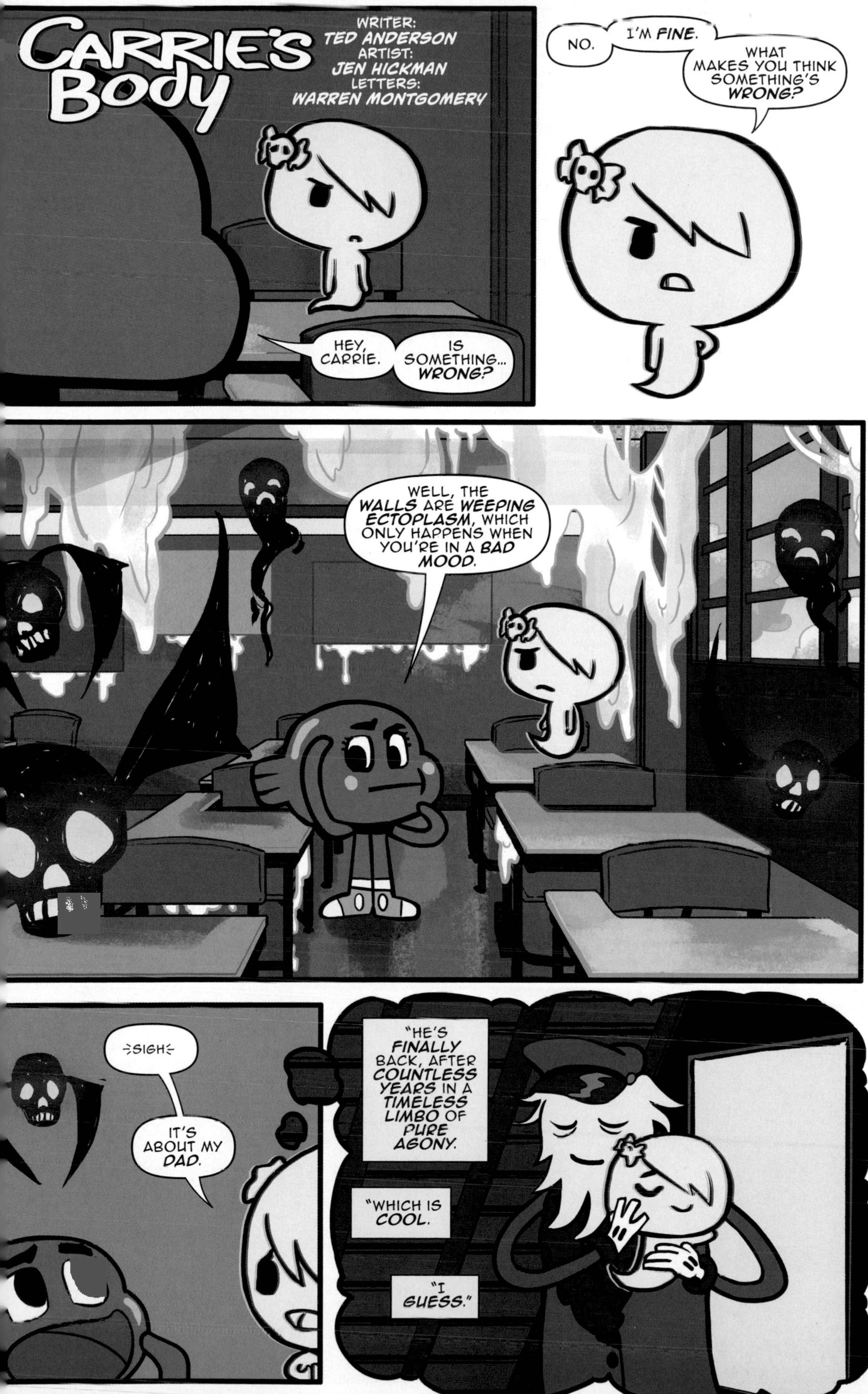
CARRIE'S Body
WRITER: TED ANDERSON
ARTIST: JEN HICKMAN
LETTERS: WARREN MONTGOMERY
HEY, CARRIE.
IS SOMETHING... WRONG?
NO.
I'M FINE.
WHAT MAKES YOU THINK SOMETHING'S WRONG?
WELL, THE WALLS ARE WEEPING ECTOPLASM, WHICH ONLY HAPPENS WHEN YOU'RE IN A BAD MOOD.
SIGH
IT'S ABOUT MY DAD.
"HE'S FINALLY BACK, AFTER COUNTLESS YEARS IN A TIMELESS LIMBO OF PURE AGONY.
"WHICH IS COOL.
"I GUESS."

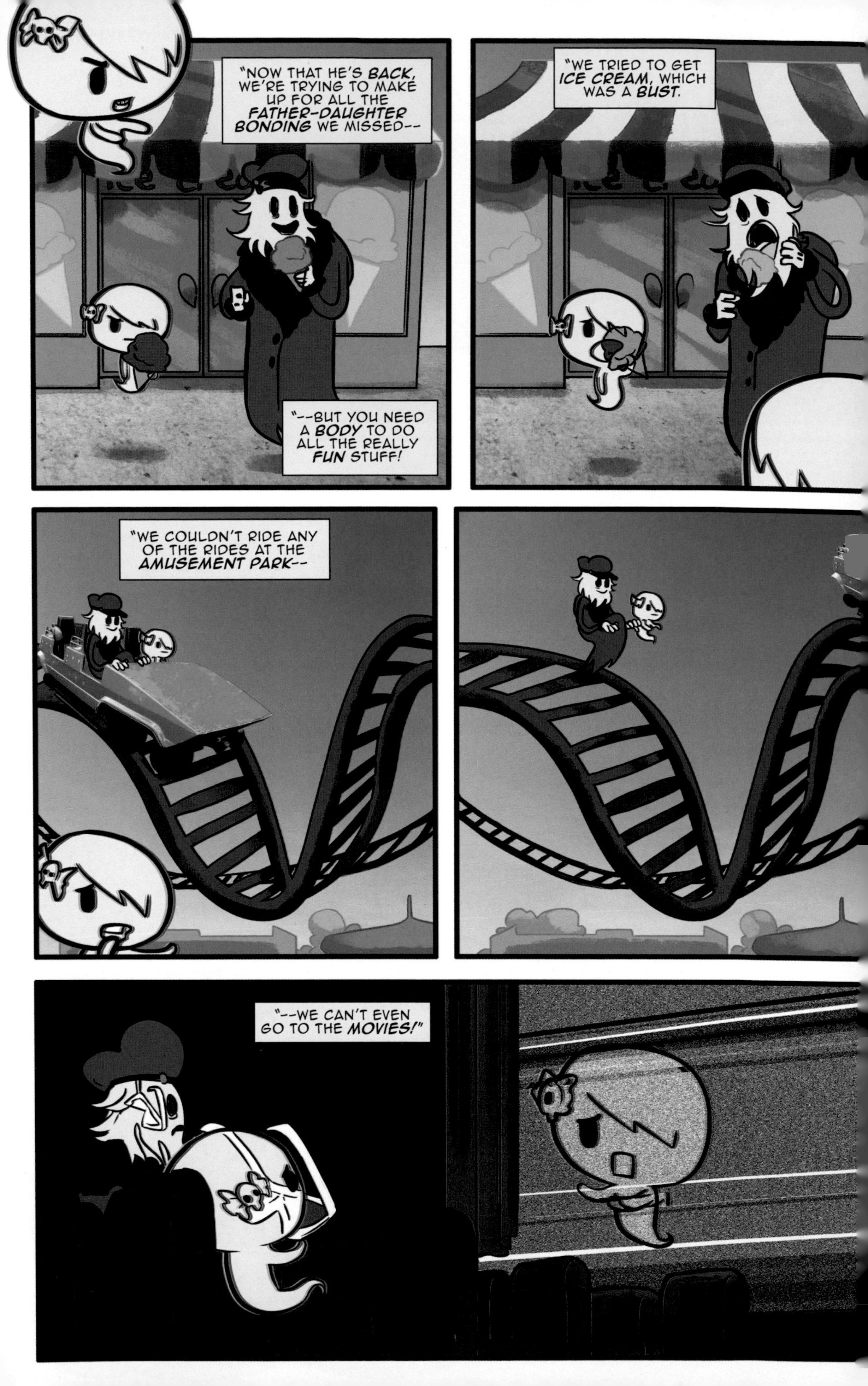
"NOW THAT HE'S BACK, WE'RE TRYING TO MAKE UP FOR ALL THE FATHER-DAUGHTER BONDING WE MISSED--
"--BUT YOU NEED A BODY TO DO ALL THE REALLY FUN STUFF!
"WE TRIED TO GET ICE CREAM, WHICH WAS A BUST.
"WE COULDN'T RIDE ANY OF THE RIDES AT THE AMUSEMENT PARK--
"--WE CAN'T EVEN GO TO THE MOVIES!"

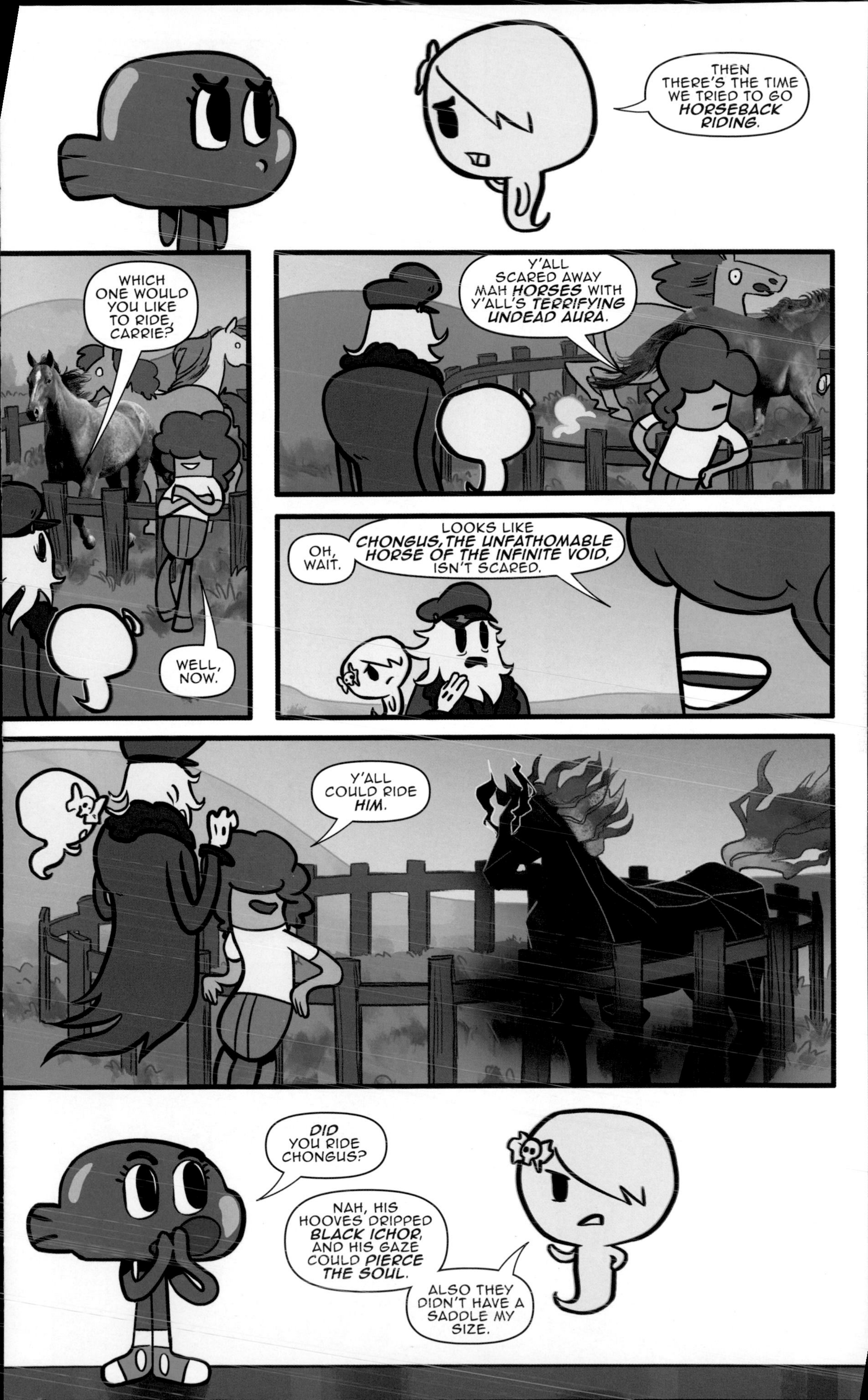

THEN THERE'S THE TIME WE TRIED TO GO HORSEBACK RIDING.
WHICH ONE WOULD YOU LIKE TO RIDE, CARRIE?
WELL, NOW.
Y'ALL SCARED AWAY MAH HORSES WITH Y'ALL'S TERRIFYING UNDEAD AURA.
OH, WAIT.
LOOKS LIKE CHONGUS, THE UNFATHOMABLE HORSE OF THE INFINITE VOID, ISN'T SCARED.
Y'ALL COULD RIDE HIM.
DID YOU RIDE CHONGUS?
NAH, HIS HOOVES DRIPPED BLACK ICHOR, AND HIS GAZE COULD PIERCE THE SOUL.
ALSO THEY DIDN'T HAVE A SADDLE MY SIZE.

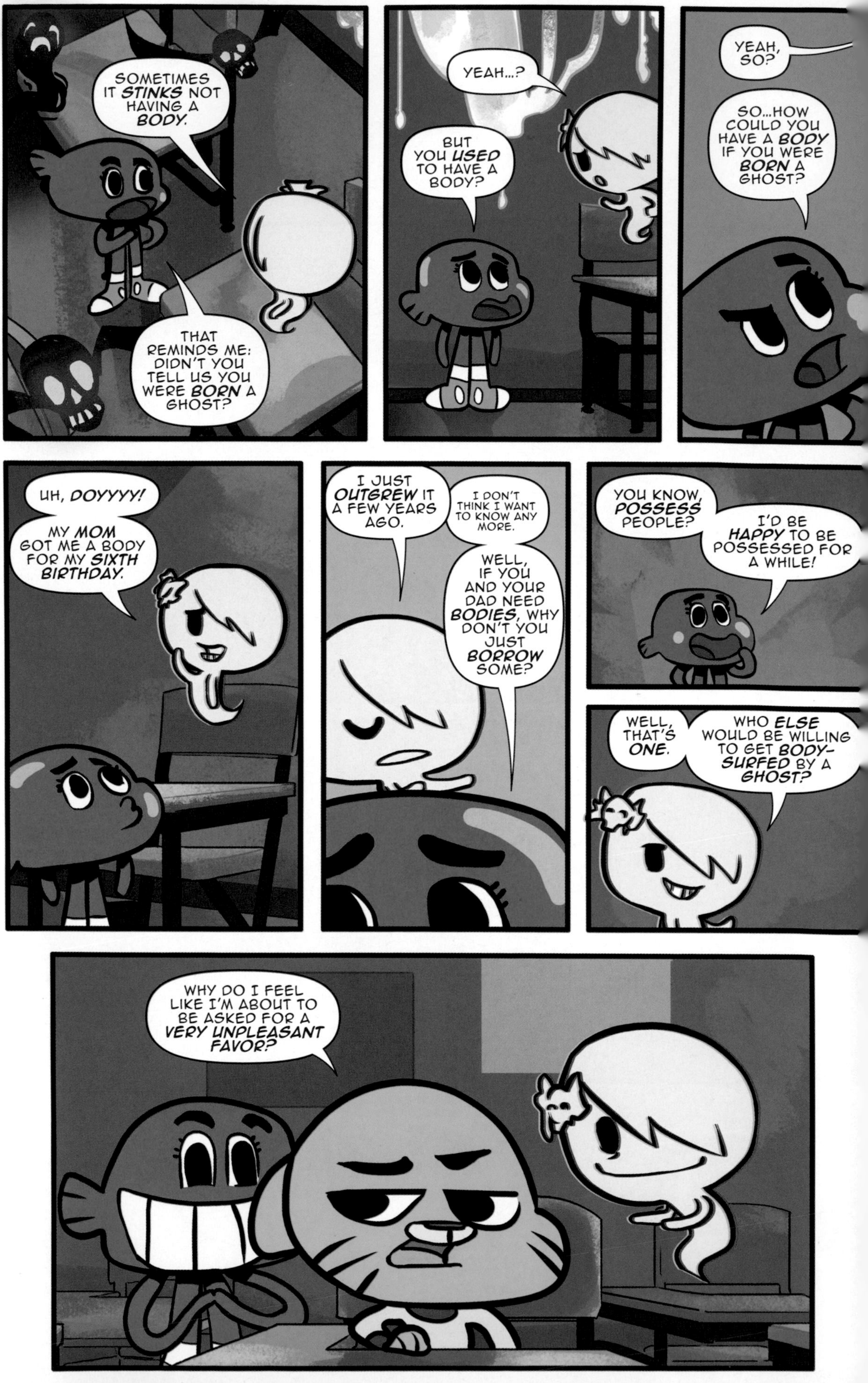
SOMETIMES IT STINKS NOT HAVING A BODY.
THAT REMINDS ME: DIDN'T YOU TELL US YOU WERE BORN A GHOST?
YEAH...?
BUT YOU USED TO HAVE A BODY?
YEAH, SO?
SO...HOW COULD YOU HAVE A BODY IF YOU WERE BORN A GHOST?
UH, DOYYYY!
MY MOM GOT ME A BODY FOR MY SIXTH BIRTHDAY.
I JUST OUTGREW IT A FEW YEARS AGO.
I DON'T THINK I WANT TO KNOW ANY MORE.
WELL, IF YOU AND YOUR DAD NEED BODIES, WHY DON'T YOU JUST BORROW SOME?
YOU KNOW, POSSESS PEOPLE?
I'D BE HAPPY TO BE POSSESSED FOR A WHILE!
WELL, THAT'S ONE.
WHO ELSE WOULD BE WILLING TO GET BODY-SURFED BY A GHOST?
WHY DO I FEEL LIKE I'M ABOUT TO BE ASKED FOR A VERY UNPLEASANT FAVOR?

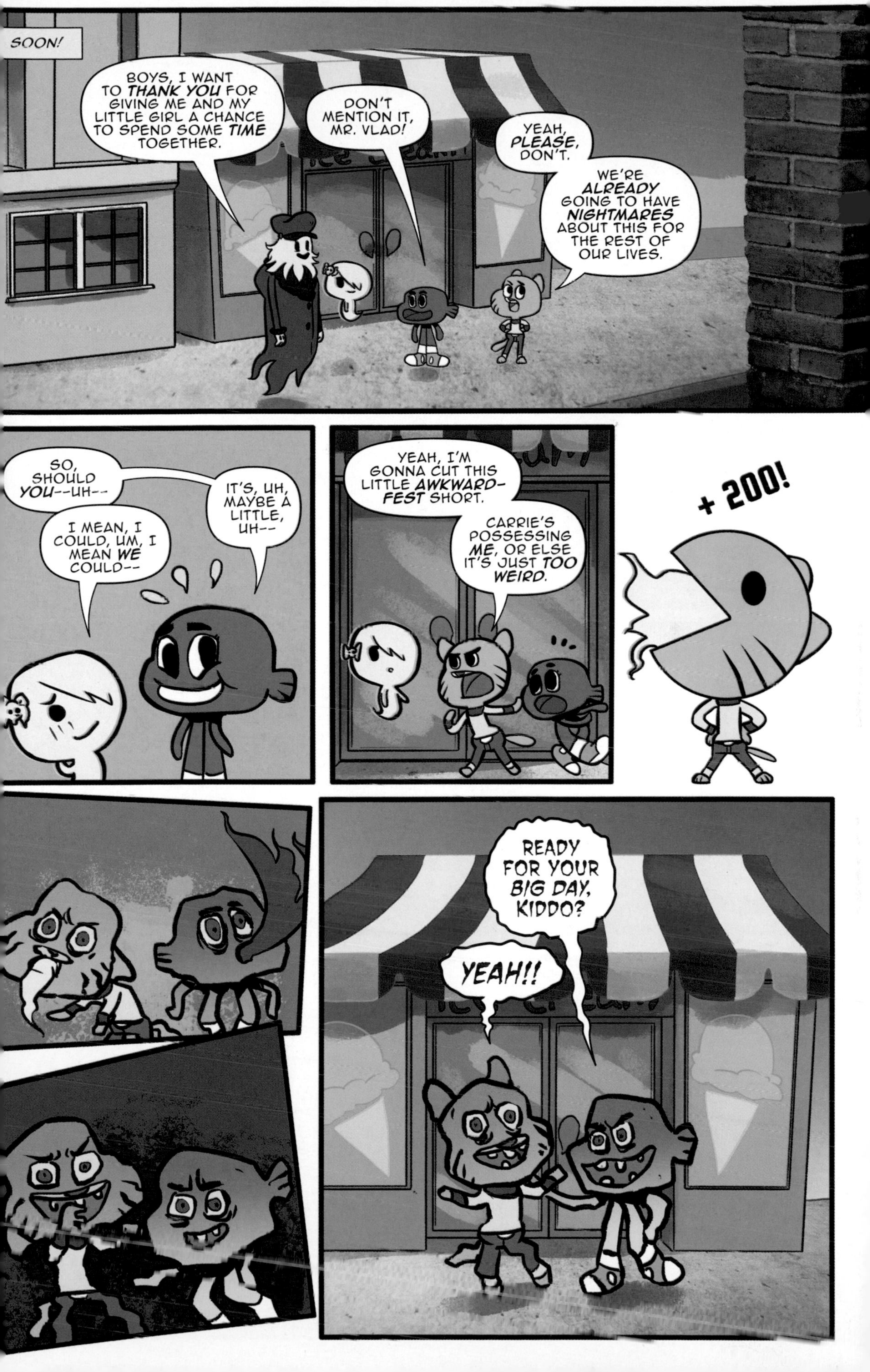
SOON!
BOYS, I WANT TO THANK YOU FOR GIVING ME AND MY LITTLE GIRL A CHANCE TO SPEND SOME TIME TOGETHER.
DON'T MENTION IT, MR. VLAD!
YEAH, PLEASE, DON'T.
WE'RE ALREADY GOING TO HAVE NIGHTMARES ABOUT THIS FOR THE REST OF OUR LIVES.
SO, SHOULD YOU--UH--
IT'S, UH, MAYBE A LITTLE, UH--
I MEAN, I COULD, UM, I MEAN WE COULD--
YEAH, I'M GONNA CUT THIS LITTLE AWKWARD-FEST SHORT.
CARRIE'S POSSESSING ME, OR ELSE IT'S JUST TOO WEIRD.
+ 200!
READY FOR YOUR BIG DAY, KIDDO?
YEAH!!

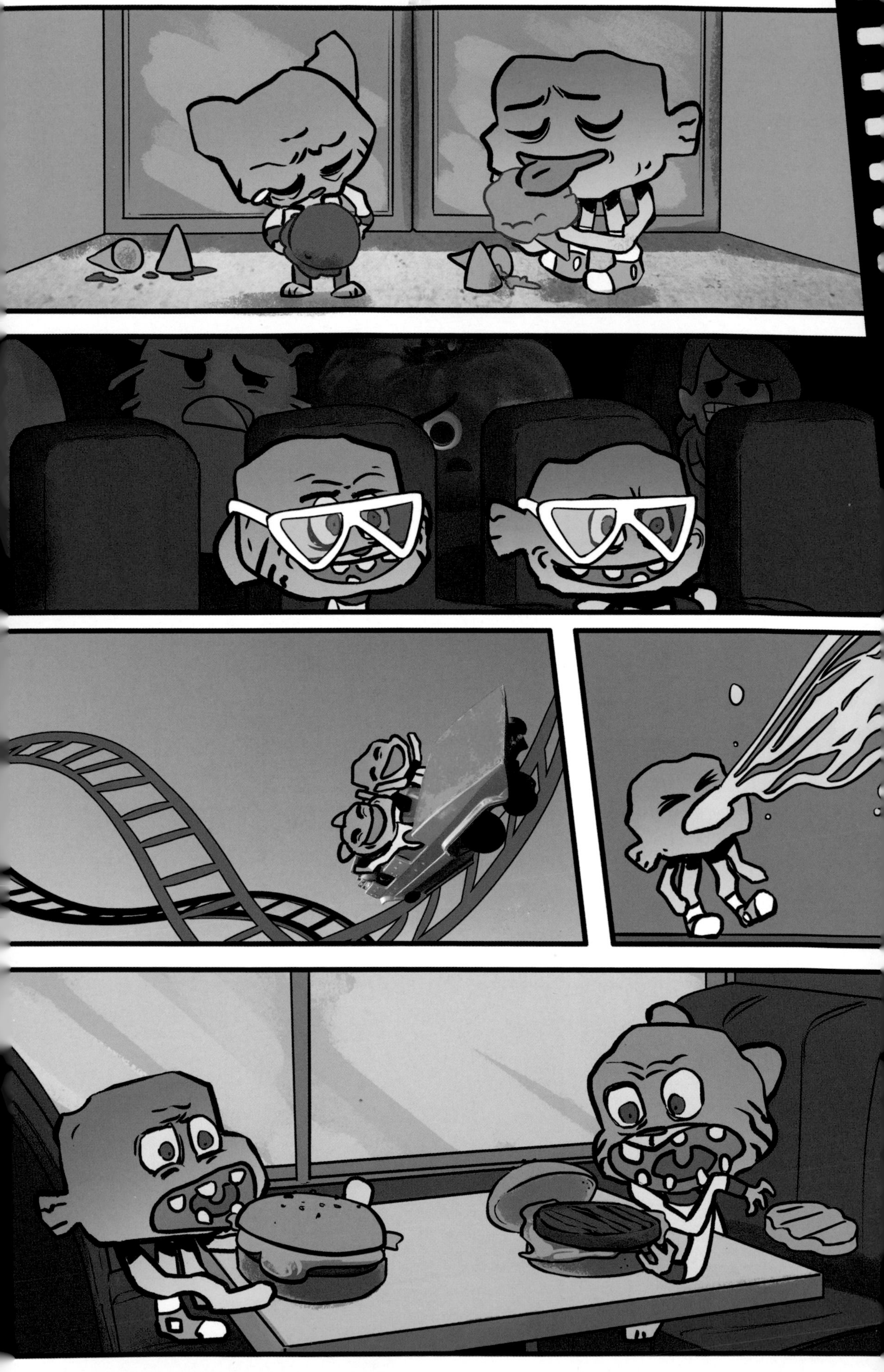

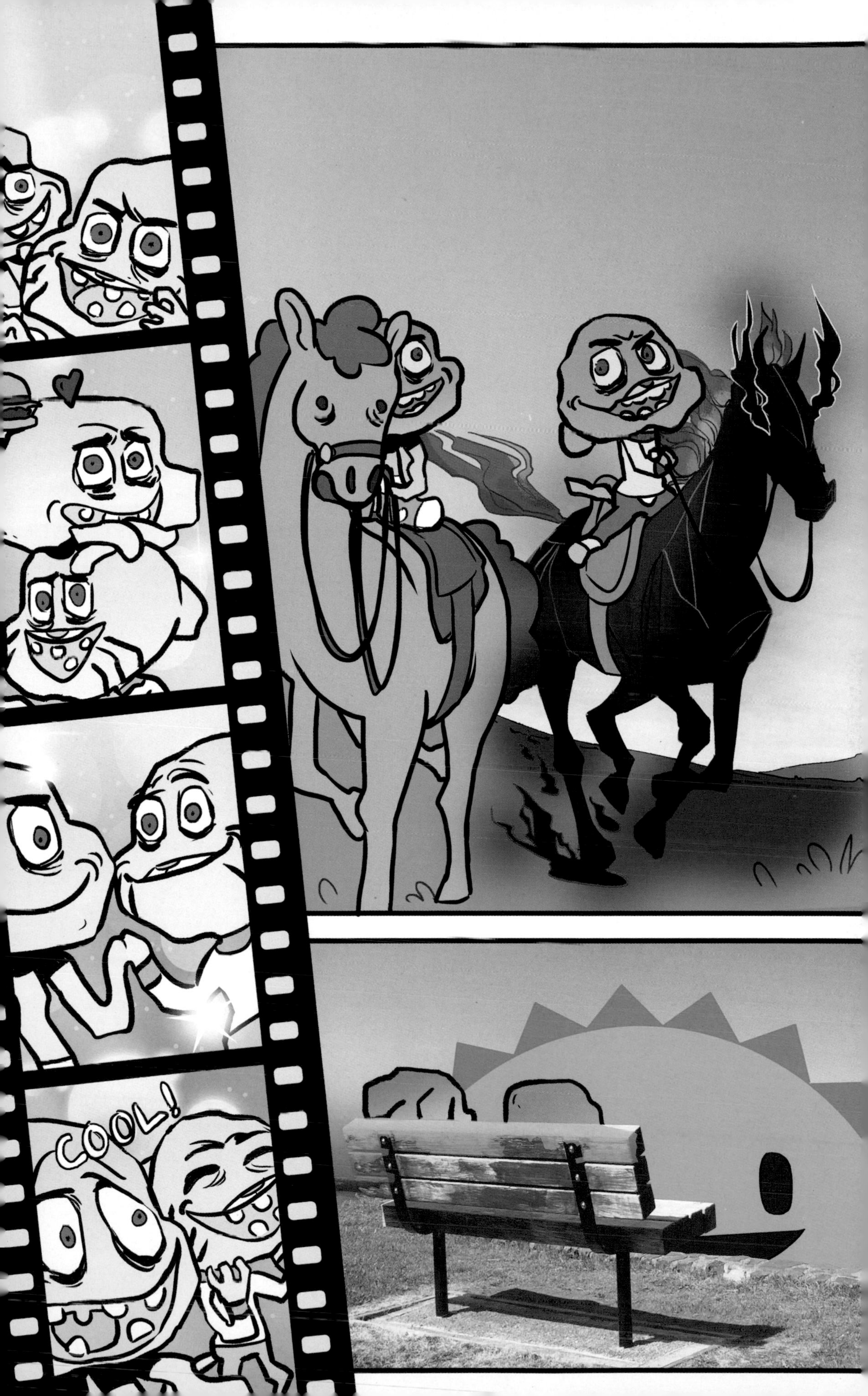
COOL!

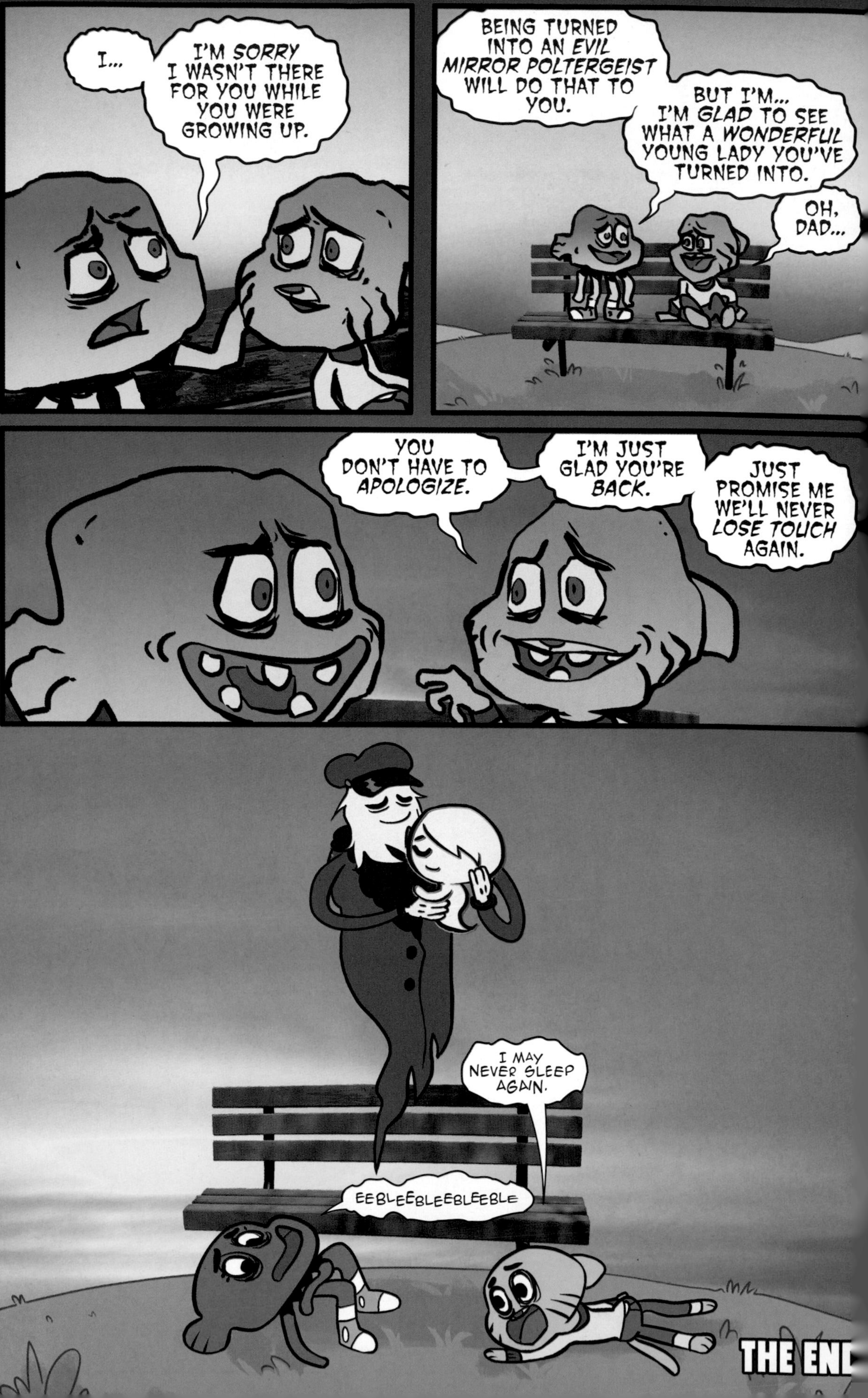
I...
I'M SORRY I WASN'T THERE FOR YOU WHILE YOU WERE GROWING UP.
BEING TURNED INTO AN EVIL MIRROR POLTERGEIST WILL DO THAT TO YOU.
BUT I'M... I'M GLAD TO SEE WHAT A WONDERFUL YOUNG LADY YOU'VE TURNED INTO.
OH, DAD...
YOU DON'T HAVE TO APOLOGIZE.
I'M JUST GLAD YOU'RE BACK.
JUST PROMISE ME WE'LL NEVER LOSE TOUCH AGAIN.
I MAY NEVER SLEEP AGAIN.
EEBLEEBLEEBLEEBLE
THE END

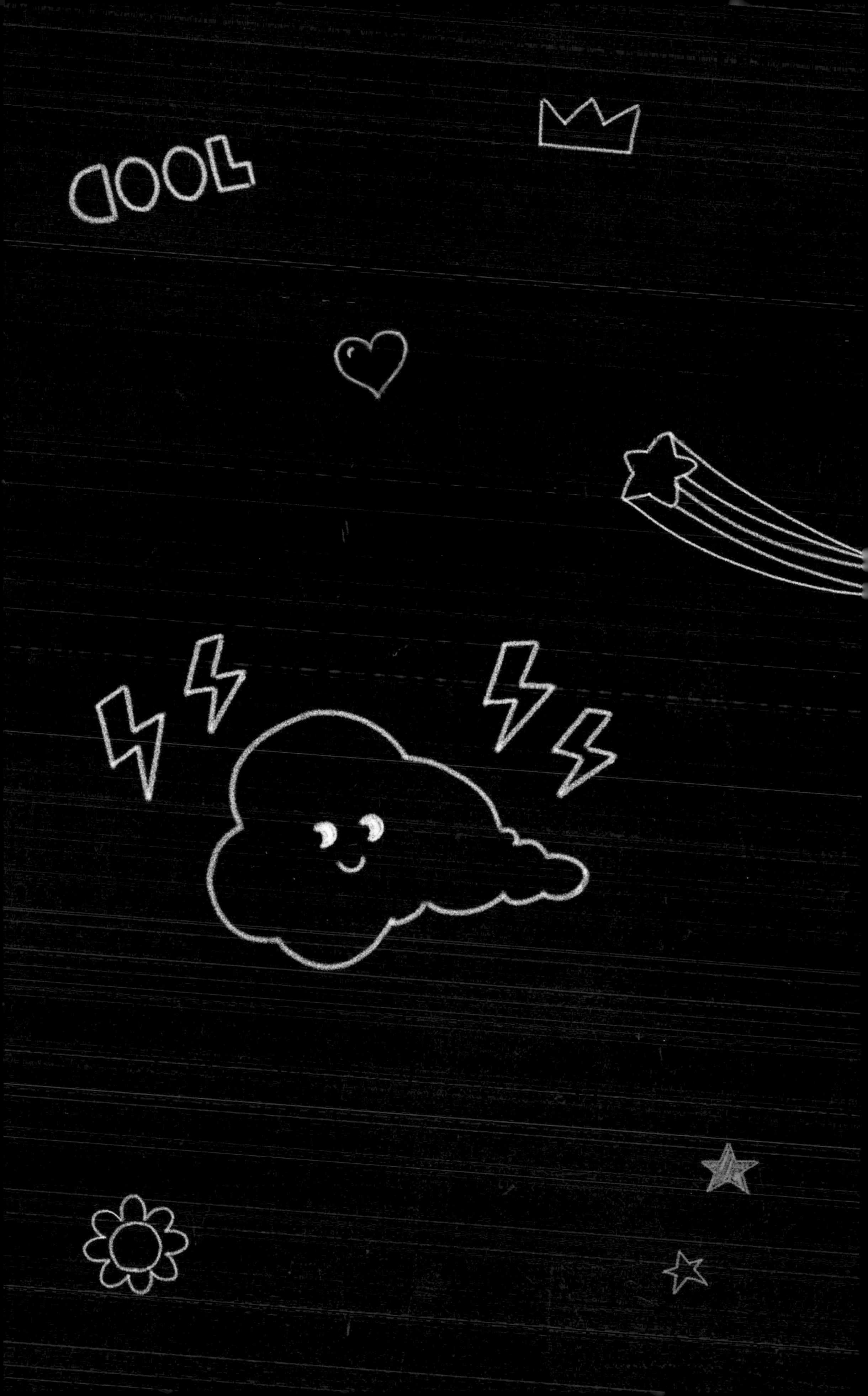
COOL

SNOW CLOSE, YETTI SO FAR

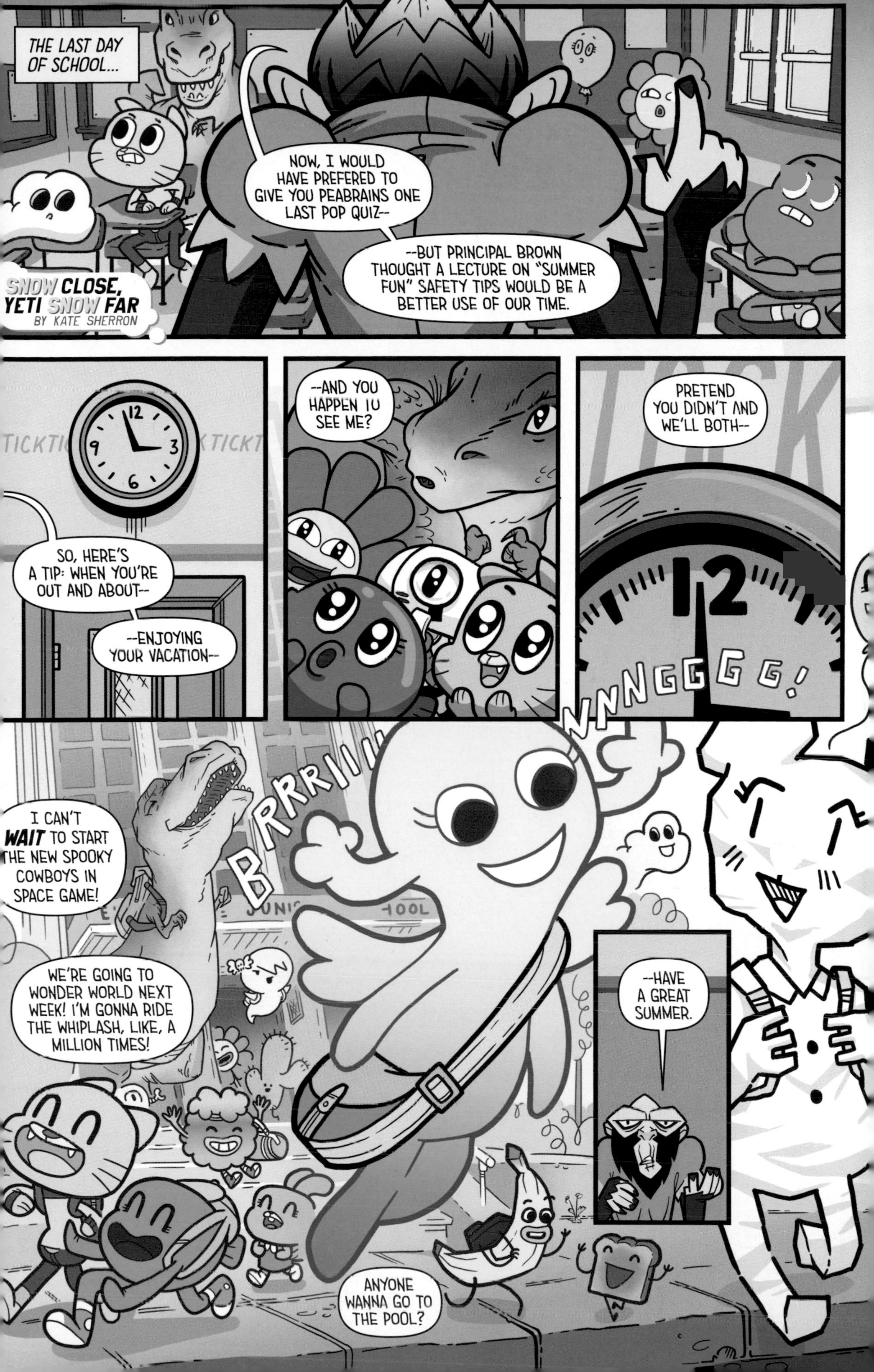
THE LAST DAY OF SCHOOL...
NOW, I WOULD HAVE PREFERED TO GIVE YOU PEABRAINS ONE LAST POP QUIZ--
--BUT PRINCIPAL BROWN THOUGHT A LECTURE ON "SUMMER FUN" SAFETY TIPS WOULD BE A BETTER USE OF OUR TIME.
SNOW CLOSE, YETI SNOW FAR
BY KATE SHERRON
TICKTICKTICKT
SO, HERE'S A TIP: WHEN YOU'RE OUT AND ABOUT--
--ENJOYING YOUR VACATION--
--AND YOU HAPPEN TO SEE ME?
PRETEND YOU DIDN'T AND WE'LL BOTH--
BRRRIIINNNGGGGG!
I CAN'T WAIT TO START THE NEW SPOOKY COWBOYS IN SPACE GAME!
WE'RE GOING TO WONDER WORLD NEXT WEEK! I'M GONNA RIDE THE WHIPLASH, LIKE, A MILLION TIMES!
--HAVE A GREAT SUMMER.
ANYONE WANNA GO TO THE POOL?

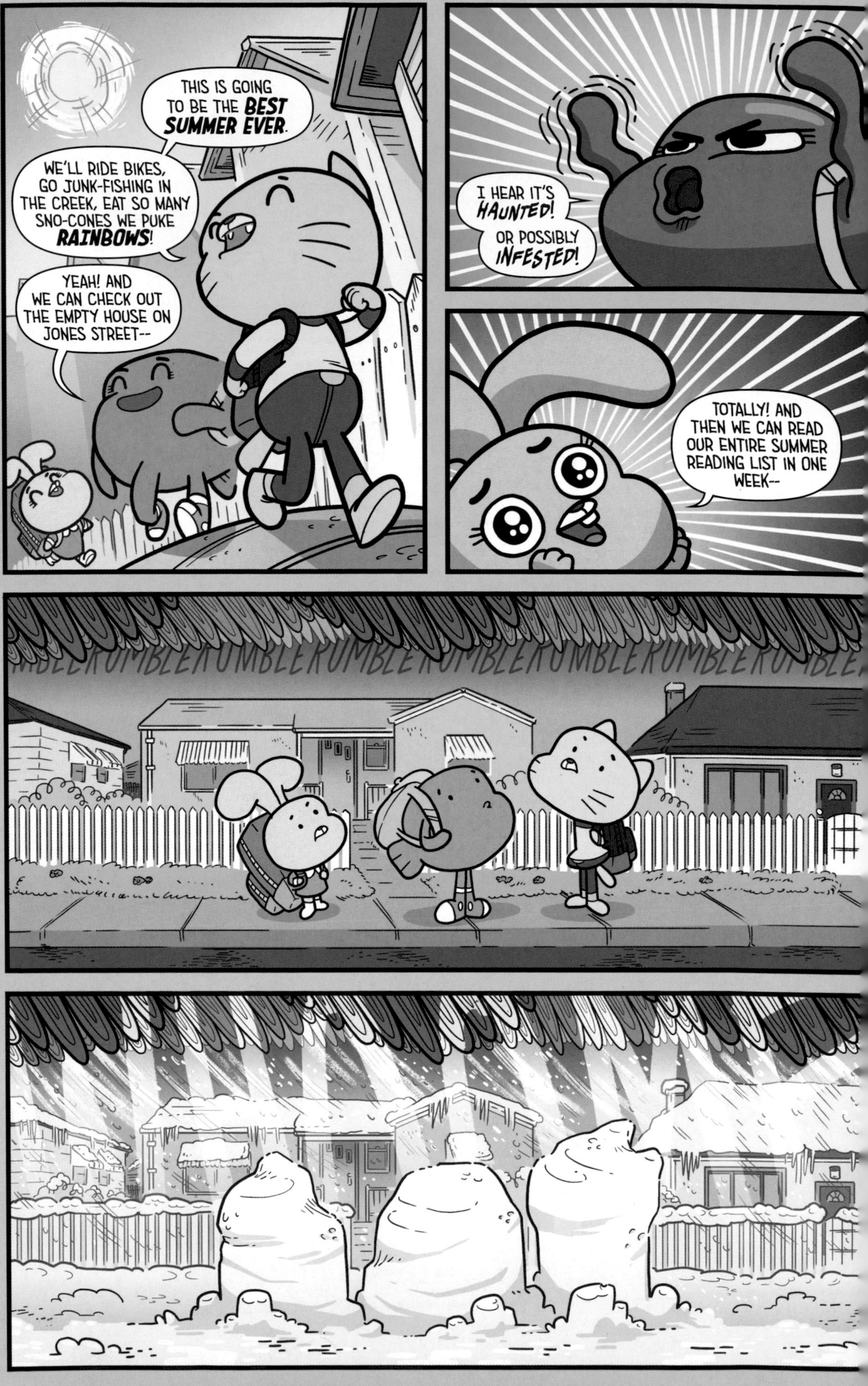
THIS IS GOING TO BE THE BEST SUMMER EVER.
WE'LL RIDE BIKES, GO JUNK-FISHING IN THE CREEK, EAT SO MANY SNO-CONES WE PUKE RAINBOWS!
YEAH! AND WE CAN CHECK OUT THE EMPTY HOUSE ON JONES STREET--
I HEAR IT'S HAUNTED!
OR POSSIBLY INFESTED!
TOTALLY! AND THEN WE CAN READ OUR ENTIRE SUMMER READING LIST IN ONE WEEK--
RUMBLERUMBLERUMBLERUMBLE

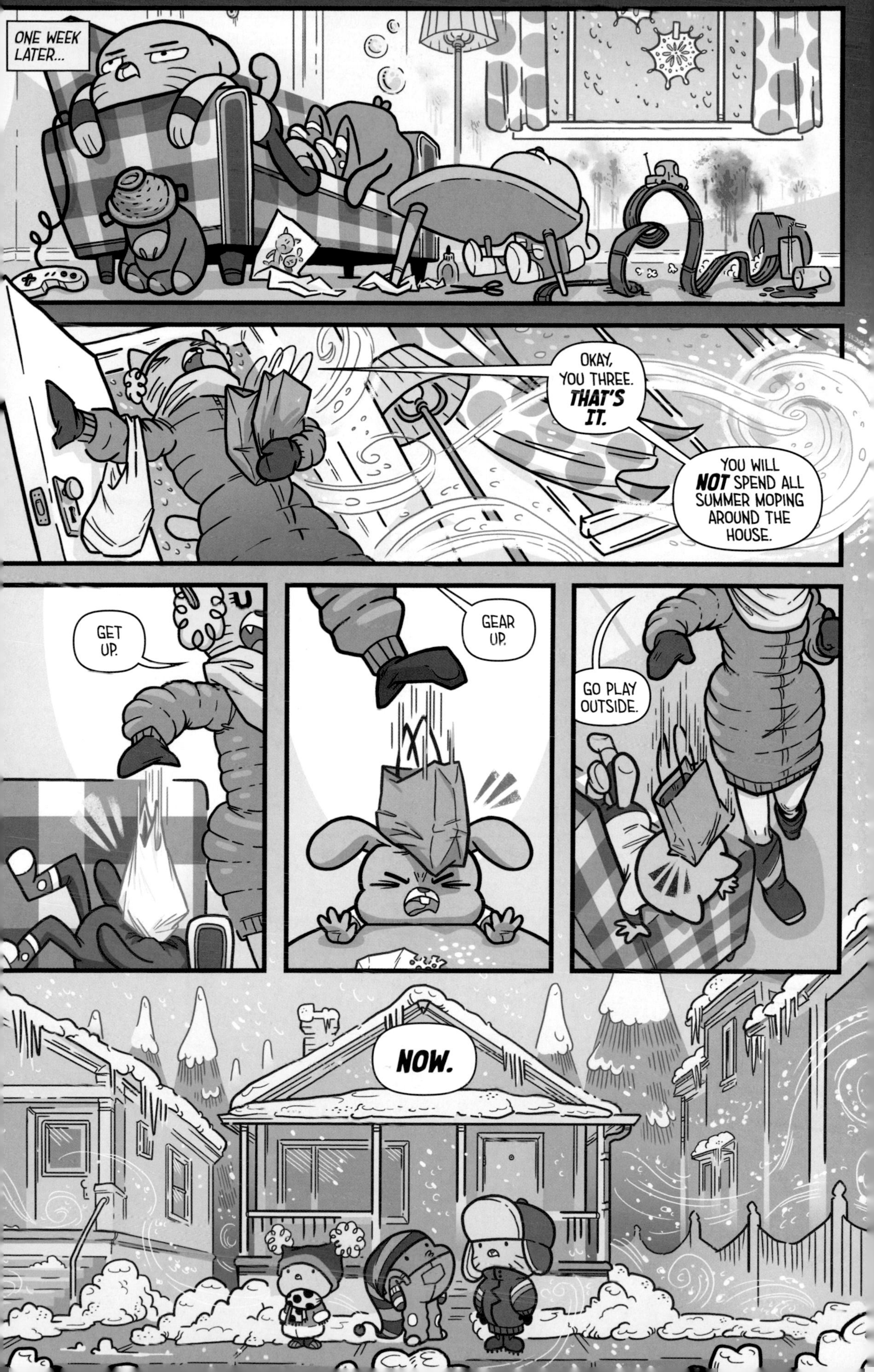
ONE WEEK LATER...
OKAY, YOU THREE. THAT'S IT.
YOU WILL NOT SPEND ALL SUMMER MOPING AROUND THE HOUSE.
GET UP.
GEAR UP.
GO PLAY OUTSIDE.
NOW.

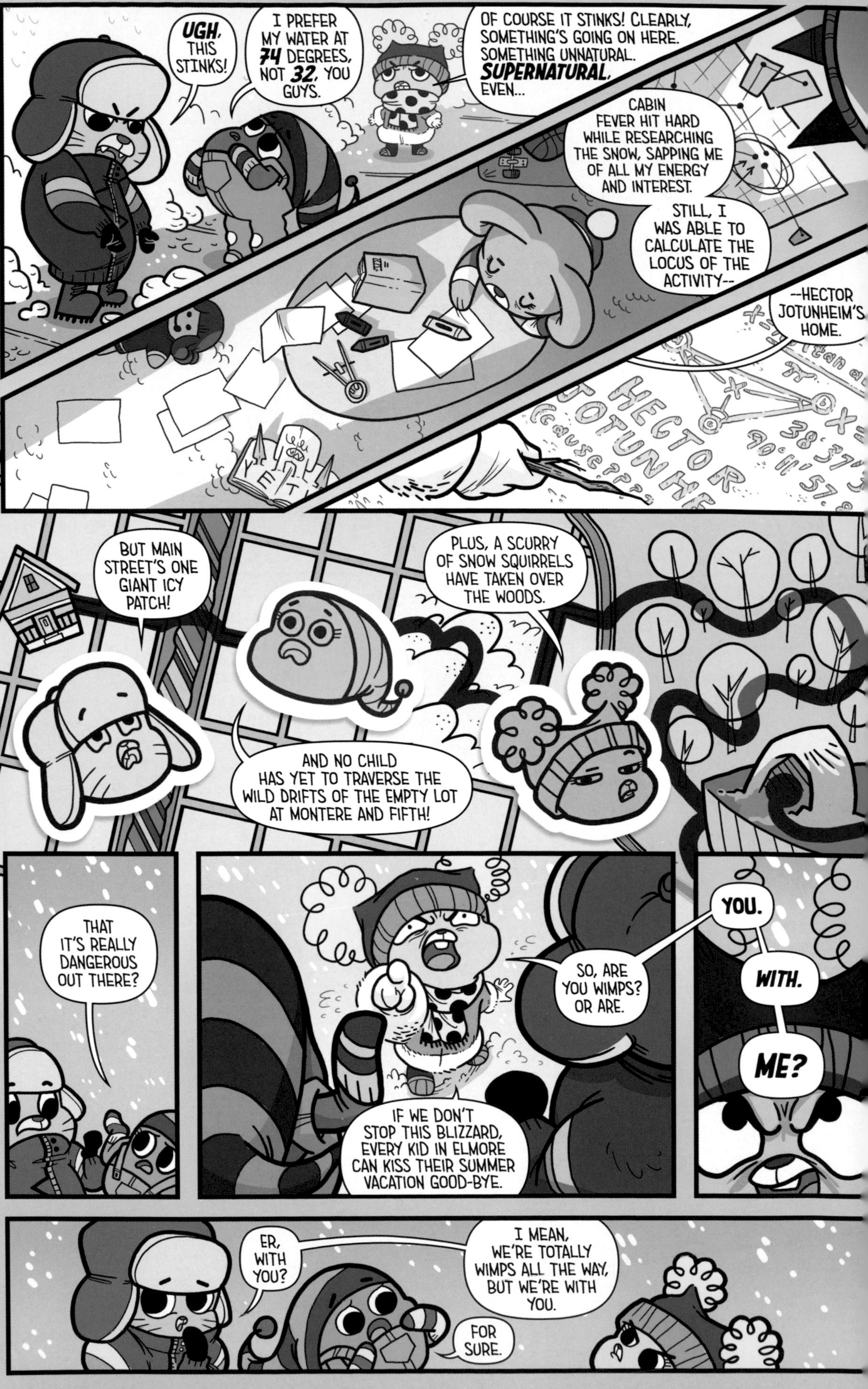

UGH, THIS STINKS!
I PREFER MY WATER AT 74 DEGREES, NOT 32, YOU GUYS.
OF COURSE IT STINKS! CLEARLY, SOMETHING'S GOING ON HERE. SOMETHING UNNATURAL. SUPERNATURAL, EVEN...
CABIN FEVER HIT HARD WHILE RESEARCHING THE SNOW, SAPPING ME OF ALL MY ENERGY AND INTEREST.
STILL, I WAS ABLE TO CALCULATE THE LOCUS OF THE ACTIVITY--
--HECTOR JOTUNHEIM'S HOME.
BUT MAIN STREET'S ONE GIANT ICY PATCH!
PLUS, A SCURRY OF SNOW SQUIRRELS HAVE TAKEN OVER THE WOODS.
AND NO CHILD HAS YET TO TRAVERSE THE WILD DRIFTS OF THE EMPTY LOT AT MONTERE AND FIFTH!
THAT IT'S REALLY DANGEROUS OUT THERE?
SO, ARE YOU WIMPS? OR ARE.
YOU.
WITH.
ME?
IF WE DON'T STOP THIS BLIZZARD, EVERY KID IN ELMORE CAN KISS THEIR SUMMER VACATION GOOD-BYE.
ER, WITH YOU?
I MEAN, WE'RE TOTALLY WIMPS ALL THE WAY, BUT WE'RE WITH YOU.
FOR SURE.

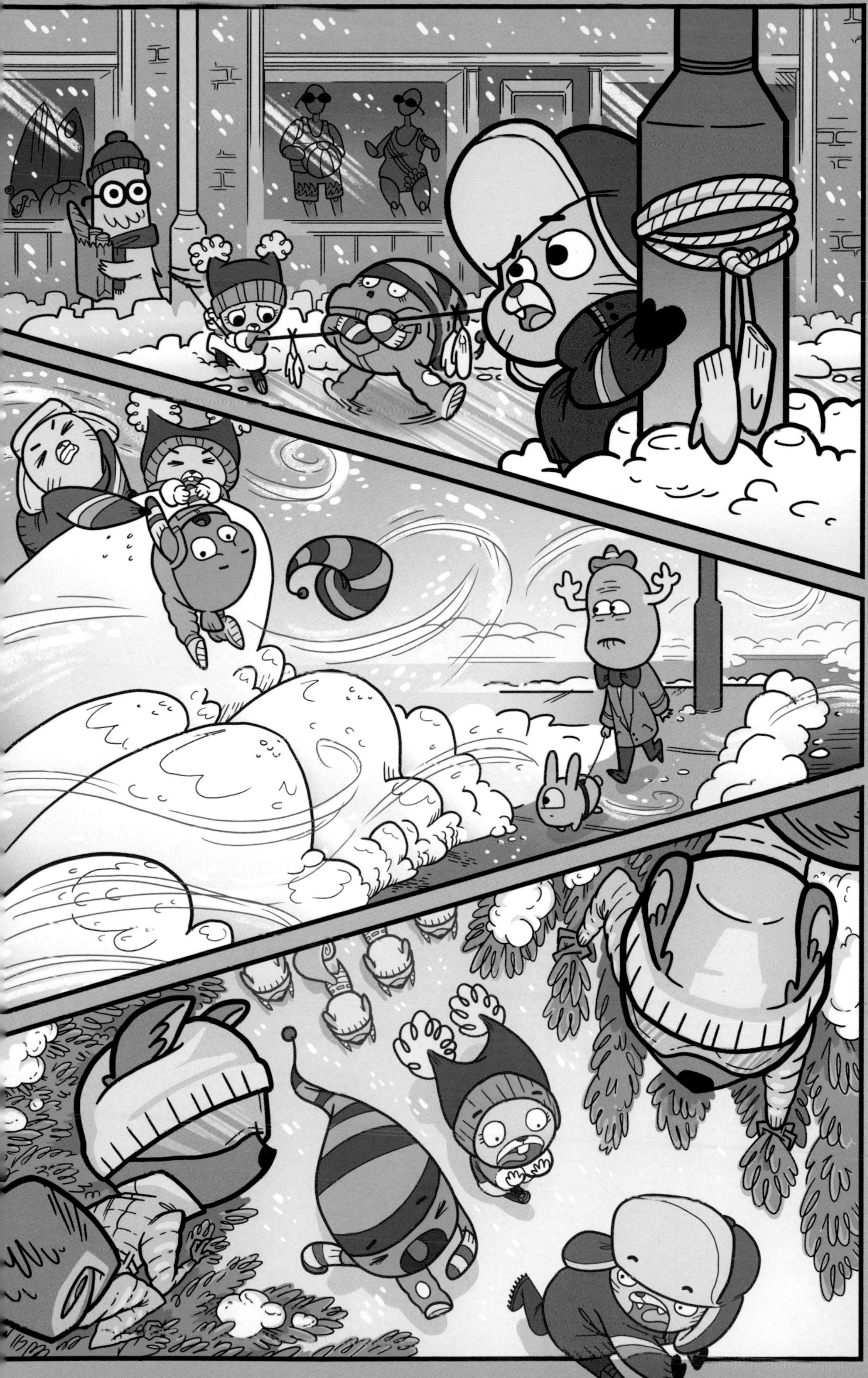

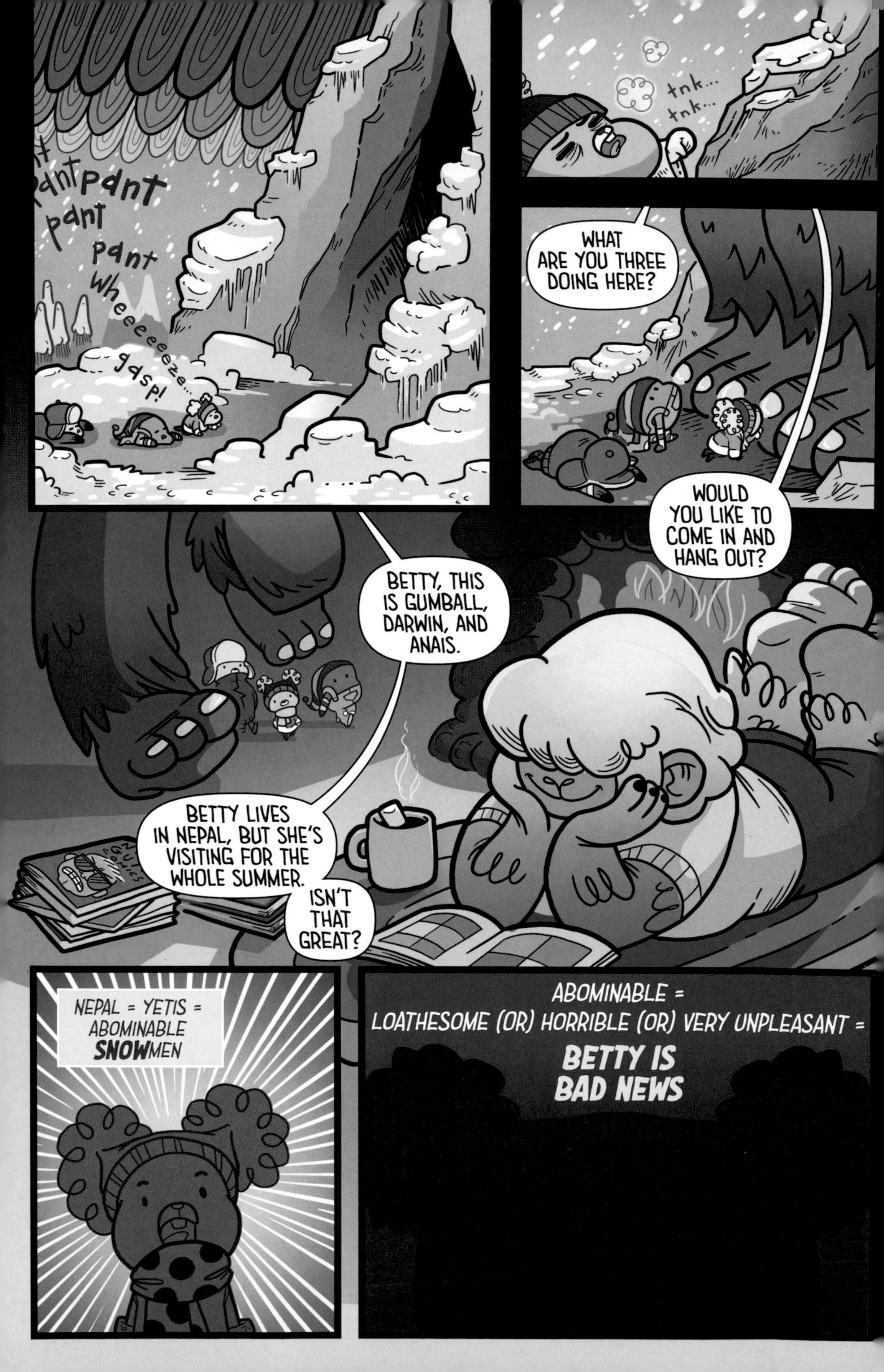
pant pant pant pant
wheeeeeeeeze...
gasp!
tnk... tnk...
WHAT ARE YOU THREE DOING HERE?
WOULD YOU LIKE TO COME IN AND HANG OUT?
BETTY, THIS IS GUMBALL, DARWIN, AND ANAIS.
BETTY LIVES IN NEPAL, BUT SHE'S VISITING FOR THE WHOLE SUMMER.
ISN'T THAT GREAT?
NEPAL = YETIS = ABOMINABLE SNOWMEN
ABOMINABLE = LOATHESOME (OR) HORRIBLE (OR) VERY UNPLEASANT =
BETTY IS BAD NEWS

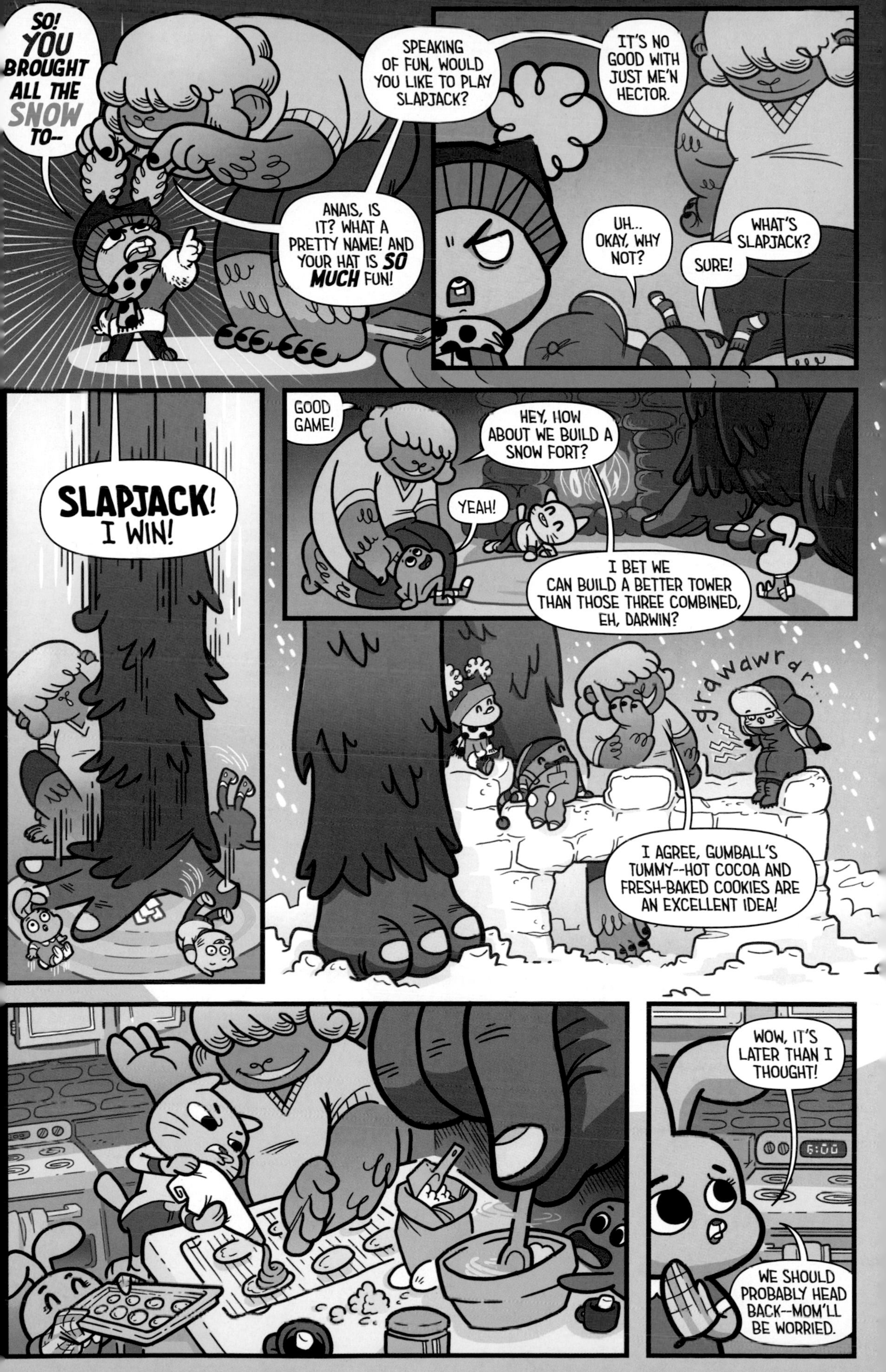
SO! YOU BROUGHT ALL THE SNOW TO--
SPEAKING OF FUN, WOULD YOU LIKE TO PLAY SLAPJACK?
ANAIS, IS IT? WHAT A PRETTY NAME! AND YOUR HAT IS SO MUCH FUN!
IT'S NO GOOD WITH JUST ME'N HECTOR.
UH... OKAY, WHY NOT?
WHAT'S SLAPJACK?
SURE!
SLAPJACK! I WIN!
GOOD GAME!
HEY, HOW ABOUT WE BUILD A SNOW FORT?
YEAH!
I BET WE CAN BUILD A BETTER TOWER THAN THOSE THREE COMBINED, EH, DARWIN?
-GRAWAWRDR...
I AGREE, GUMBALL'S TUMMY--HOT COCOA AND FRESH-BAKED COOKIES ARE AN EXCELLENT IDEA!
WOW, IT'S LATER THAN I THOUGHT!
6:00
WE SHOULD PROBABLY HEAD BACK--MOM'LL BE WORRIED.

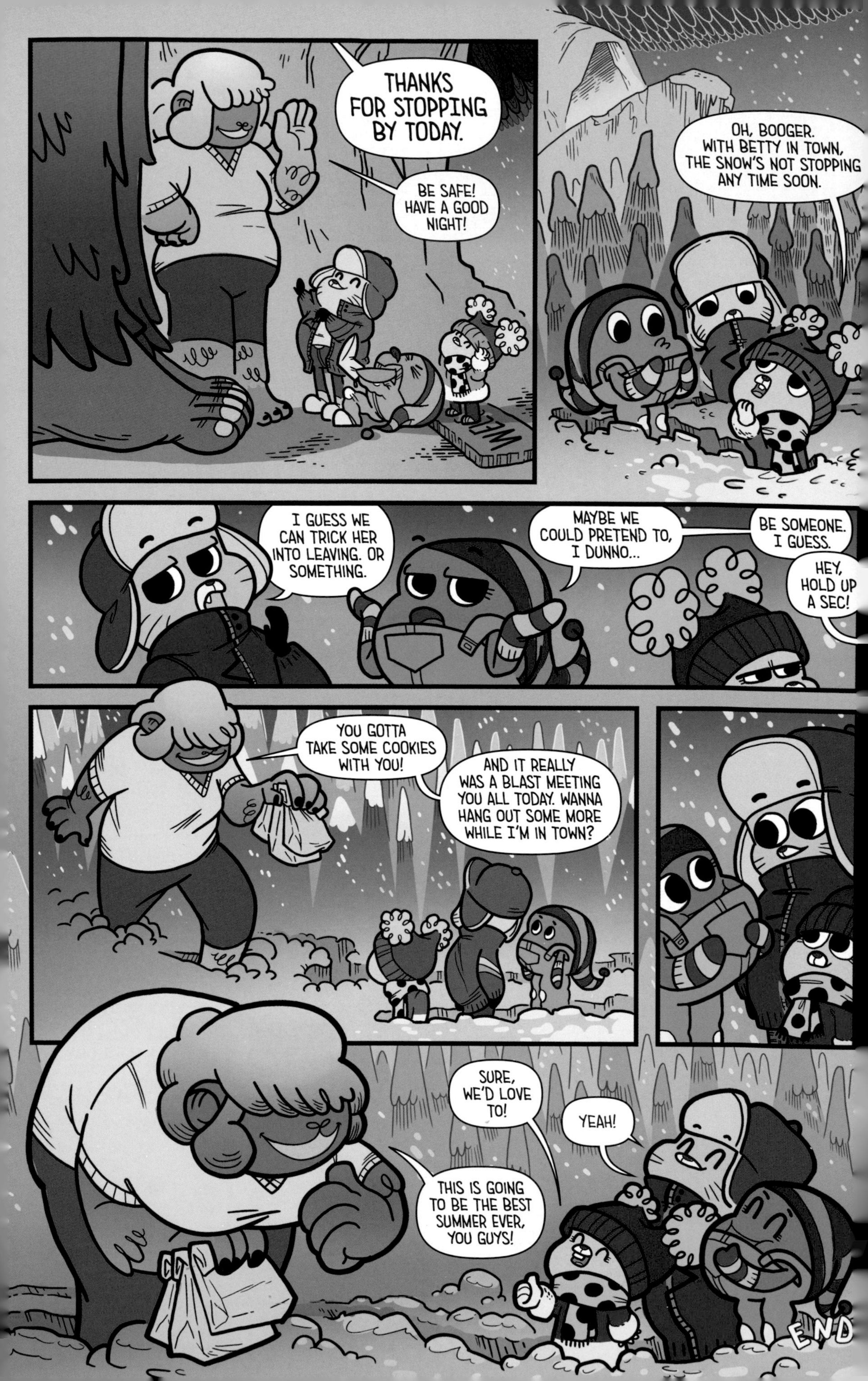
THANKS FOR STOPPING BY TODAY.
BE SAFE! HAVE A GOOD NIGHT!
OH, BOOGER. WITH BETTY IN TOWN, THE SNOW'S NOT STOPPING ANY TIME SOON.
I GUESS WE CAN TRICK HER INTO LEAVING. OR SOMETHING.
MAYBE WE COULD PRETEND TO, I DUNNO...
BE SOMEONE. I GUESS.
HEY, HOLD UP A SEC!
YOU GOTTA TAKE SOME COOKIES WITH YOU!
AND IT REALLY WAS A BLAST MEETING YOU ALL TODAY. WANNA HANG OUT SOME MORE WHILE I'M IN TOWN?
SURE, WE'D LOVE TO!
YEAH!
THIS IS GOING TO BE THE BEST SUMMER EVER, YOU GUYS!
END

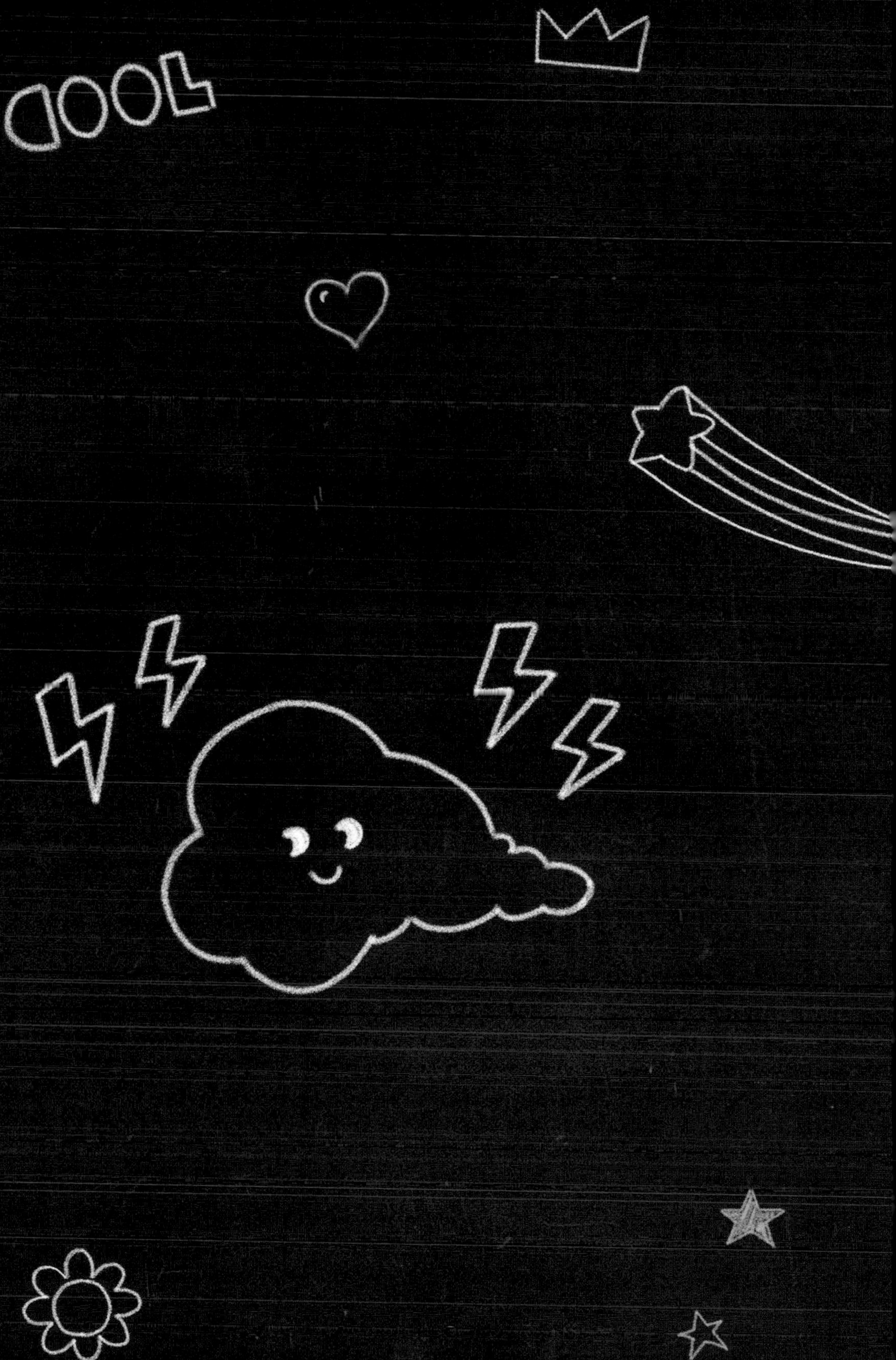
COOL

THE BIKE

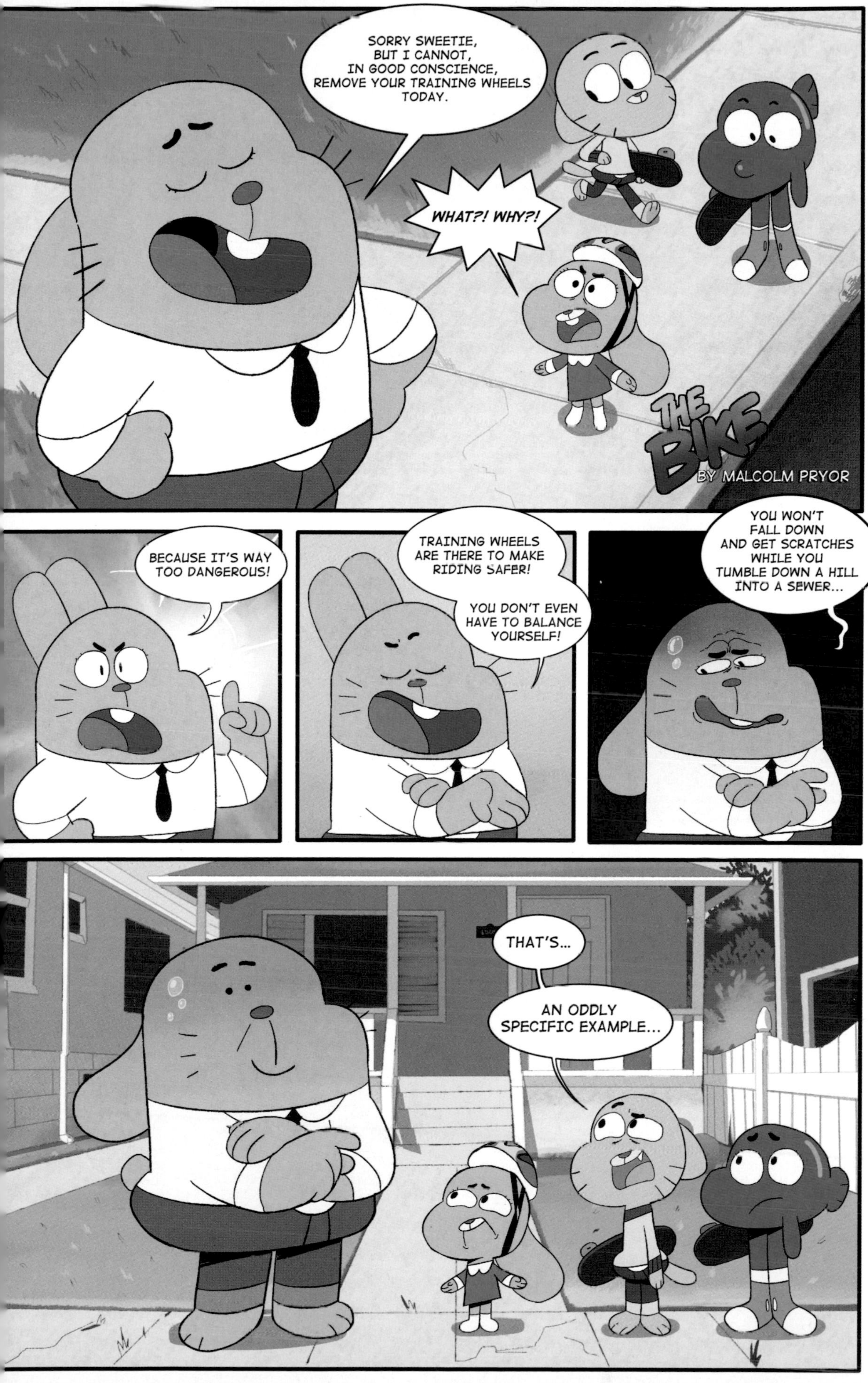
SORRY SWEETIE, BUT I CANNOT, IN GOOD CONSCIENCE, REMOVE YOUR TRAINING WHEELS TODAY.
WHAT?! WHY?!
THE BIKE
BY MALCOLM PRYOR
BECAUSE IT'S WAY TOO DANGEROUS!
TRAINING WHEELS ARE THERE TO MAKE RIDING SAFER!
YOU DON'T EVEN HAVE TO BALANCE YOURSELF!
YOU WON'T FALL DOWN AND GET SCRATCHES WHILE YOU TUMBLE DOWN A HILL INTO A SEWER...
THAT'S...
AN ODDLY SPECIFIC EXAMPLE...

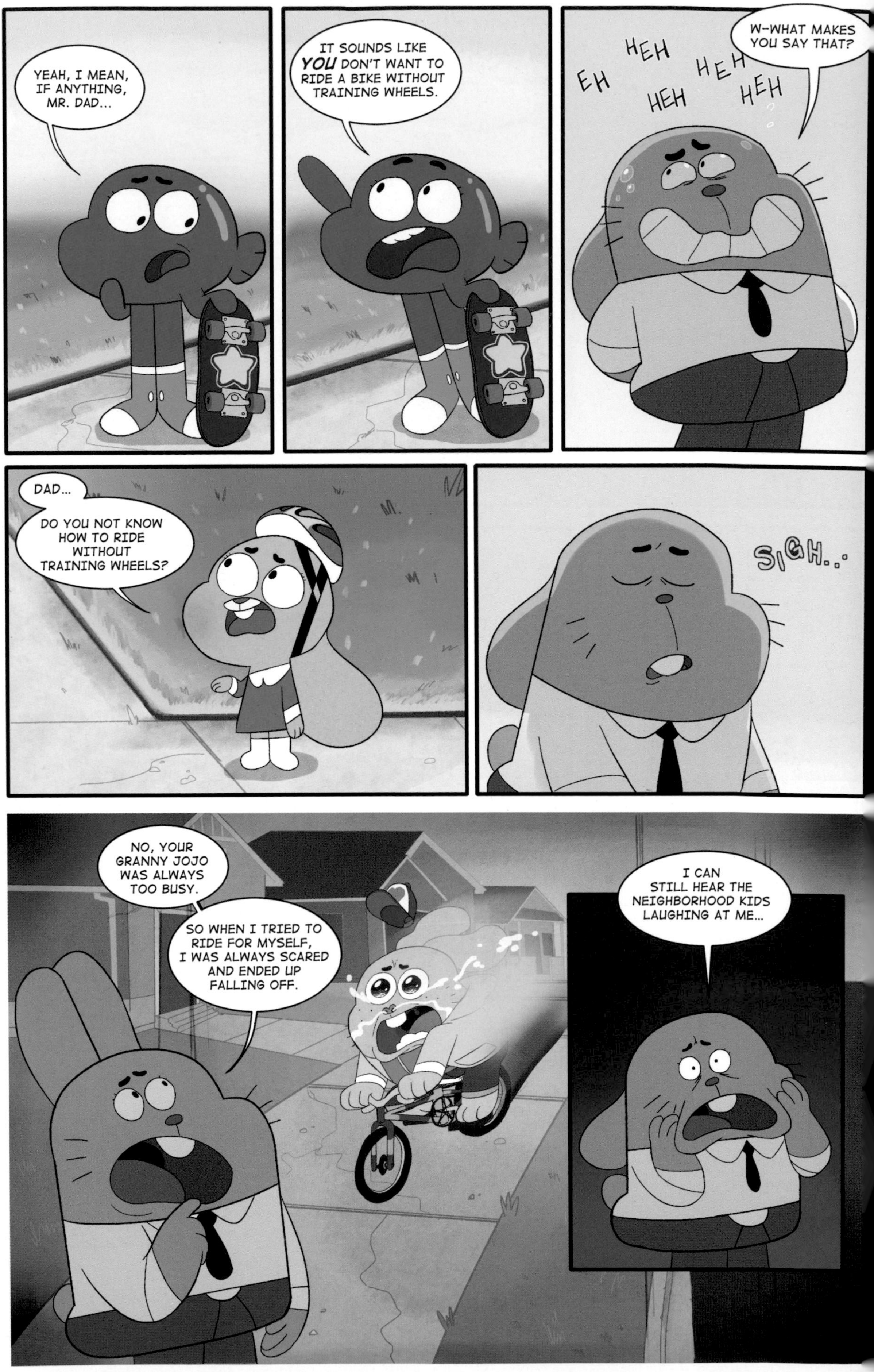
YEAH, I MEAN, IF ANYTHING, MR. DAD...
IT SOUNDS LIKE YOU DON'T WANT TO RIDE A BIKE WITHOUT TRAINING WHEELS.
EH HEH HEH HEH HEH
W-WHAT MAKES YOU SAY THAT?
DAD...
DO YOU NOT KNOW HOW TO RIDE WITHOUT TRAINING WHEELS?
SIGH...
NO, YOUR GRANNY JOJO WAS ALWAYS TOO BUSY.
SO WHEN I TRIED TO RIDE FOR MYSELF, I WAS ALWAYS SCARED AND ENDED UP FALLING OFF.
I CAN STILL HEAR THE NEIGHBORHOOD KIDS LAUGHING AT ME...

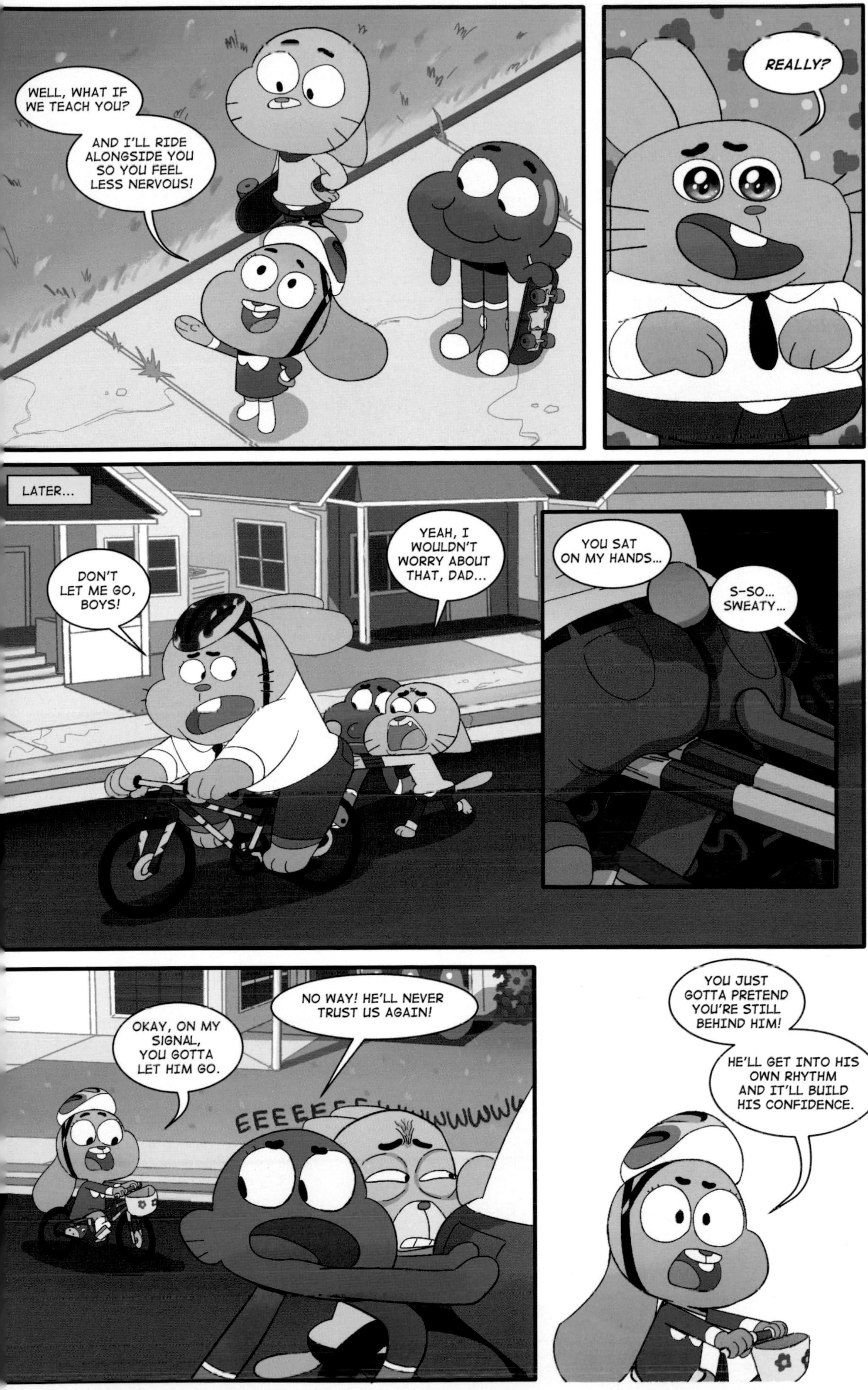
WELL, WHAT IF WE TEACH YOU?
AND I'LL RIDE ALONGSIDE YOU SO YOU FEEL LESS NERVOUS!
REALLY?
LATER...
DON'T LET ME GO, BOYS!
YEAH, I WOULDN'T WORRY ABOUT THAT, DAD...
YOU SAT ON MY HANDS...
S-SO... SWEATY...
OKAY, ON MY SIGNAL, YOU GOTTA LET HIM GO.
NO WAY! HE'LL NEVER TRUST US AGAIN!
YOU JUST GOTTA PRETEND YOU'RE STILL BEHIND HIM!
HE'LL GET INTO HIS OWN RHYTHM AND IT'LL BUILD HIS CONFIDENCE.

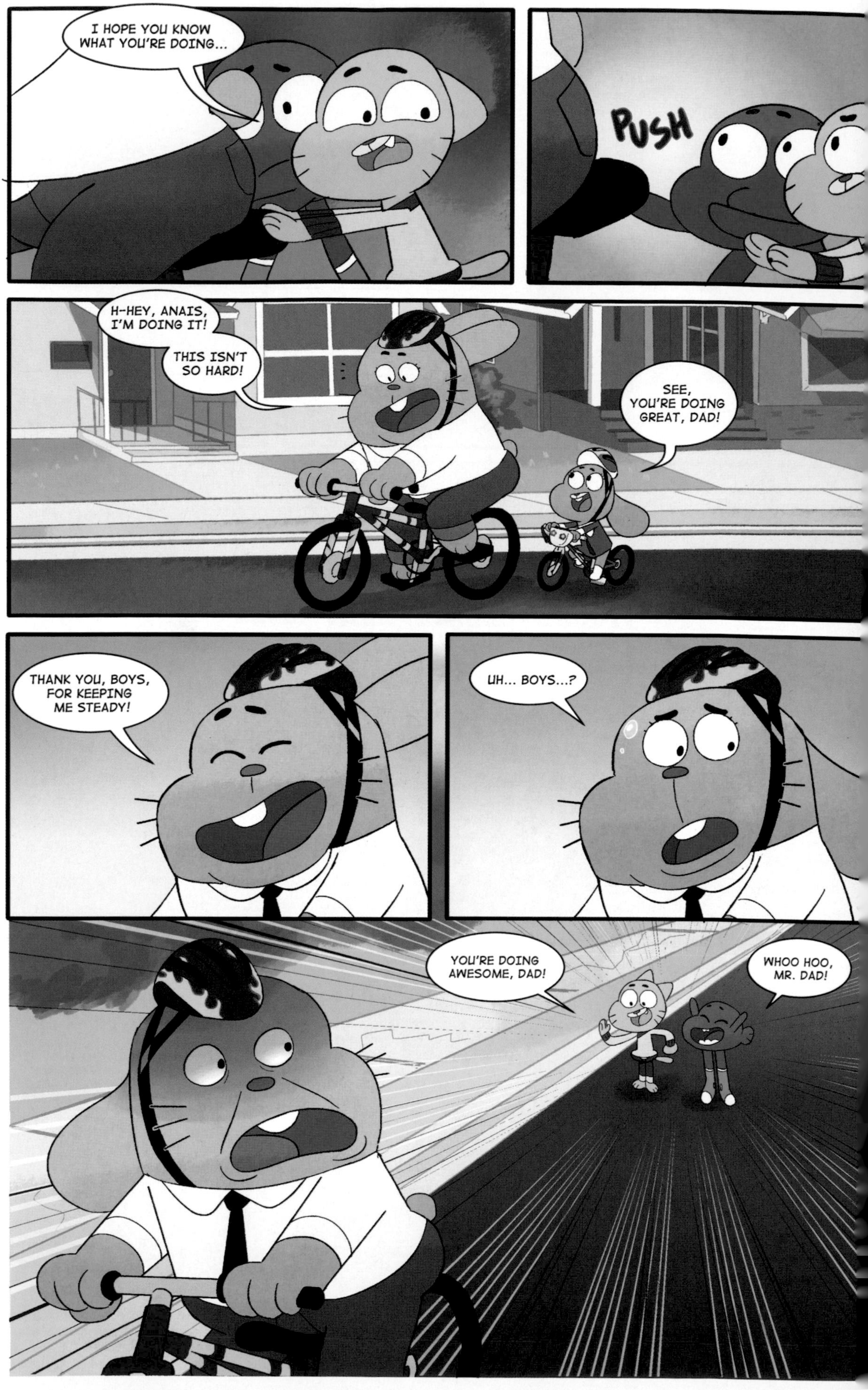
I HOPE YOU KNOW WHAT YOU'RE DOING...
PUSH
H-HEY, ANAIS, I'M DOING IT!
THIS ISN'T SO HARD!
SEE, YOU'RE DOING GREAT, DAD!
THANK YOU, BOYS, FOR KEEPING ME STEADY!
UH... BOYS...?
YOU'RE DOING AWESOME, DAD!
WHOO HOO, MR. DAD!

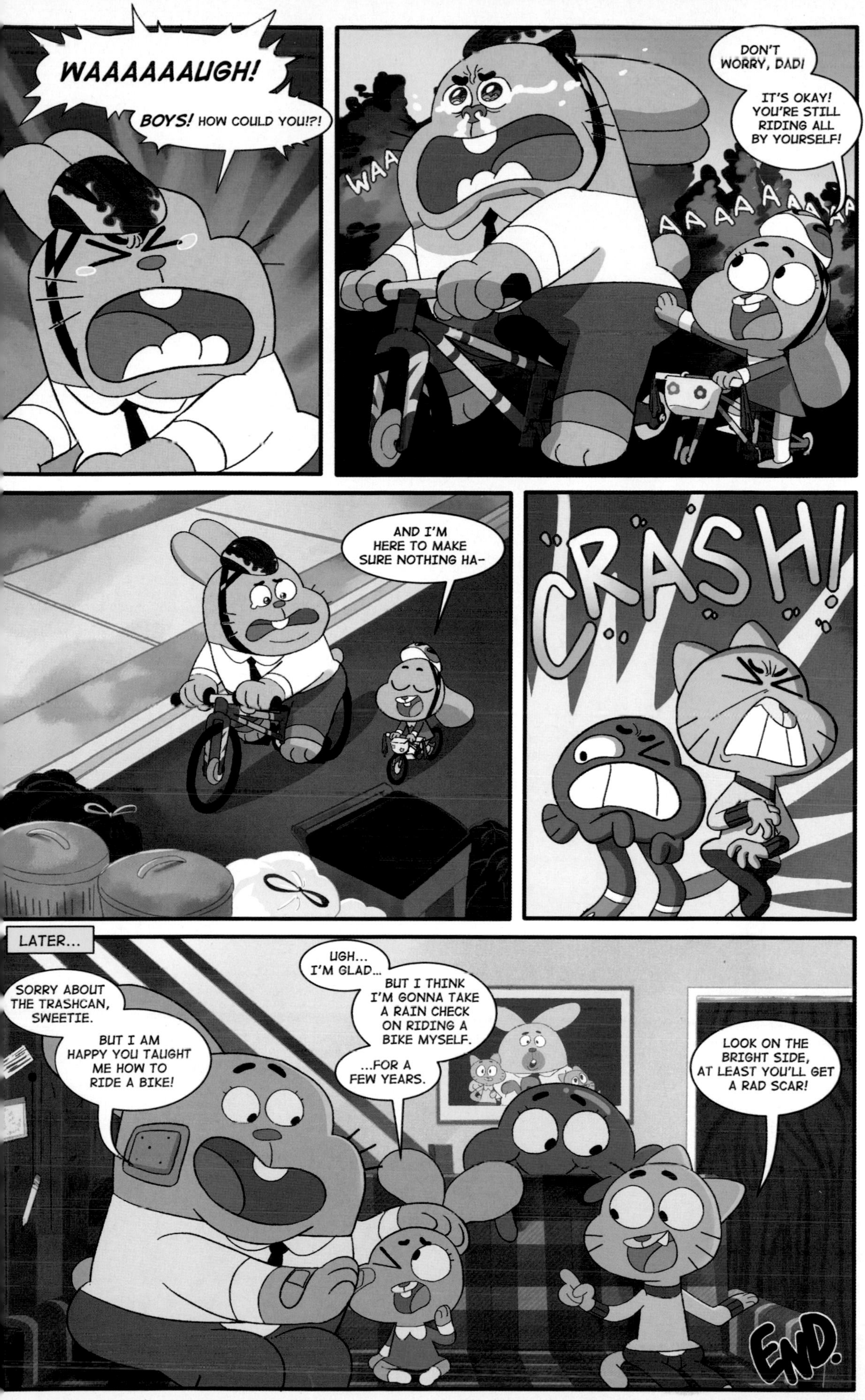
WAAAAAAUGH!
BOYS! HOW COULD YOU!?!
DON'T WORRY, DAD!
IT'S OKAY! YOU'RE STILL RIDING ALL BY YOURSELF!
WAA
AAAAAAA
AND I'M HERE TO MAKE SURE NOTHING HA-
CRASH!
LATER...
SORRY ABOUT THE TRASHCAN, SWEETIE.
BUT I AM HAPPY YOU TAUGHT ME HOW TO RIDE A BIKE!
UGH... I'M GLAD... BUT I THINK I'M GONNA TAKE A RAIN CHECK ON RIDING A BIKE MYSELF.
...FOR A FEW YEARS.
LOOK ON THE BRIGHT SIDE, AT LEAST YOU'LL GET A RAD SCAR!
END.

THE HOST

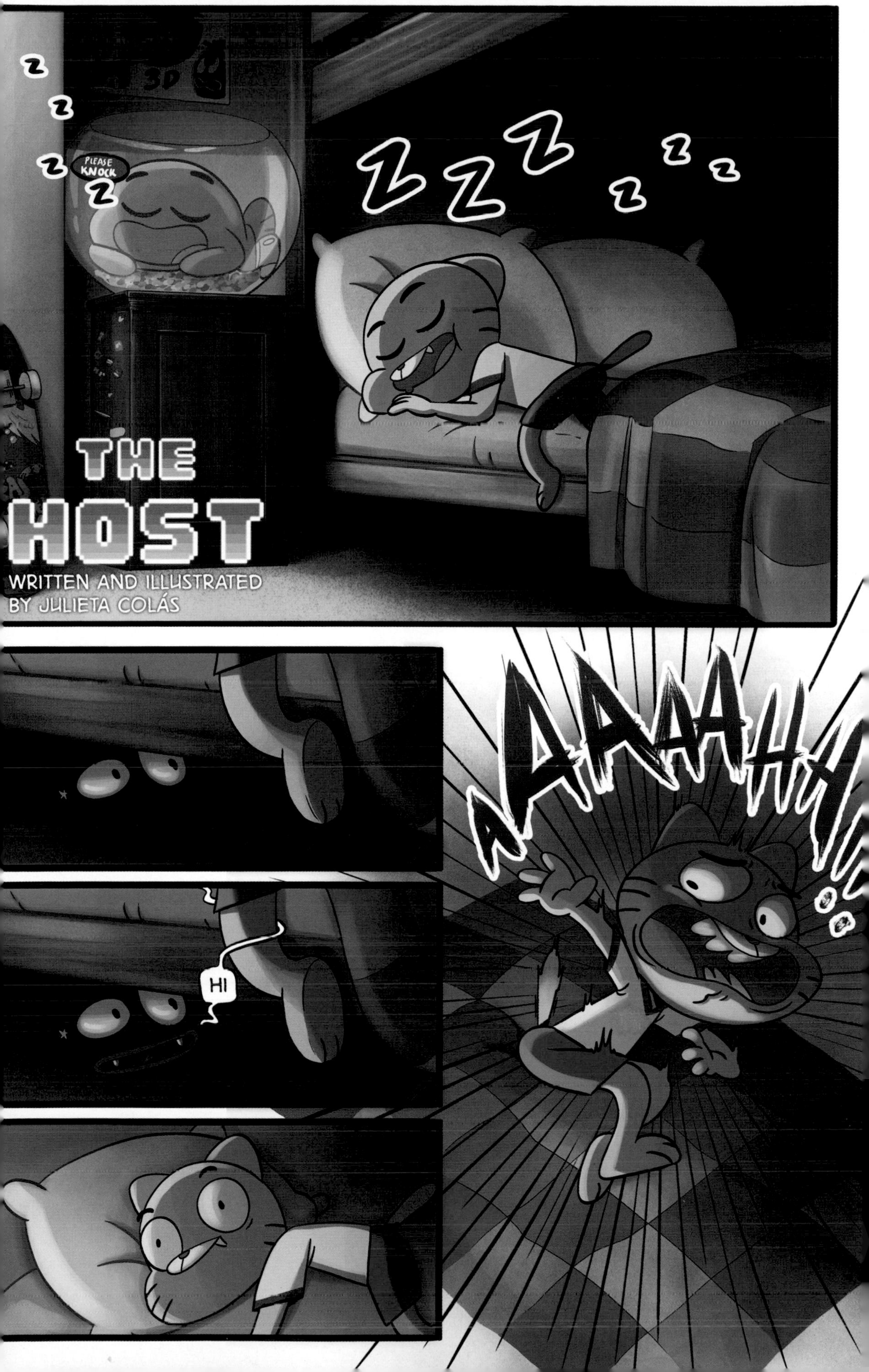
3D
Z
Z
Z
PLEASE KNOCK
Z
ZZZ
ZZZ
THE HOST
WRITTEN AND ILLUSTRATED
BY JULIETA COLÁS
HI
AAAAHH!!

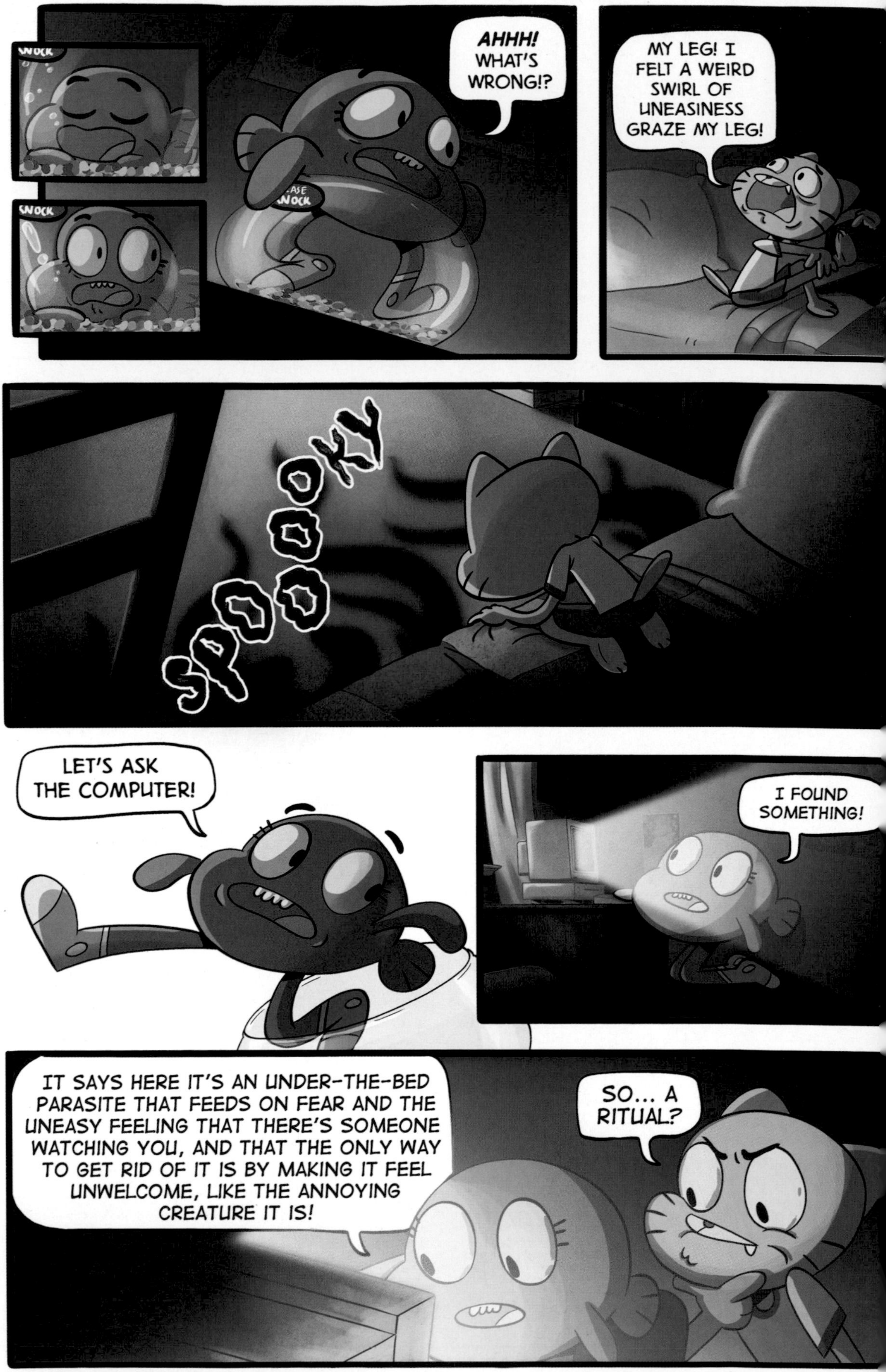
SNOCK
SNOCK
AHHH! WHAT'S WRONG!?
...ASE SNOCK
MY LEG! I FELT A WEIRD SWIRL OF UNEASINESS GRAZE MY LEG!
SPOOOOKY
LET'S ASK THE COMPUTER!
I FOUND SOMETHING!
IT SAYS HERE IT'S AN UNDER-THE-BED PARASITE THAT FEEDS ON FEAR AND THE UNEASY FEELING THAT THERE'S SOMEONE WATCHING YOU, AND THAT THE ONLY WAY TO GET RID OF IT IS BY MAKING IT FEEL UNWELCOME, LIKE THE ANNOYING CREATURE IT IS!
SO... A RITUAL?

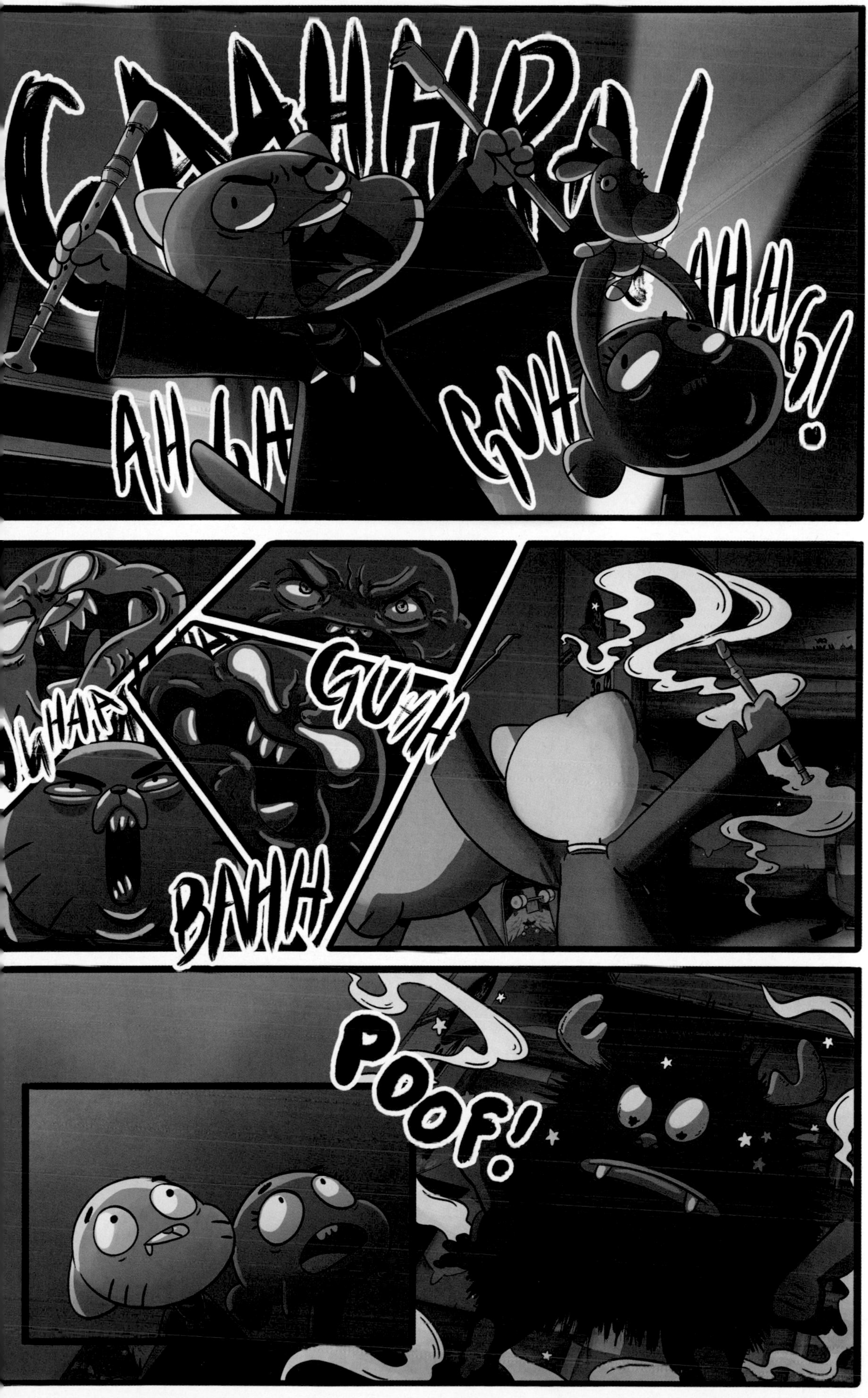
GUH
BAHH
POOF!

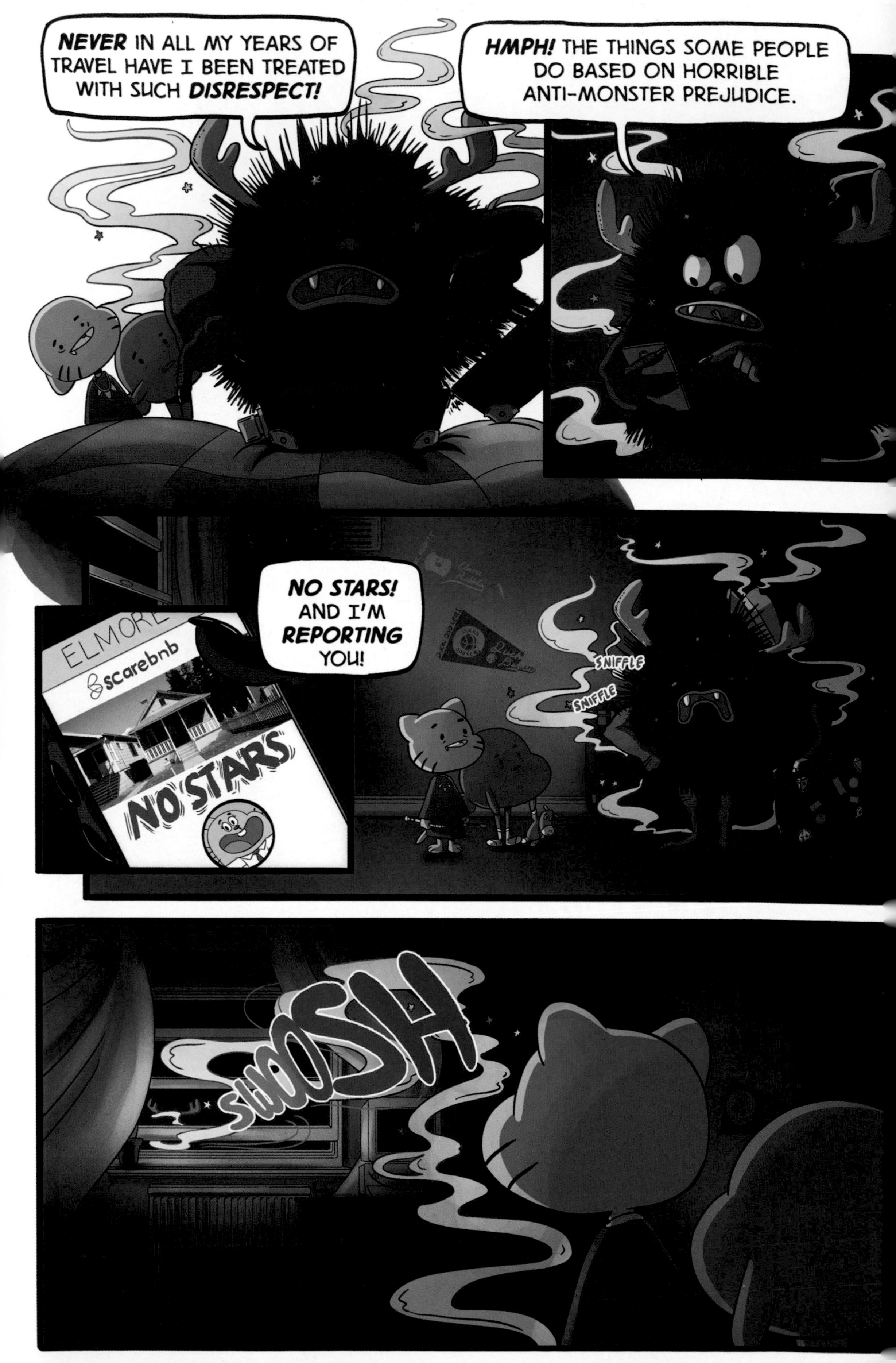
NEVER IN ALL MY YEARS OF TRAVEL HAVE I BEEN TREATED WITH SUCH DISRESPECT!
HMPH! THE THINGS SOME PEOPLE DO BASED ON HORRIBLE ANTI-MONSTER PREJUDICE.
ELMORE
scarebnb
NO STARS
NO STARS! AND I'M REPORTING YOU!
SNIFFLE
SNIFFLE
SWOOSH

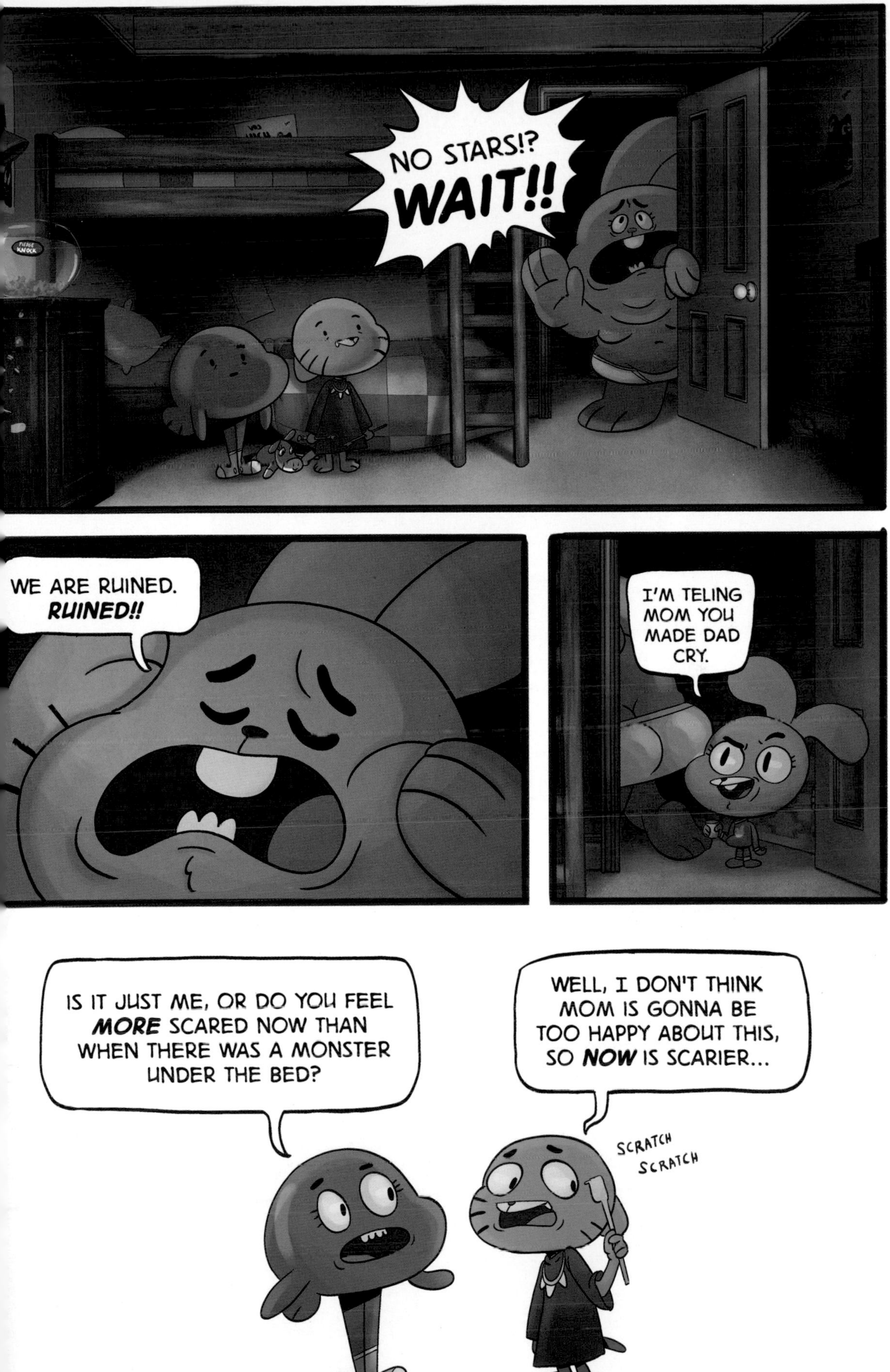
PLEASE KNOCK
NO STARS!? WAIT!!
WE ARE RUINED. RUINED!!
I'M TELING MOM YOU MADE DAD CRY.
IS IT JUST ME, OR DO YOU FEEL MORE SCARED NOW THAN WHEN THERE WAS A MONSTER UNDER THE BED?
WELL, I DON'T THINK MOM IS GONNA BE TOO HAPPY ABOUT THIS, SO NOW IS SCARIER...
SCRATCH SCRATCH

THE END.

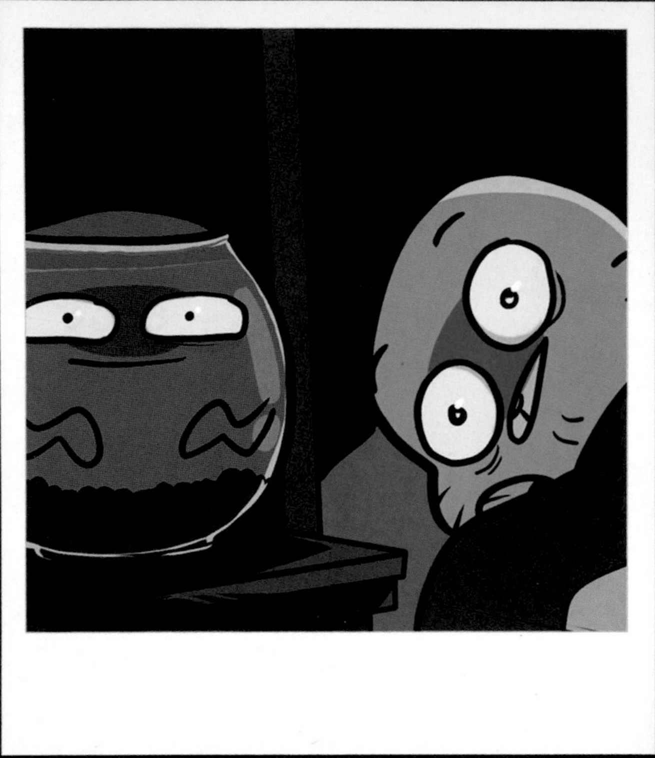

THE HAUNTENING

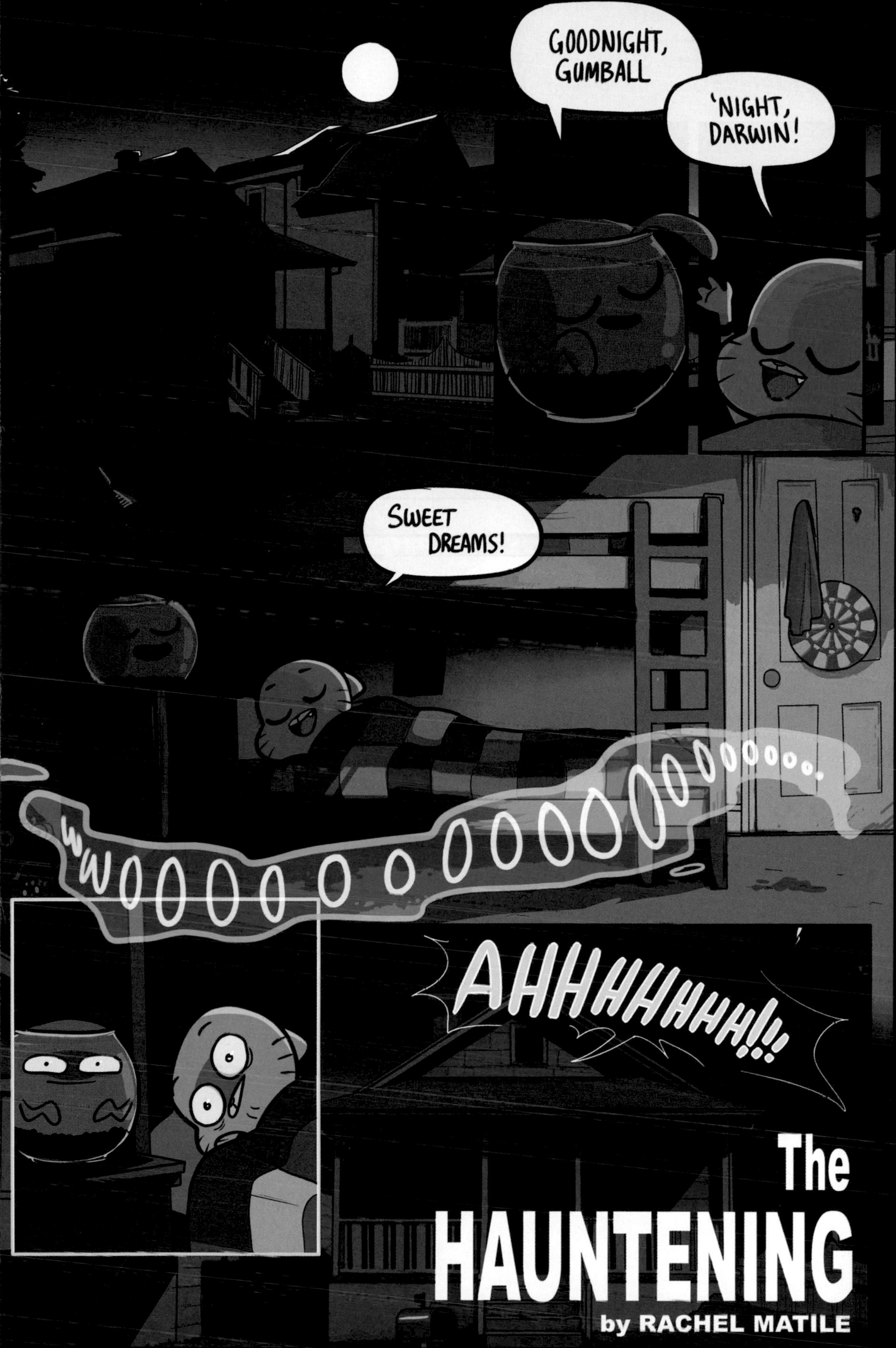
GOODNIGHT, GUMBALL
'NIGHT, DARWIN!
SWEET DREAMS!
WWOOOOOOOOOOOOOOOOoooo...
AHHHHHHH!!!
The HAUNTENING
by RACHEL MATILE

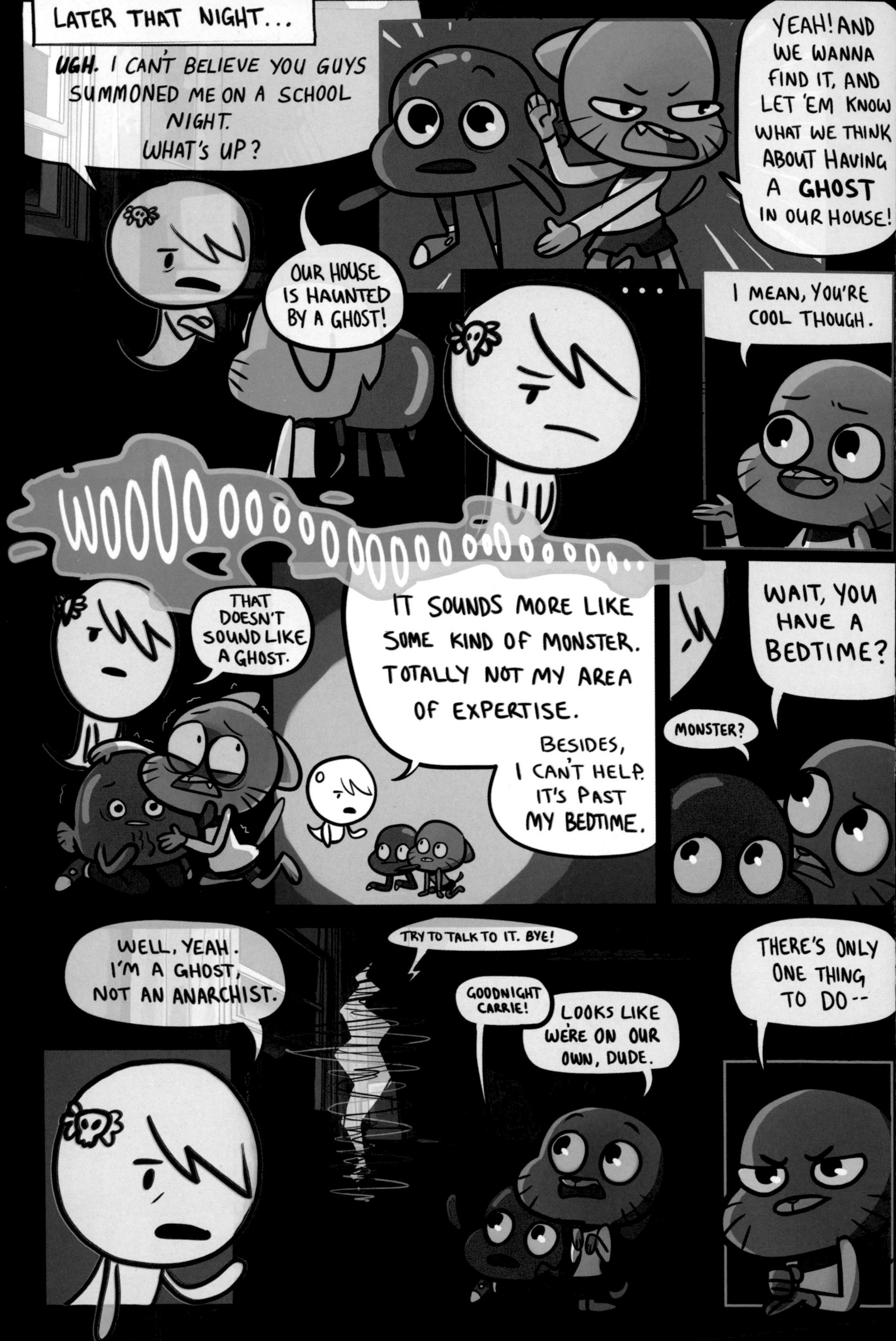
LATER THAT NIGHT...
UGH. I CAN'T BELIEVE YOU GUYS SUMMONED ME ON A SCHOOL NIGHT. WHAT'S UP?
OUR HOUSE IS HAUNTED BY A GHOST!
YEAH! AND WE WANNA FIND IT, AND LET 'EM KNOW WHAT WE THINK ABOUT HAVING A GHOST IN OUR HOUSE!
...
I MEAN, YOU'RE COOL THOUGH.
WOOOOOOOOOOOOOOOOOO...
THAT DOESN'T SOUND LIKE A GHOST.
IT SOUNDS MORE LIKE SOME KIND OF MONSTER. TOTALLY NOT MY AREA OF EXPERTISE.
BESIDES, I CAN'T HELP. IT'S PAST MY BEDTIME.
MONSTER?
WAIT, YOU HAVE A BEDTIME?
WELL, YEAH. I'M A GHOST, NOT AN ANARCHIST.
TRY TO TALK TO IT. BYE!
GOODNIGHT CARRIE!
LOOKS LIKE WE'RE ON OUR OWN, DUDE.
THERE'S ONLY ONE THING TO DO--

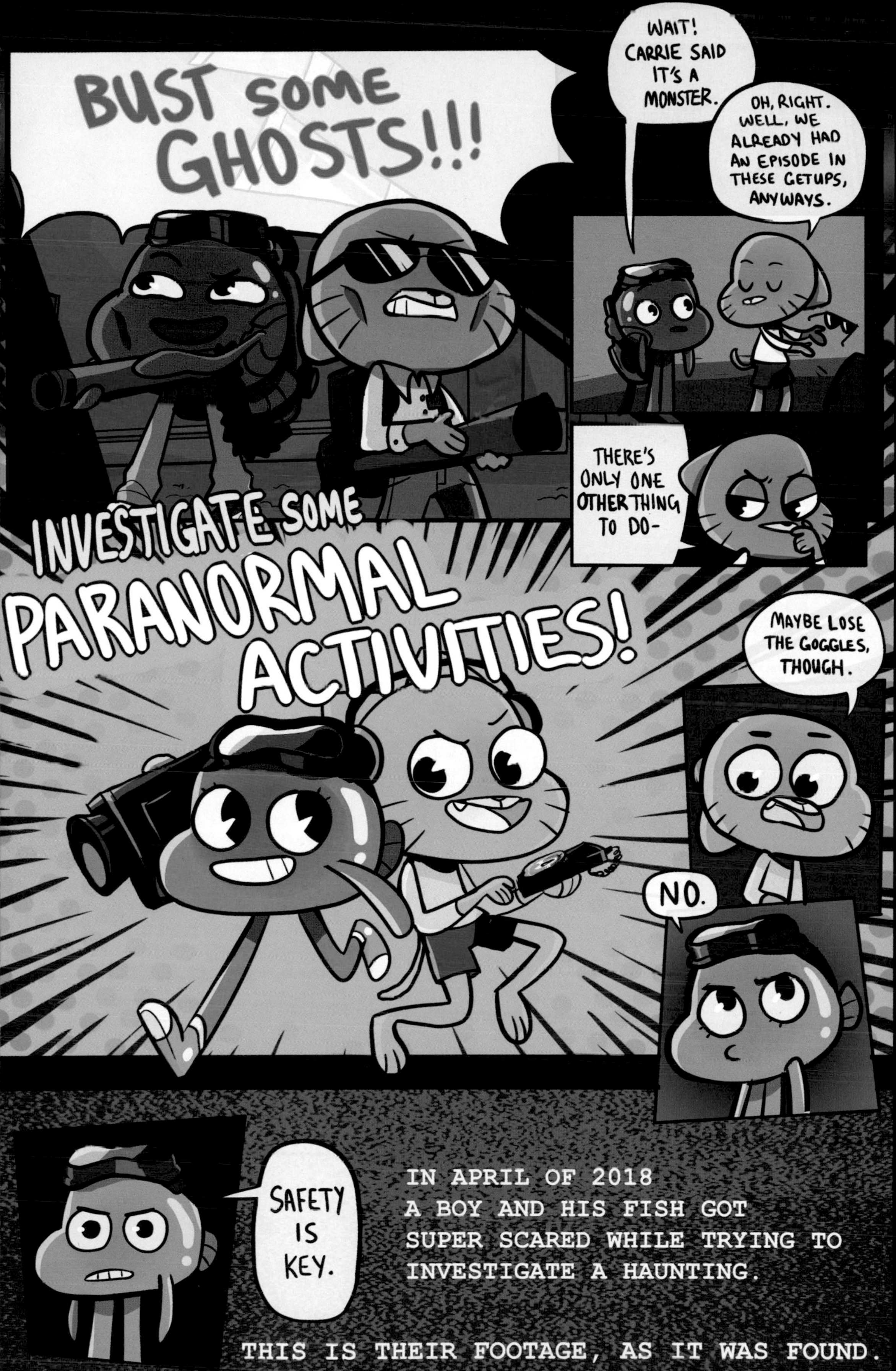
BUST SOME GHOSTS!!!
WAIT! CARRIE SAID IT'S A MONSTER.
OH, RIGHT. WELL, WE ALREADY HAD AN EPISODE IN THESE GETUPS, ANYWAYS.
THERE'S ONLY ONE OTHER THING TO DO-
INVESTIGATE SOME PARANORMAL ACTIVITIES!
MAYBE LOSE THE GOGGLES, THOUGH.
NO.
SAFETY IS KEY.
IN APRIL OF 2018
A BOY AND HIS FISH GOT
SUPER SCARED WHILE TRYING TO
INVESTIGATE A HAUNTING.
THIS IS THEIR FOOTAGE, AS IT WAS FOUND.

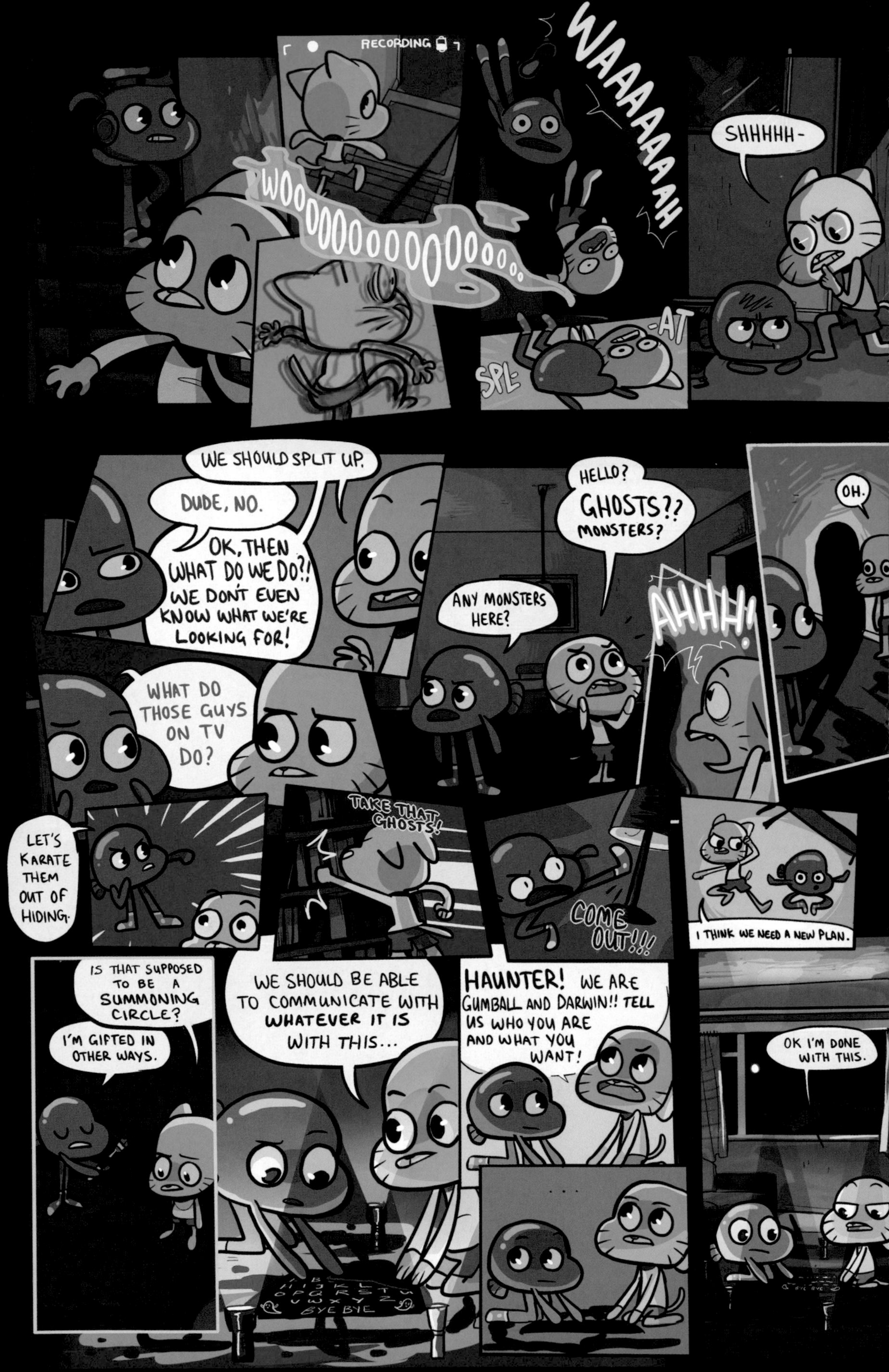
RECORDING
WOOOOOOOOOOOOOOooooo
WAAAAAAAAH
SPL-
-AT
SHHHHH-
WE SHOULD SPLIT UP.
DUDE, NO.
OK, THEN WHAT DO WE DO?! WE DON'T EVEN KNOW WHAT WE'RE LOOKING FOR!
WHAT DO THOSE GUYS ON TV DO?
HELLO? GHOSTS?? MONSTERS?
ANY MONSTERS HERE?
AHHH!
OH.
LET'S KARATE THEM OUT OF HIDING.
TAKE THAT GHOSTS!
COME OUT!!!
I THINK WE NEED A NEW PLAN.
IS THAT SUPPOSED TO BE A SUMMONING CIRCLE?
I'M GIFTED IN OTHER WAYS.
WE SHOULD BE ABLE TO COMMUNICATE WITH WHATEVER IT IS WITH THIS...
BYE BYE
HAUNTER! WE ARE GUMBALL AND DARWIN!! TELL US WHO YOU ARE AND WHAT YOU WANT!
...
OK I'M DONE WITH THIS.

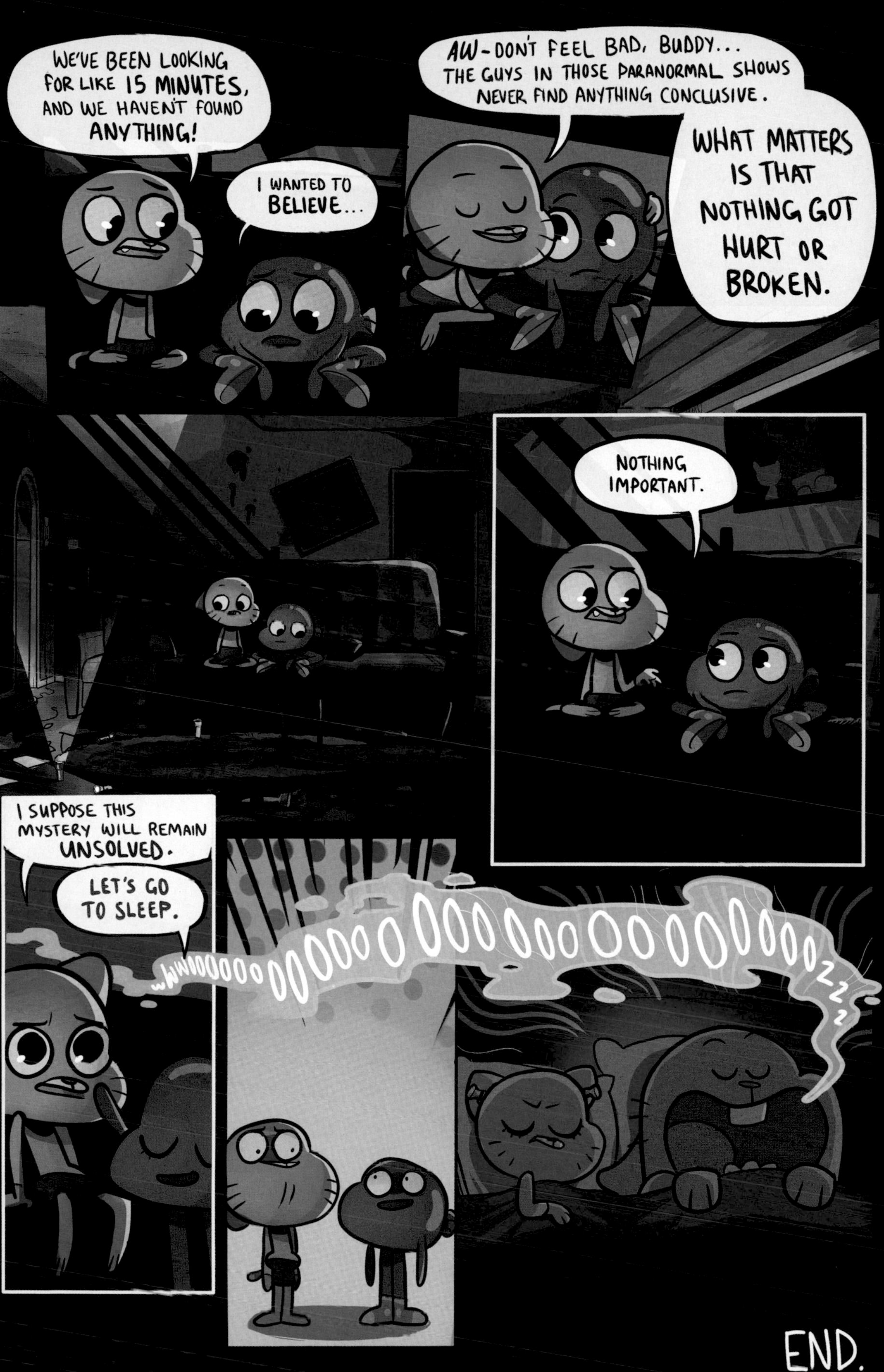
WE'VE BEEN LOOKING FOR LIKE 15 MINUTES, AND WE HAVEN'T FOUND ANYTHING!
I WANTED TO BELIEVE...
AW- DON'T FEEL BAD, BUDDY... THE GUYS IN THOSE PARANORMAL SHOWS NEVER FIND ANYTHING CONCLUSIVE.
WHAT MATTERS IS THAT NOTHING GOT HURT OR BROKEN.
NOTHING IMPORTANT.
I SUPPOSE THIS MYSTERY WILL REMAIN UNSOLVED.
LET'S GO TO SLEEP.
..WOOOOOOOOOOOOOOOOOOOOOOOOOOOOOOZZZ
END.

SCIENCE FAIR SHENANIGANS

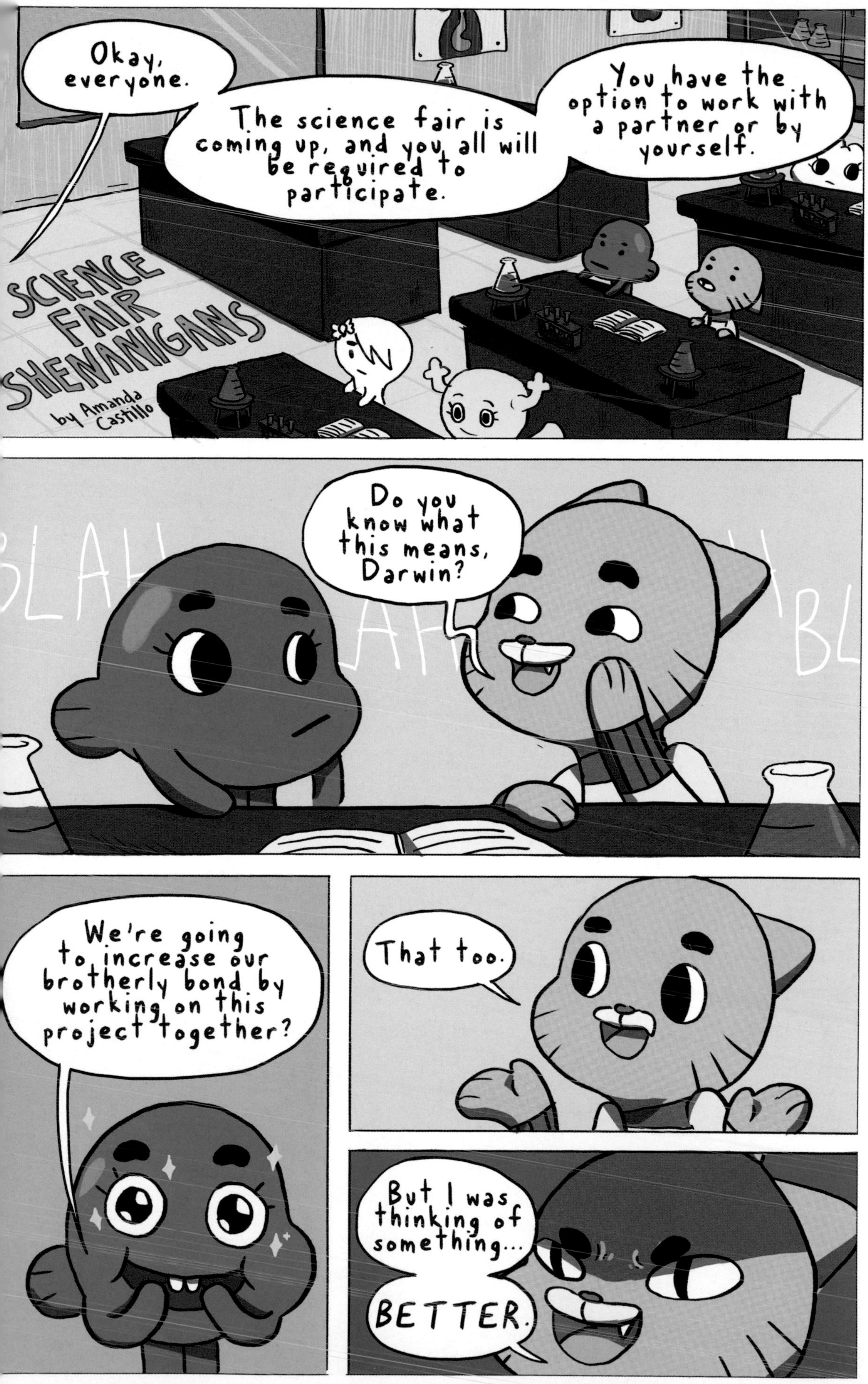
Okay, everyone.
The science fair is coming up, and you all will be required to participate.
You have the option to work with a partner or by yourself.
SCIENCE FAIR SHENANIGANS
by Amanda Castillo
Do you know what this means, Darwin?
We're going to increase our brotherly bond by working on this project together?
That too.
But I was thinking of something...
BETTER.

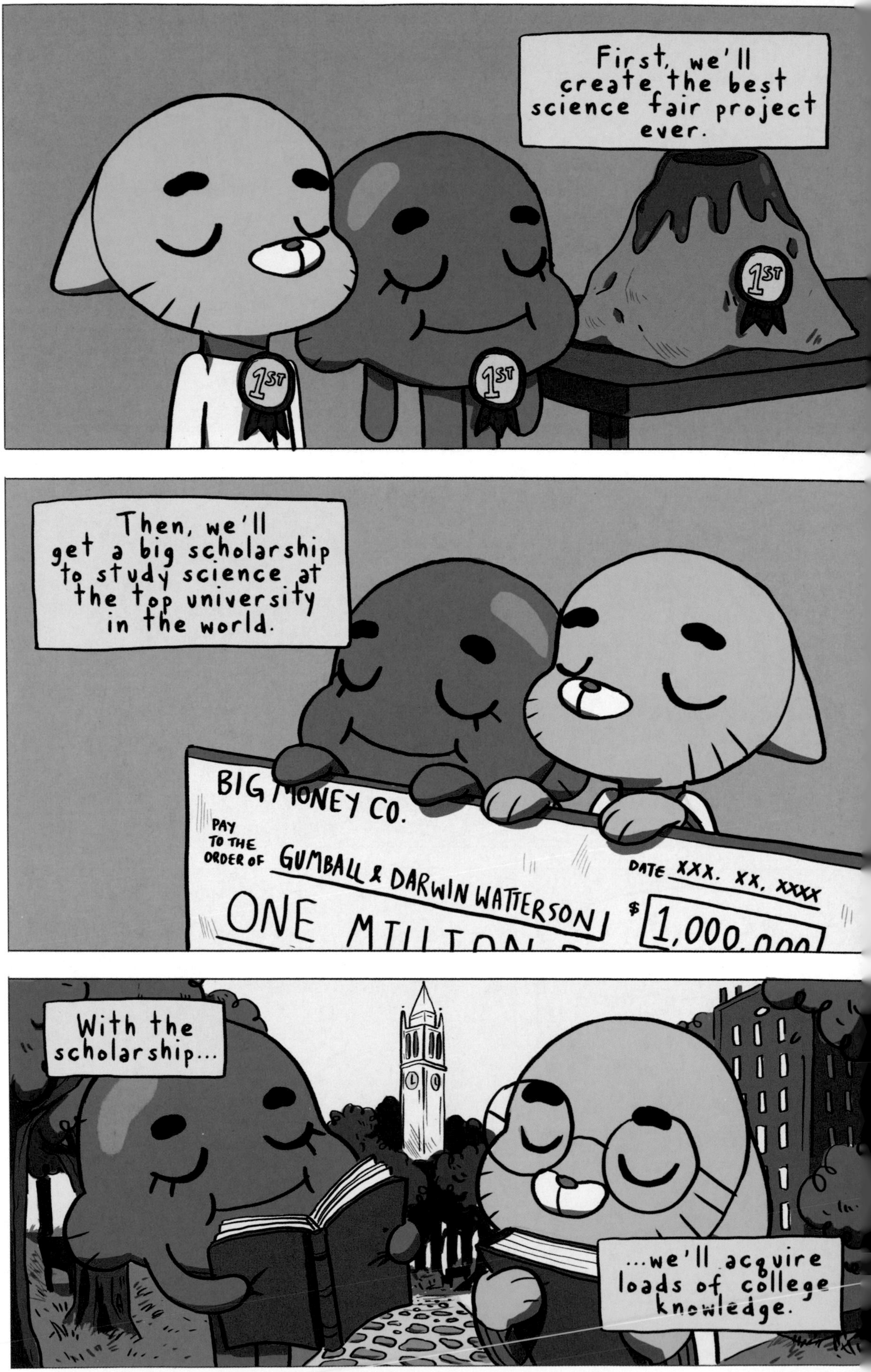
First, we'll create the best science fair project ever.
1ST
1ST
1ST
Then, we'll get a big scholarship to study science at the top university in the world.
BIG MONEY CO.
PAY TO THE ORDER OF GUMBALL & DARWIN WATTERSON
DATE XXX. XX, XXXX
ONE
$ 1,000,000
With the scholarship...
...we'll acquire loads of college knowledge.

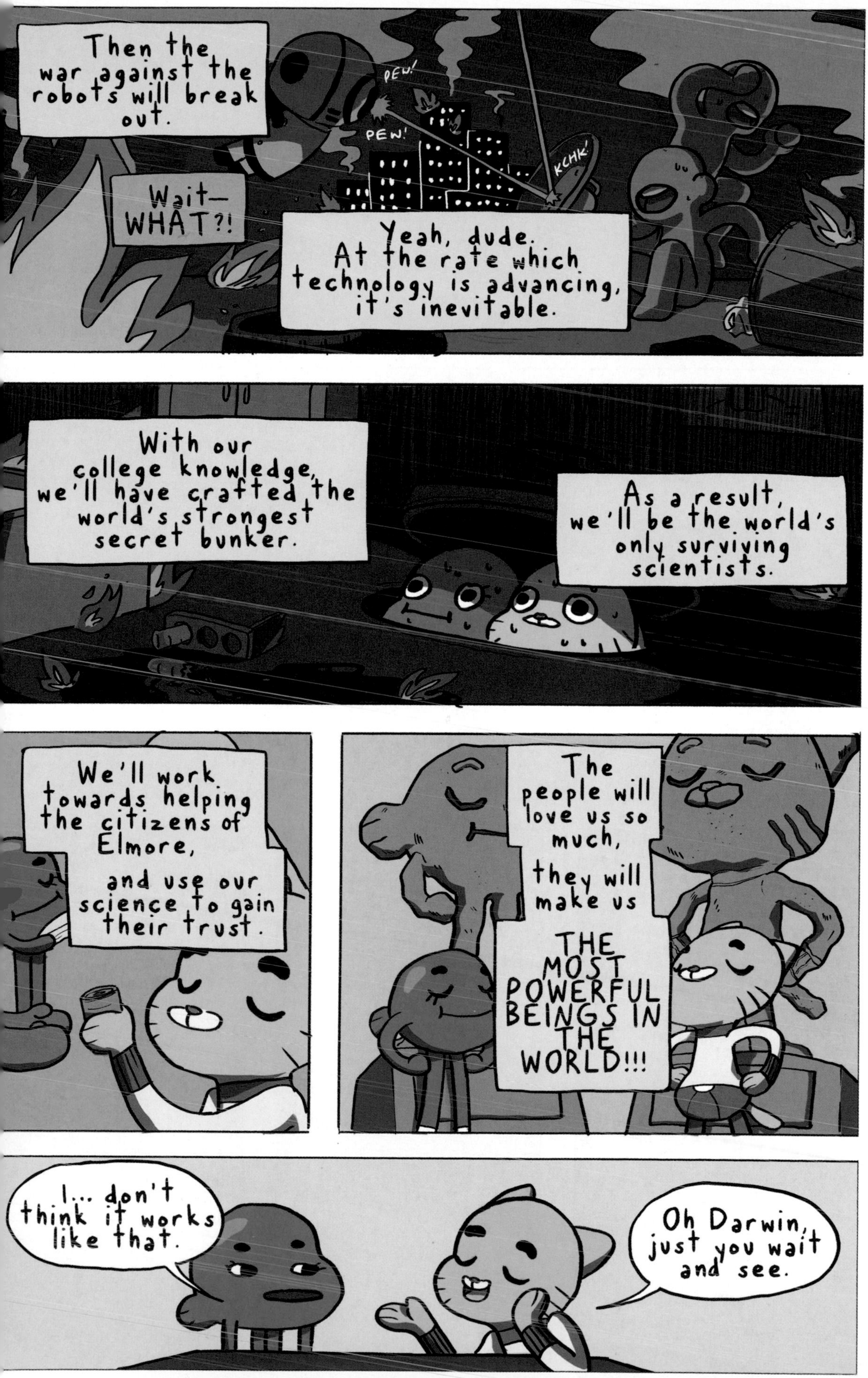
Then the war against the robots will break out.
PEW!
PEW!
KCHK!
Wait— WHAT?!
Yeah, dude. At the rate which technology is advancing, it's inevitable.
With our college knowledge, we'll have crafted the world's strongest secret bunker.
As a result, we'll be the world's only surviving scientists.
We'll work towards helping the citizens of Elmore,
and use our science to gain their trust.
The people will love us so much,
they will make us
THE MOST POWERFUL BEINGS IN THE WORLD!!!
I... don't think it works like that.
Oh Darwin, just you wait and see.

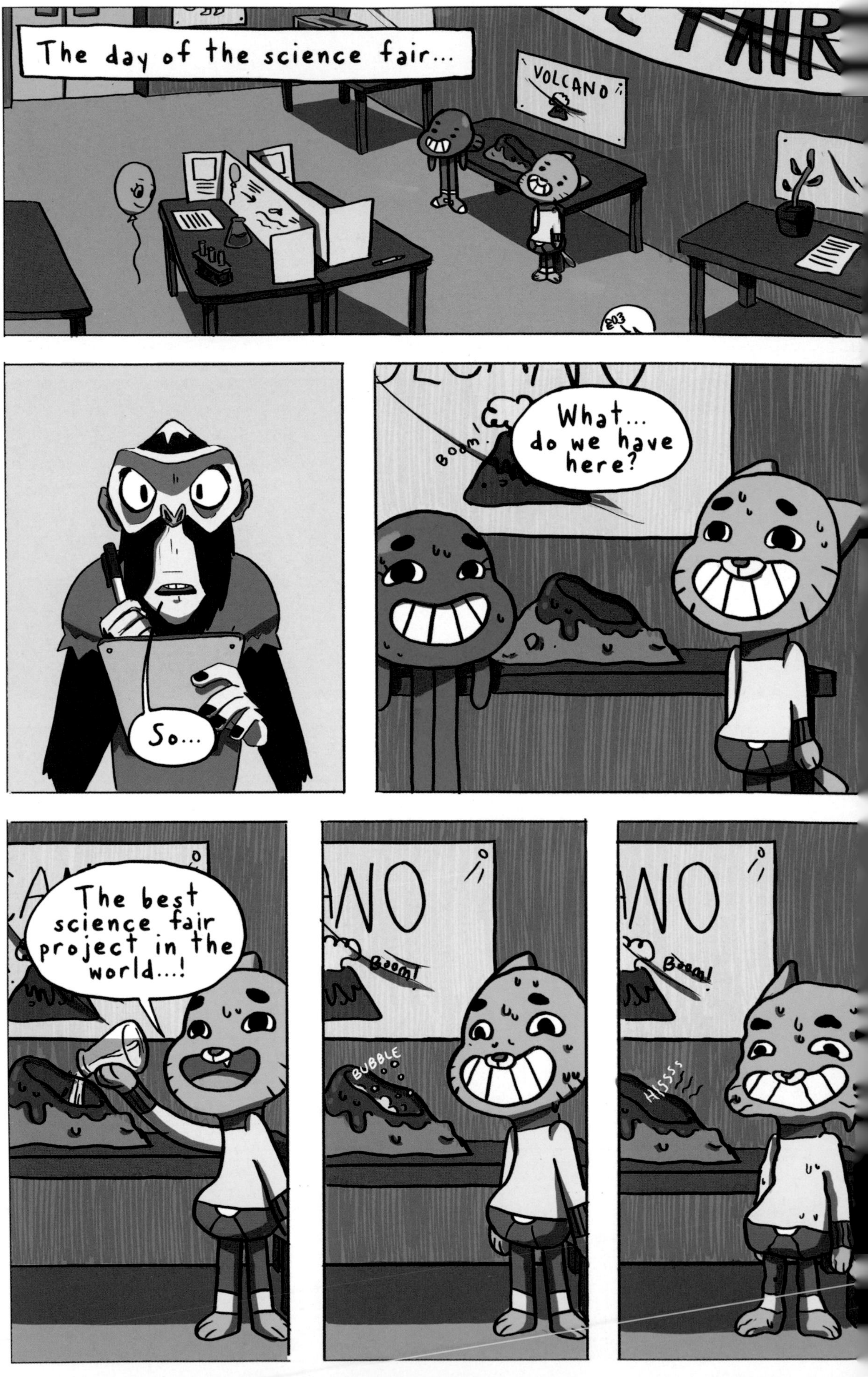
The day of the science fair...
VOLCANO
So...
What... do we have here?
The best science fair project in the world...!
BUBBLE
HISSSS

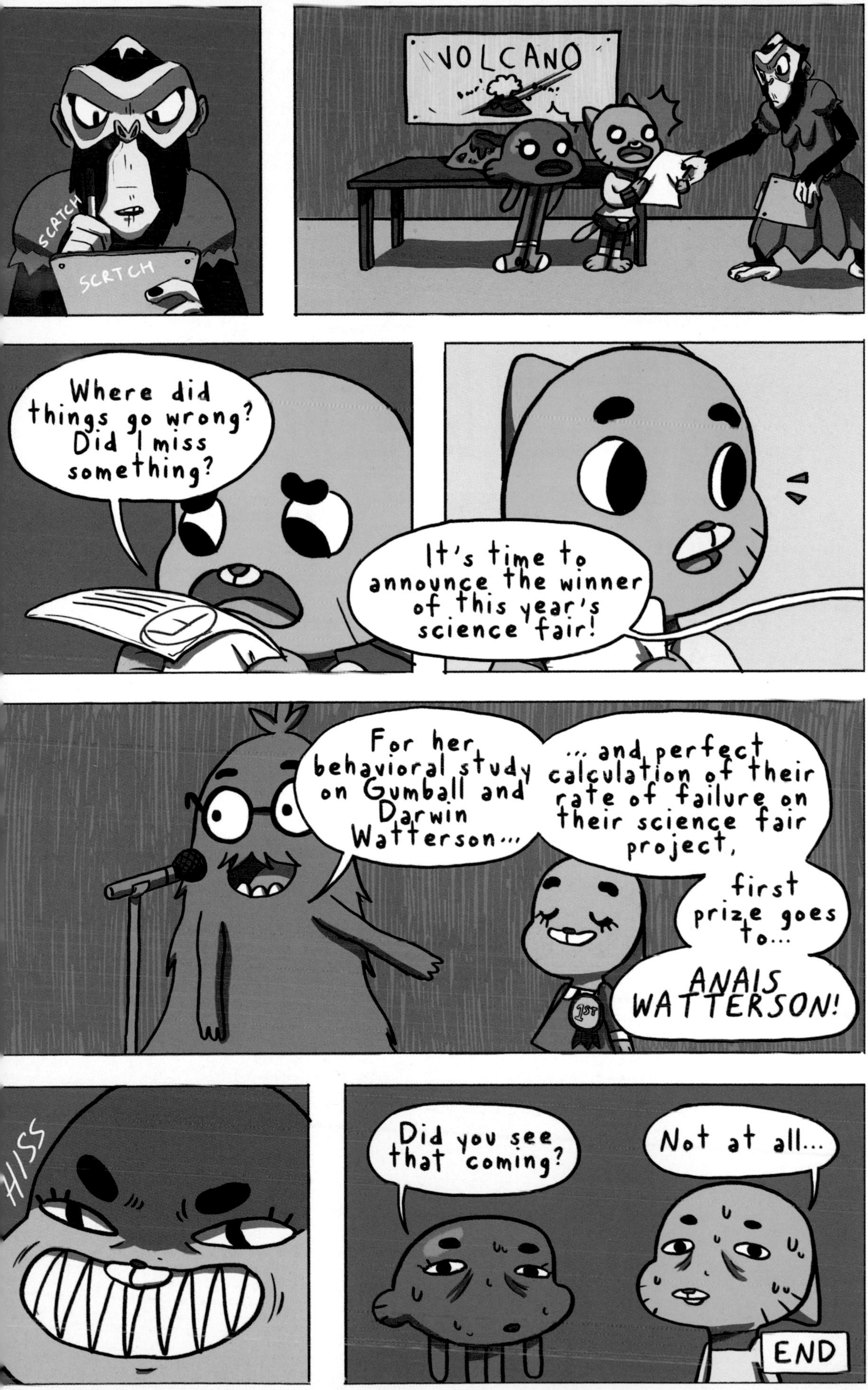
SCRATCH
SCRTCH
VOLCANO
Where did things go wrong? Did I miss something?
It's time to announce the winner of this year's science fair!
For her behavioral study on Gumball and Darwin Watterson...
... and perfect calculation of their rate of failure on their science fair project,
first prize goes to...
ANAIS WATTERSON!
1ST
HISS
Did you see that coming?
Not at all...
END

BFFS

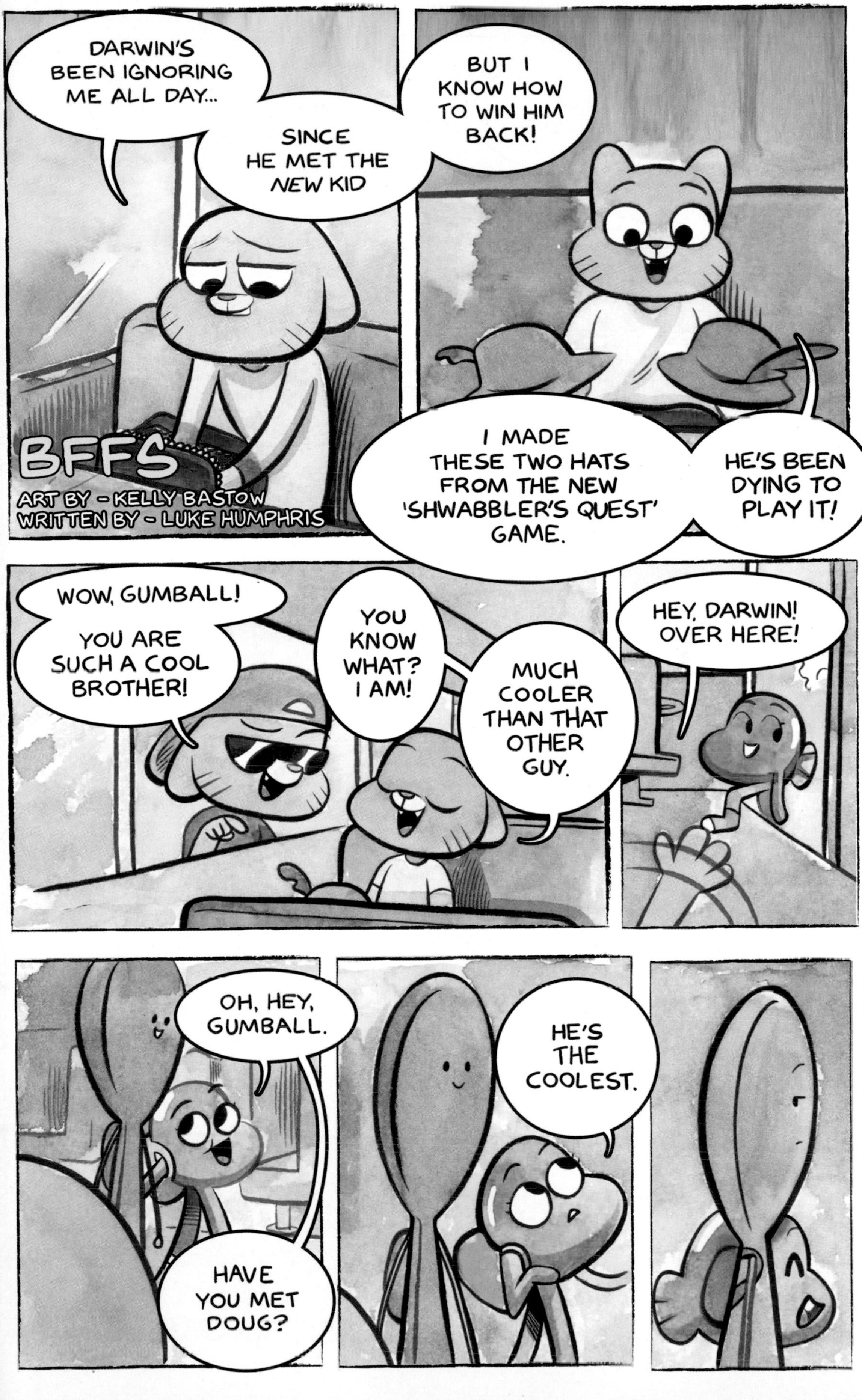
DARWIN'S BEEN IGNORING ME ALL DAY...
SINCE HE MET THE *NEW* KID
BUT I KNOW HOW TO WIN HIM BACK!
BFFS
ART BY - KELLY BASTOW
WRITTEN BY - LUKE HUMPHRIS
I MADE THESE TWO HATS FROM THE NEW 'SHWABBLER'S QUEST' GAME.
HE'S BEEN DYING TO PLAY IT!
WOW, GUMBALL!
YOU ARE SUCH A COOL BROTHER!
YOU KNOW WHAT? I AM!
MUCH COOLER THAN THAT OTHER GUY.
HEY, DARWIN! OVER HERE!
OH, HEY, GUMBALL.
HAVE YOU MET DOUG?
HE'S THE COOLEST.

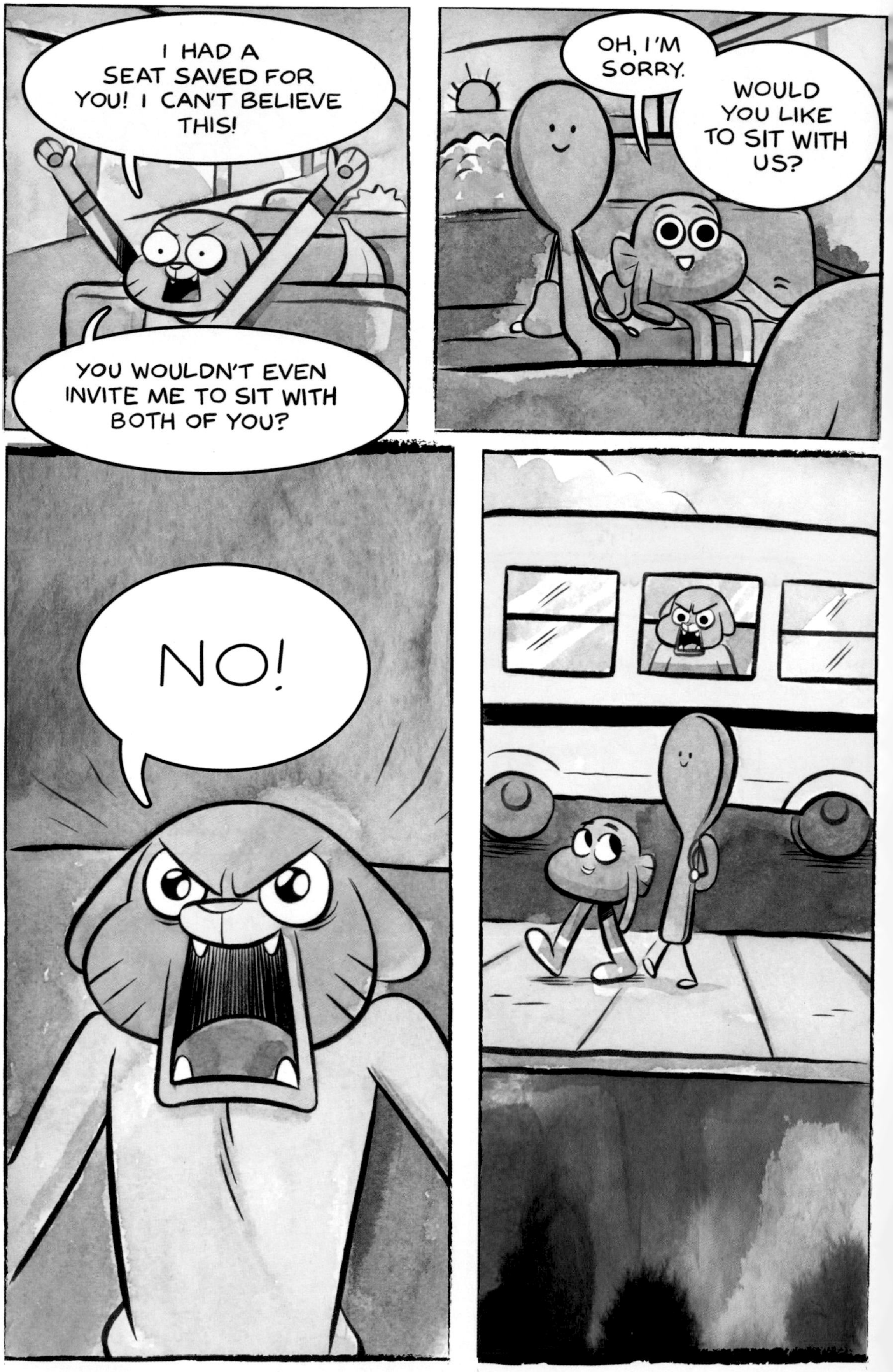
I HAD A SEAT SAVED FOR YOU! I CAN'T BELIEVE THIS!
YOU WOULDN'T EVEN INVITE ME TO SIT WITH BOTH OF YOU?
OH, I'M SORRY.
WOULD YOU LIKE TO SIT WITH US?
NO!

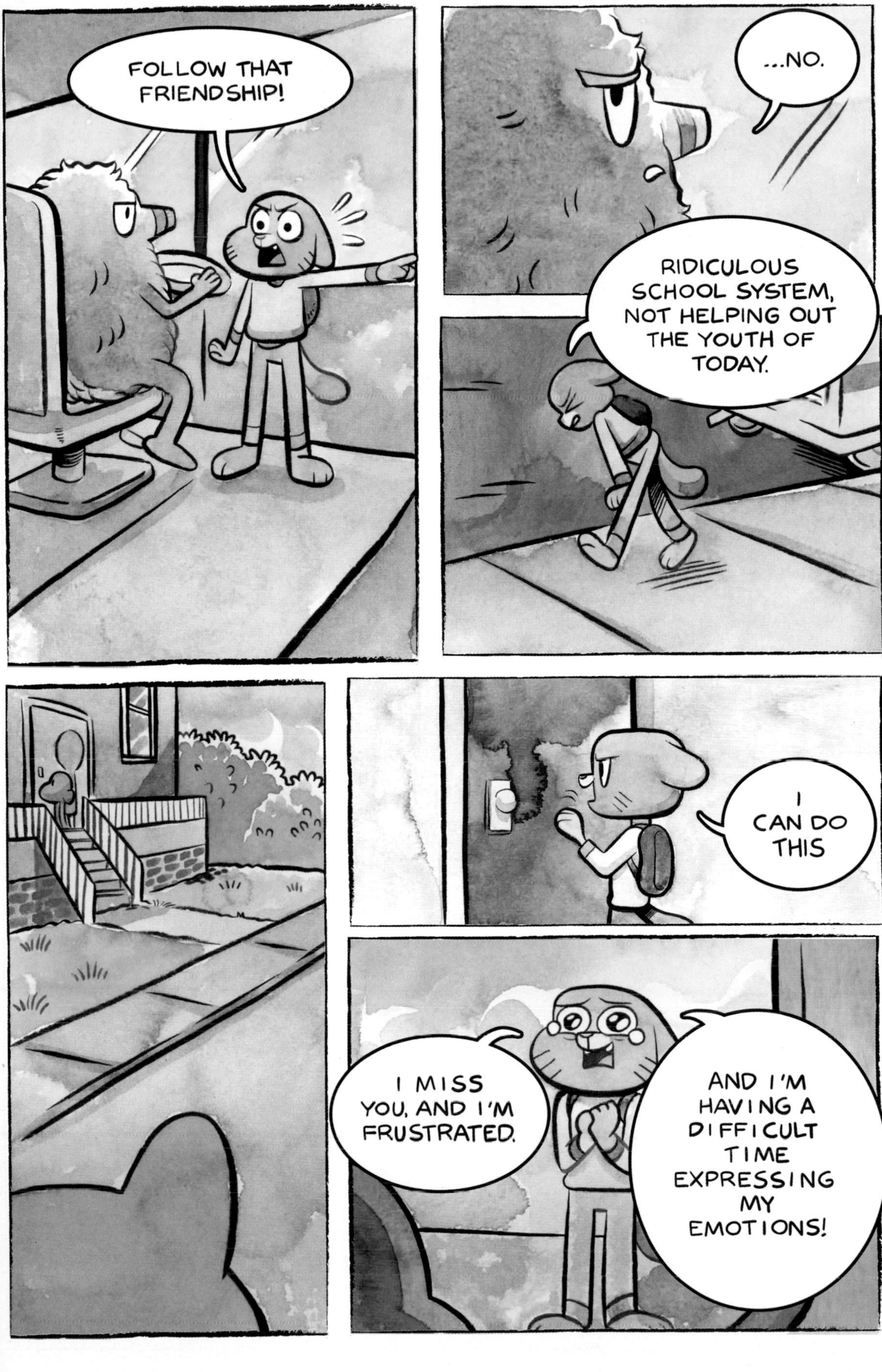
FOLLOW THAT FRIENDSHIP!
...NO.
RIDICULOUS SCHOOL SYSTEM, NOT HELPING OUT THE YOUTH OF TODAY.
I CAN DO THIS
I MISS YOU, AND I'M FRUSTRATED.
AND I'M HAVING A DIFFICULT TIME EXPRESSING MY EMOTIONS!

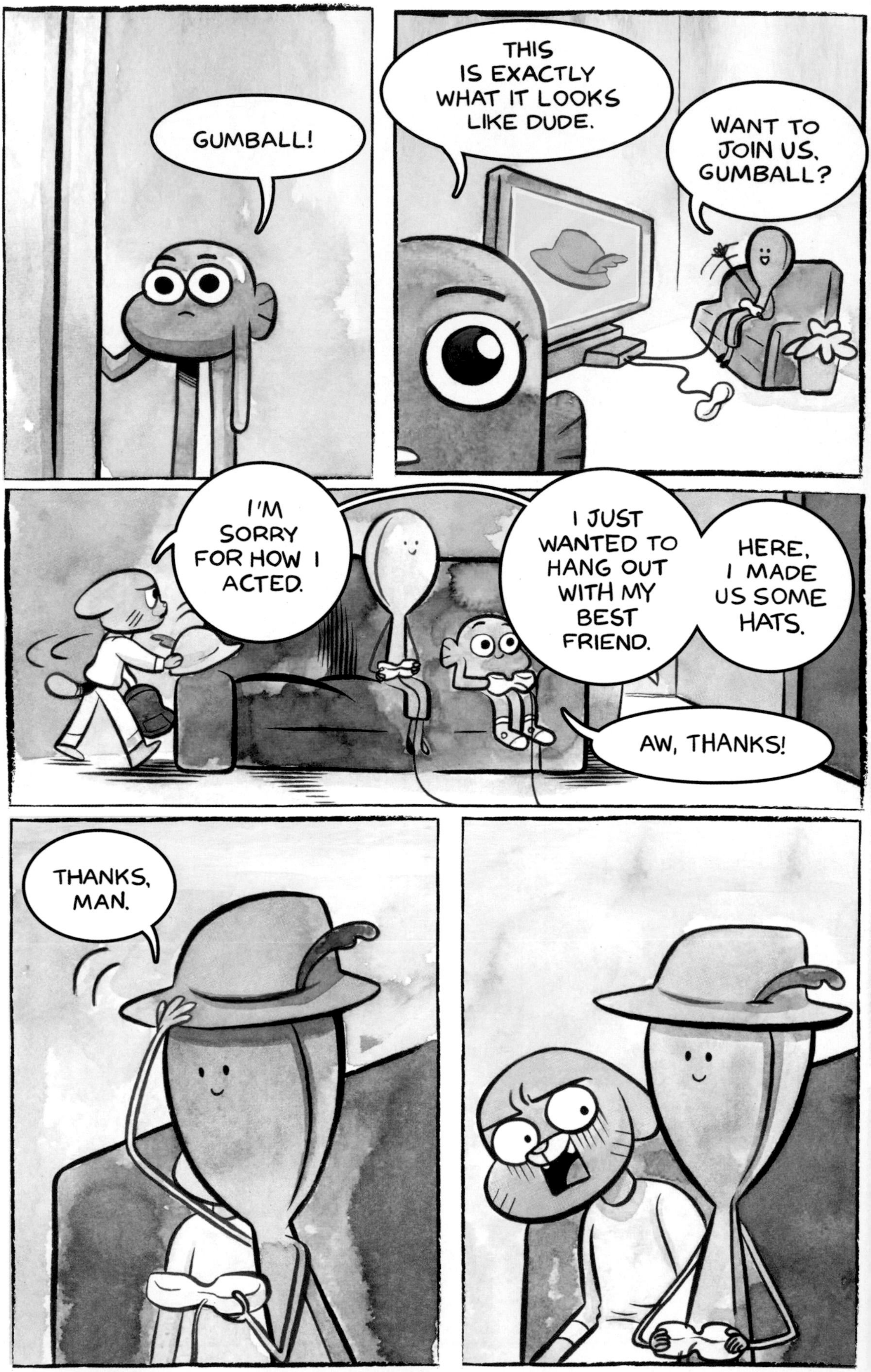
GUMBALL!
THIS IS EXACTLY WHAT IT LOOKS LIKE DUDE.
WANT TO JOIN US, GUMBALL?
I'M SORRY FOR HOW I ACTED.
I JUST WANTED TO HANG OUT WITH MY BEST FRIEND.
HERE, I MADE US SOME HATS.
AW, THANKS!
THANKS, MAN.

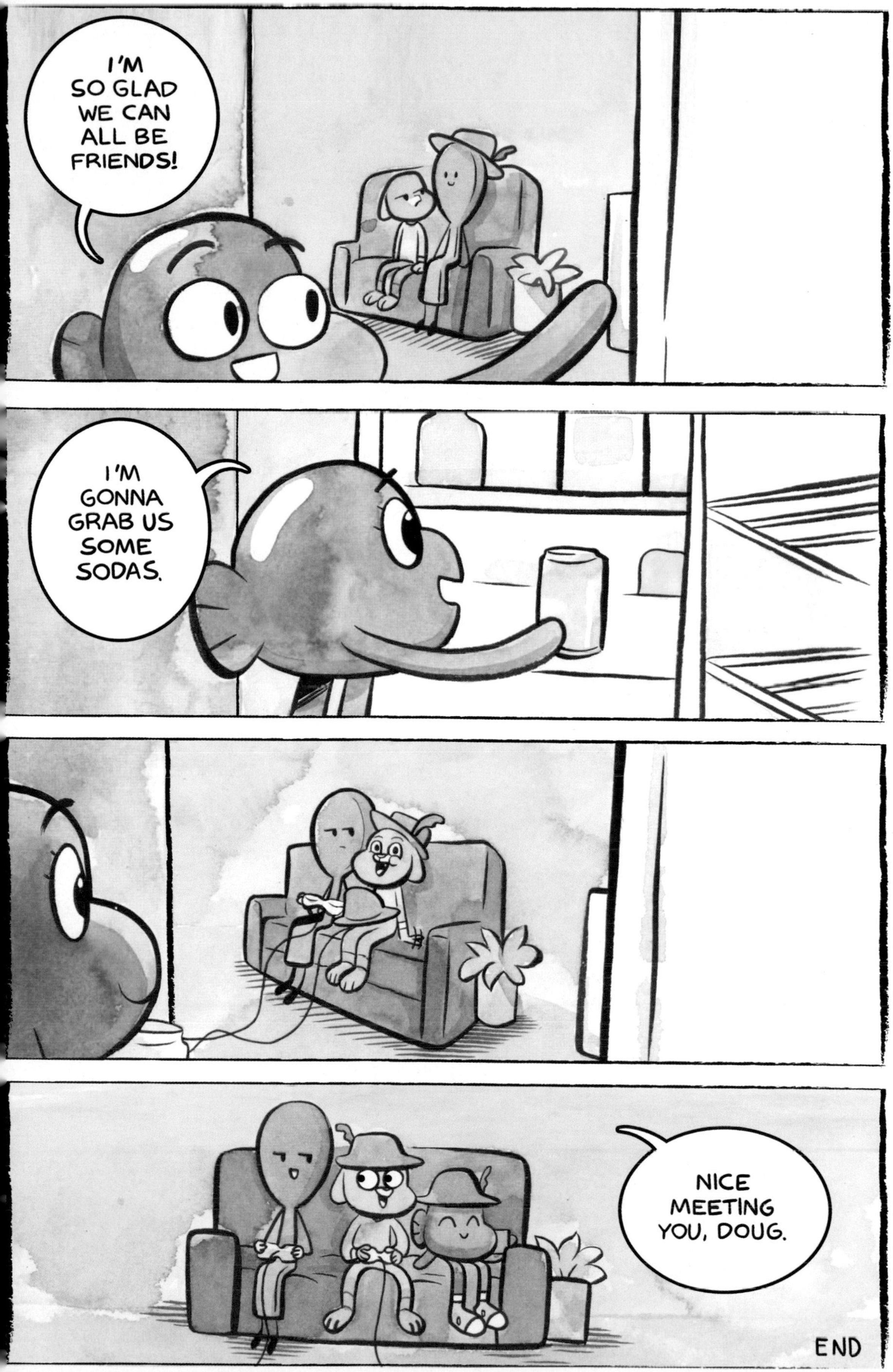
I'M SO GLAD WE CAN ALL BE FRIENDS!
I'M GONNA GRAB US SOME SODAS.
NICE MEETING YOU, DOUG.
END

THE TRICK

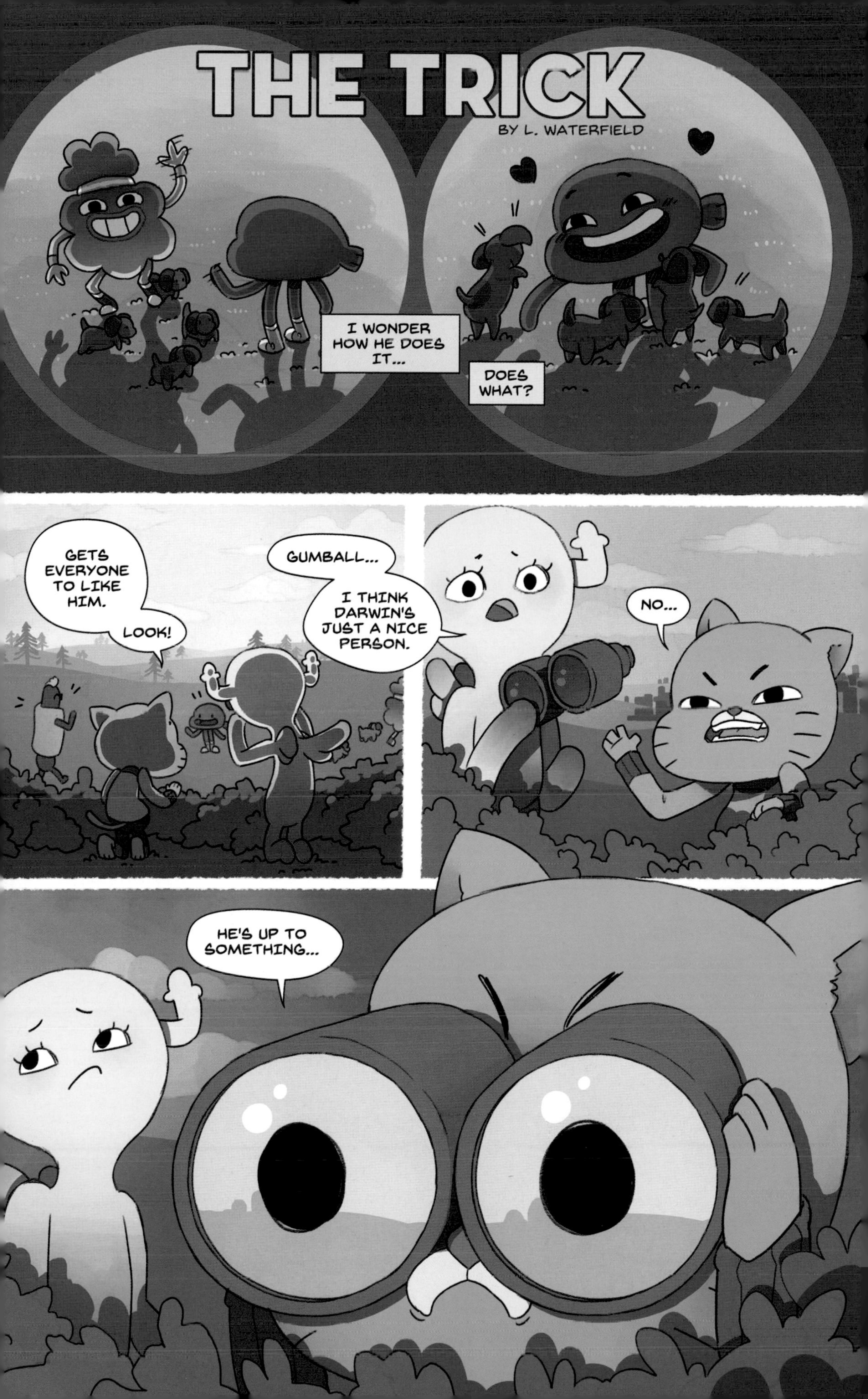
THE TRICK
BY L. WATERFIELD
I WONDER HOW HE DOES IT...
DOES WHAT?
GETS EVERYONE TO LIKE HIM.
LOOK!
GUMBALL...
I THINK DARWIN'S JUST A NICE PERSON.
NO...
HE'S UP TO SOMETHING...

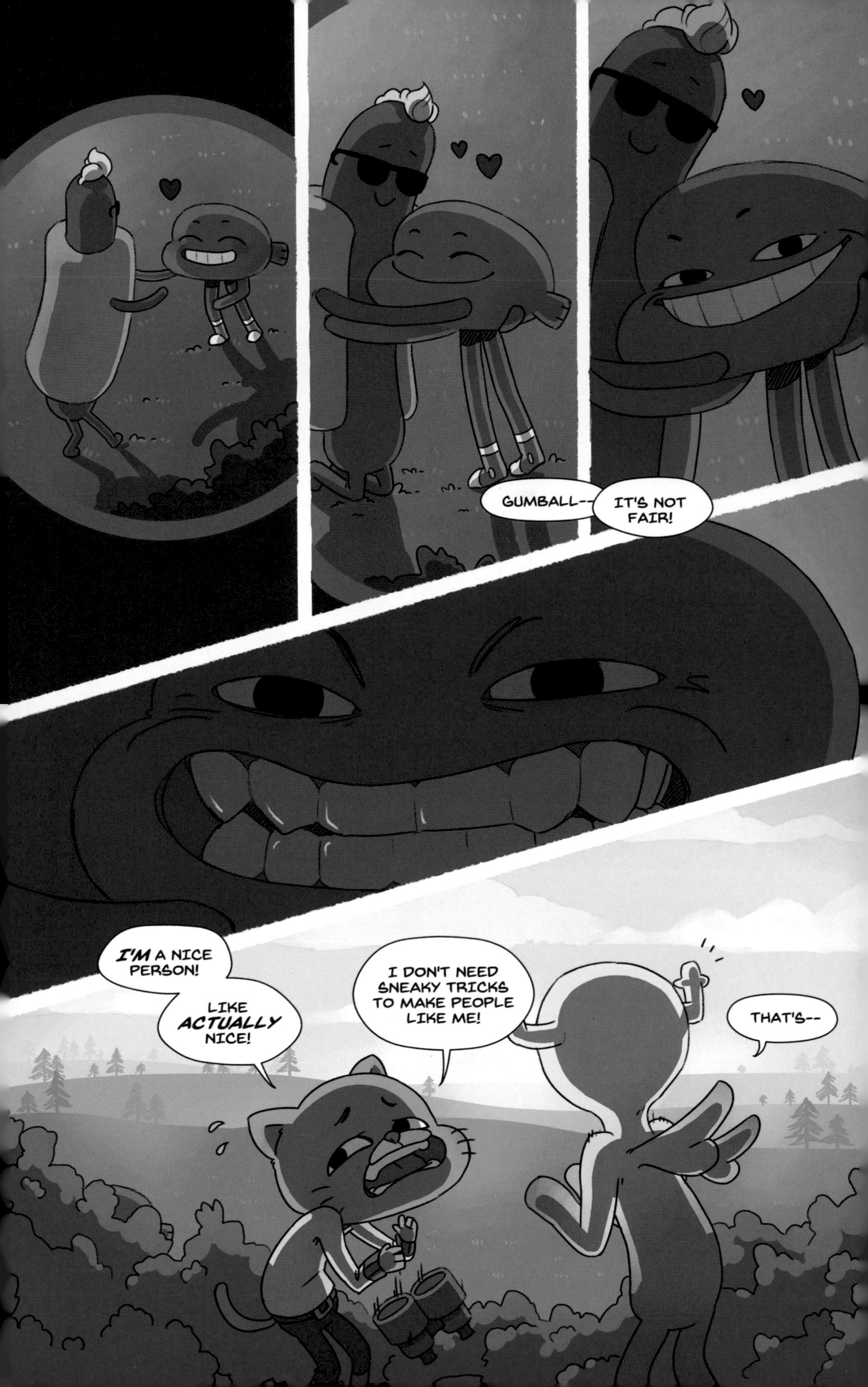
GUMBALL--
IT'S NOT FAIR!
I'M A NICE PERSON!
LIKE ACTUALLY NICE!
I DON'T NEED SNEAKY TRICKS TO MAKE PEOPLE LIKE ME!
THAT'S--

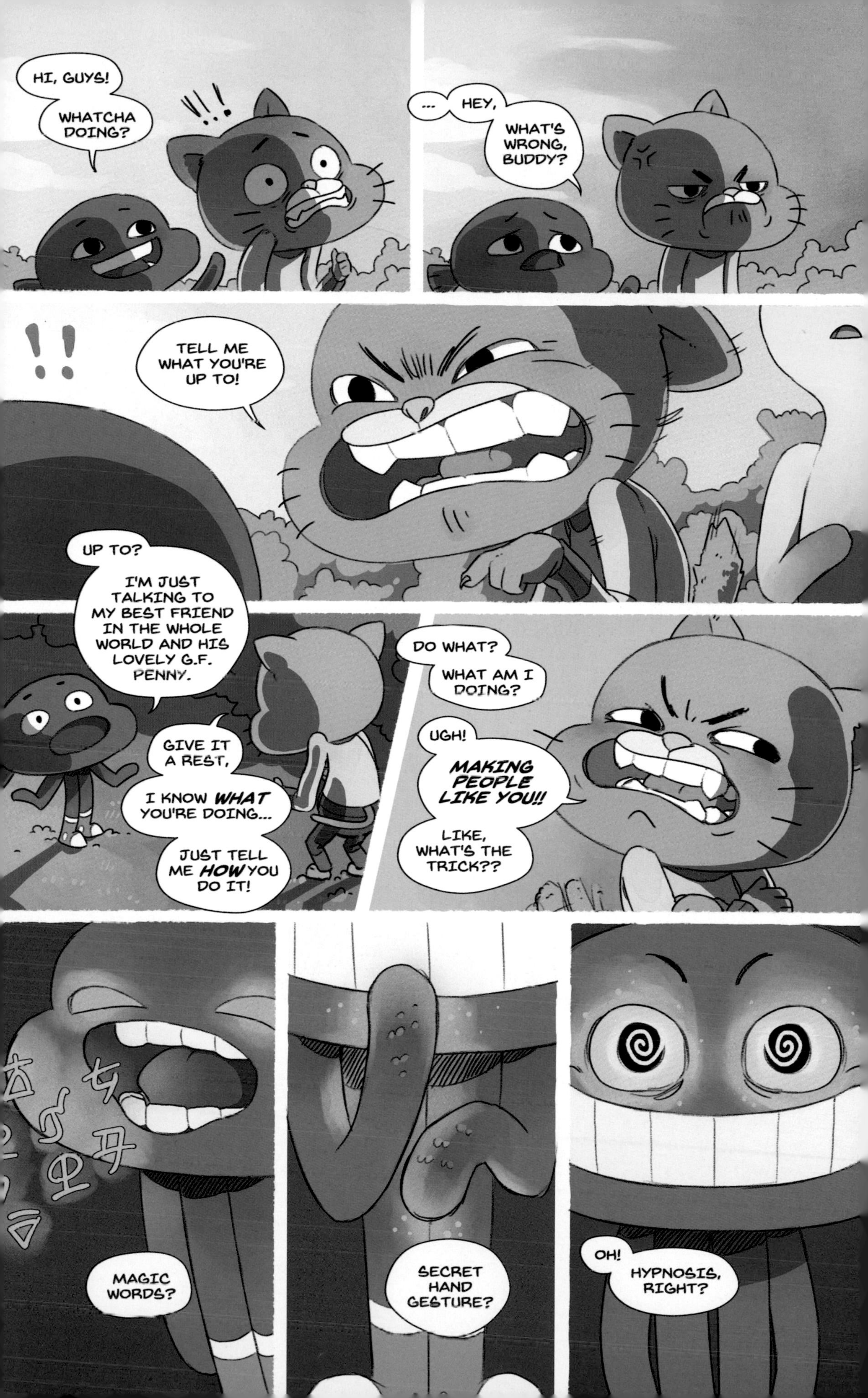
HI, GUYS!
WHATCHA DOING?
!!!..
... HEY,
WHAT'S WRONG, BUDDY?
!!
TELL ME WHAT YOU'RE UP TO!
UP TO?
I'M JUST TALKING TO MY BEST FRIEND IN THE WHOLE WORLD AND HIS LOVELY G.F. PENNY.
GIVE IT A REST,
I KNOW WHAT YOU'RE DOING...
JUST TELL ME HOW YOU DO IT!
DO WHAT?
WHAT AM I DOING?
UGH!
MAKING PEOPLE LIKE YOU!!
LIKE, WHAT'S THE TRICK??
MAGIC WORDS?
SECRET HAND GESTURE?
OH!
HYPNOSIS, RIGHT?

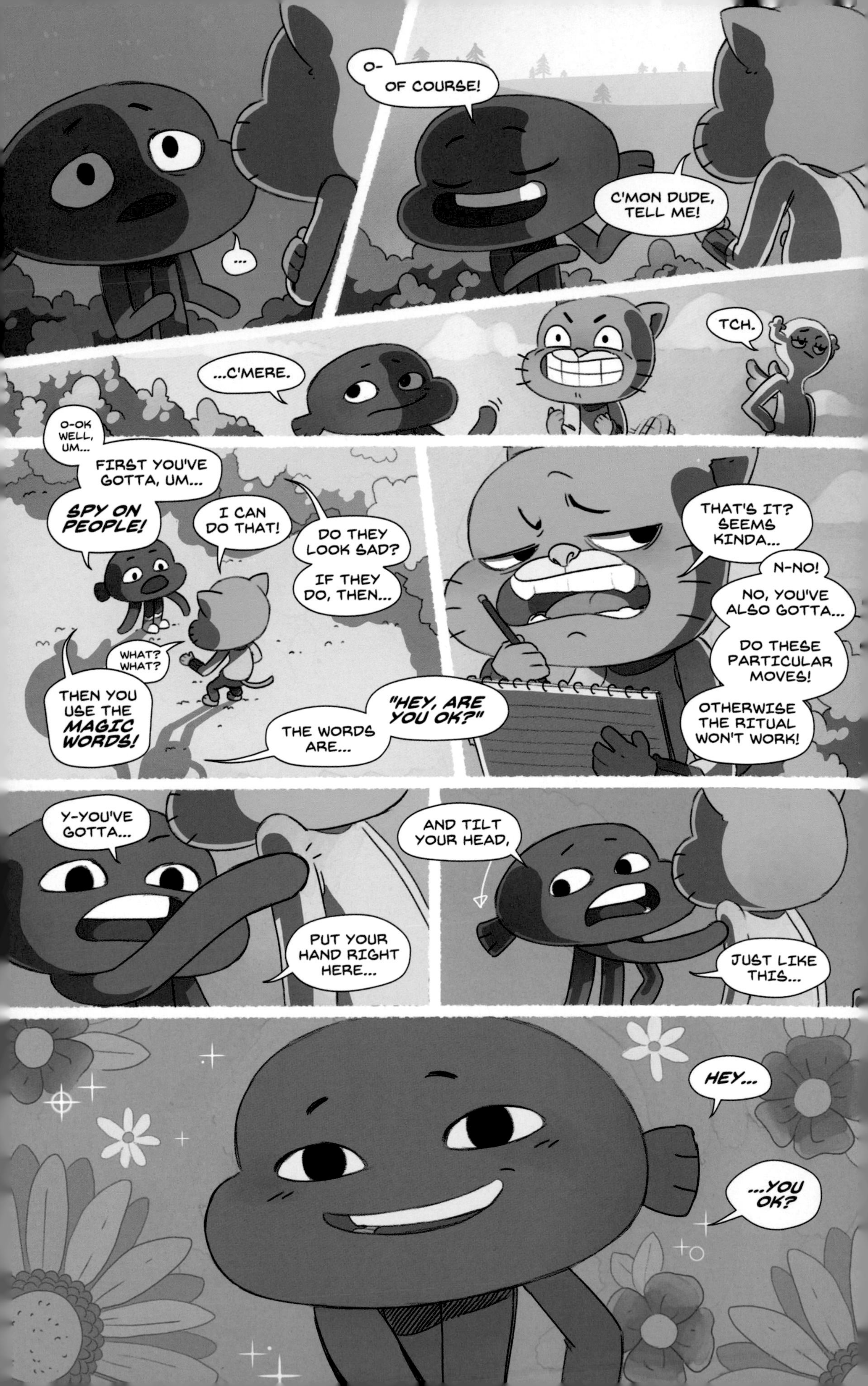
...
O-
OF COURSE!
C'MON DUDE, TELL ME!
...C'MERE.
TCH.
O-OK WELL, UM...
FIRST YOU'VE GOTTA, UM...
SPY ON PEOPLE!
I CAN DO THAT!
DO THEY LOOK SAD?
IF THEY DO, THEN...
WHAT? WHAT?
THEN YOU USE THE MAGIC WORDS!
THE WORDS ARE...
"HEY, ARE YOU OK?"
THAT'S IT? SEEMS KINDA...
N-NO!
NO, YOU'VE ALSO GOTTA...
DO THESE PARTICULAR MOVES!
OTHERWISE THE RITUAL WON'T WORK!
Y-YOU'VE GOTTA...
PUT YOUR HAND RIGHT HERE...
AND TILT YOUR HEAD,
JUST LIKE THIS...
HEY...
...YOU OK?

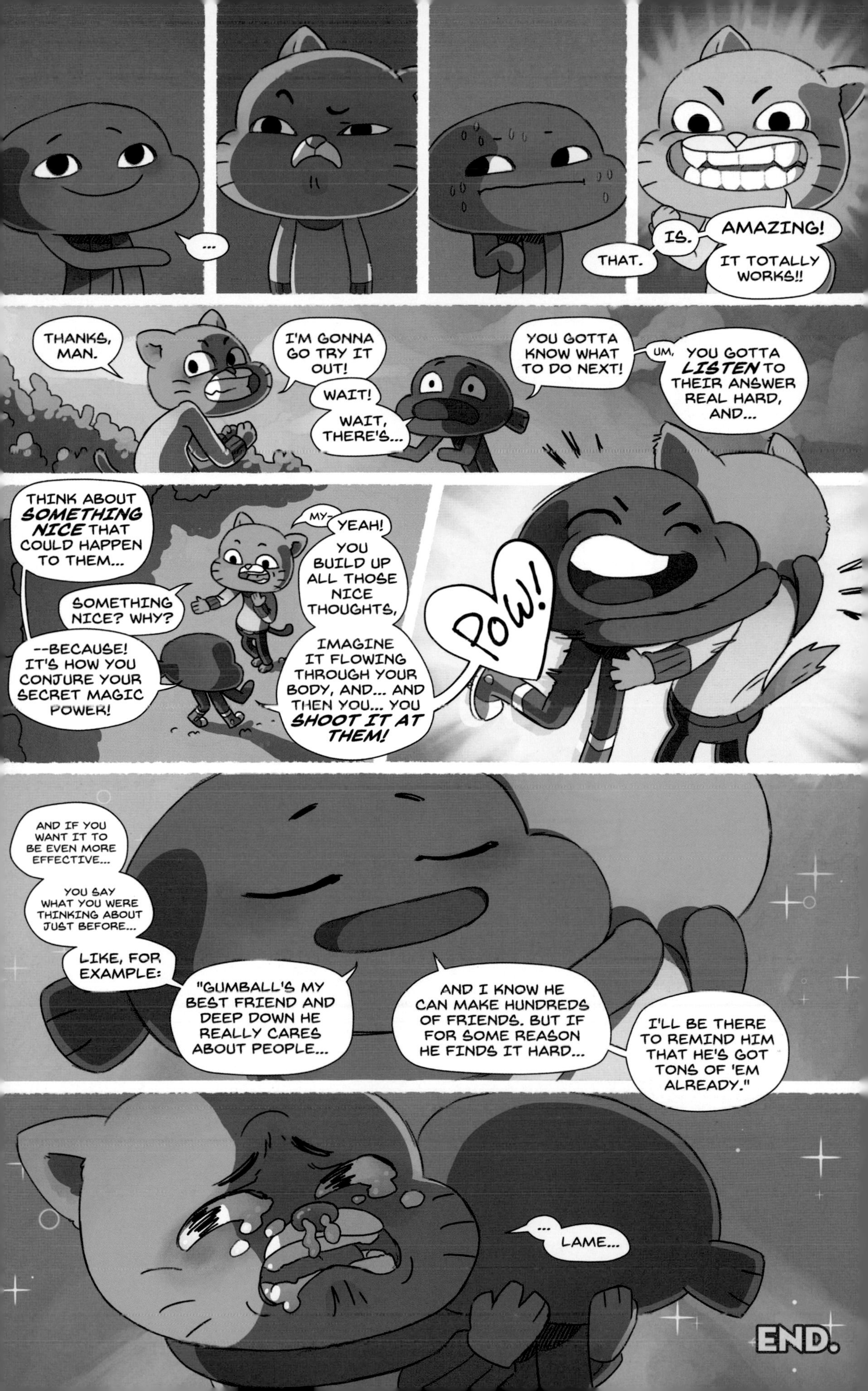
...
THAT.
IS.
AMAZING!
IT TOTALLY WORKS!!
THANKS, MAN.
I'M GONNA GO TRY IT OUT!
WAIT!
WAIT, THERE'S...
YOU GOTTA KNOW WHAT TO DO NEXT!
UM,
YOU GOTTA LISTEN TO THEIR ANSWER REAL HARD, AND...
THINK ABOUT SOMETHING NICE THAT COULD HAPPEN TO THEM...
SOMETHING NICE? WHY?
--BECAUSE! IT'S HOW YOU CONJURE YOUR SECRET MAGIC POWER!
MY-
YEAH!
YOU BUILD UP ALL THOSE NICE THOUGHTS,
IMAGINE IT FLOWING THROUGH YOUR BODY, AND... AND THEN YOU... YOU SHOOT IT AT THEM!
POW!
AND IF YOU WANT IT TO BE EVEN MORE EFFECTIVE...
YOU SAY WHAT YOU WERE THINKING ABOUT JUST BEFORE...
LIKE, FOR EXAMPLE:
"GUMBALL'S MY BEST FRIEND AND DEEP DOWN HE REALLY CARES ABOUT PEOPLE...
AND I KNOW HE CAN MAKE HUNDREDS OF FRIENDS. BUT IF FOR SOME REASON HE FINDS IT HARD...
I'LL BE THERE TO REMIND HIM THAT HE'S GOT TONS OF 'EM ALREADY."
... LAME...
END.

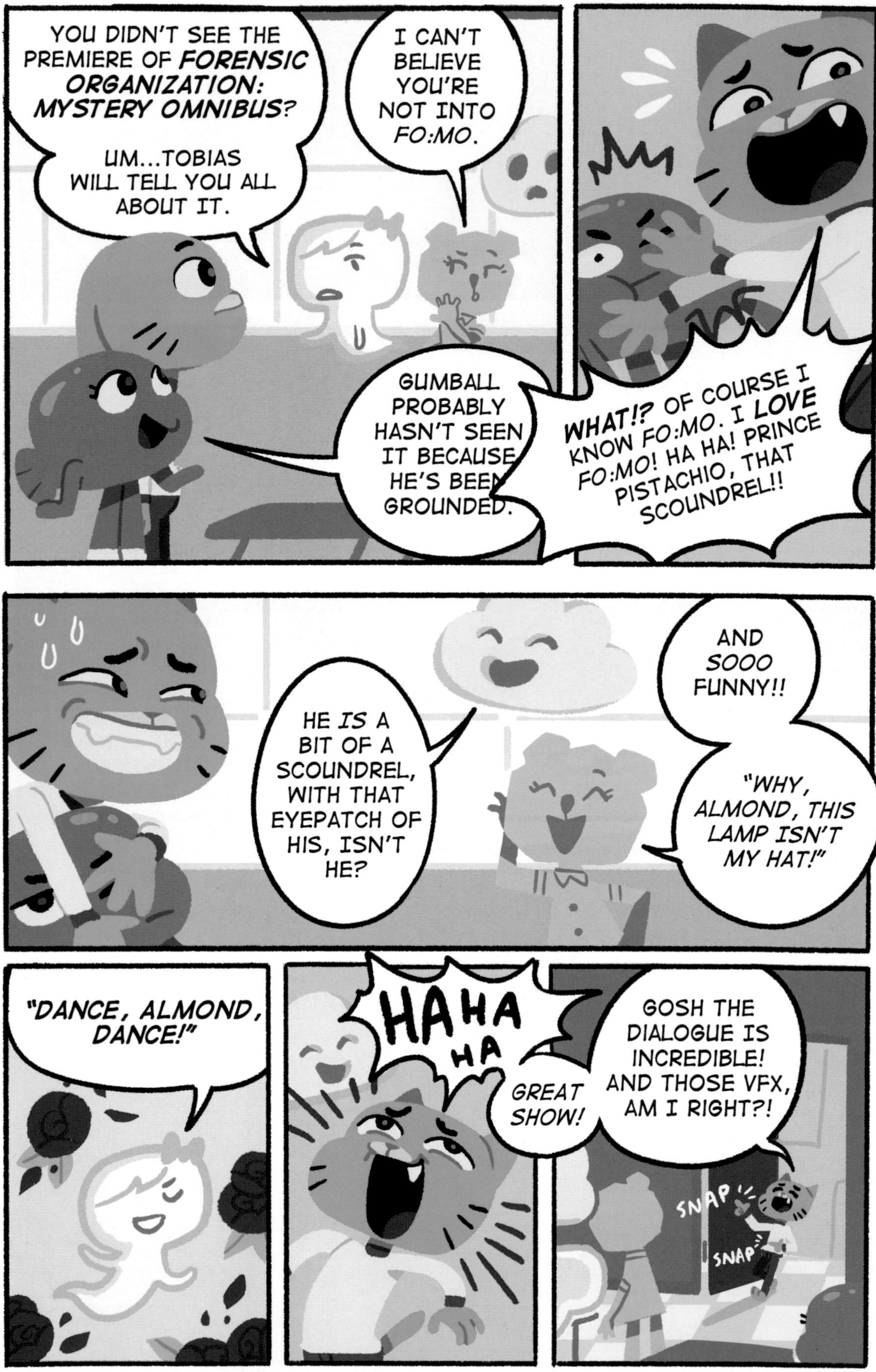

YOU DIDN'T SEE THE PREMIERE OF FORENSIC ORGANIZATION: MYSTERY OMNIBUS?
UM...TOBIAS WILL TELL YOU ALL ABOUT IT.
I CAN'T BELIEVE YOU'RE NOT INTO FO:MO.
GUMBALL PROBABLY HASN'T SEEN IT BECAUSE HE'S BEEN GROUNDED.
WHAT!? OF COURSE I KNOW FO:MO. I LOVE FO:MO! HA HA! PRINCE PISTACHIO, THAT SCOUNDREL!!
HE IS A BIT OF A SCOUNDREL, WITH THAT EYEPATCH OF HIS, ISN'T HE?
AND SOOO FUNNY!!
"WHY, ALMOND, THIS LAMP ISN'T MY HAT!"
"DANCE, ALMOND, DANCE!"
HAHA HA
GREAT SHOW!
GOSH THE DIALOGUE IS INCREDIBLE! AND THOSE VFX, AM I RIGHT?!
SNAP
SNAP

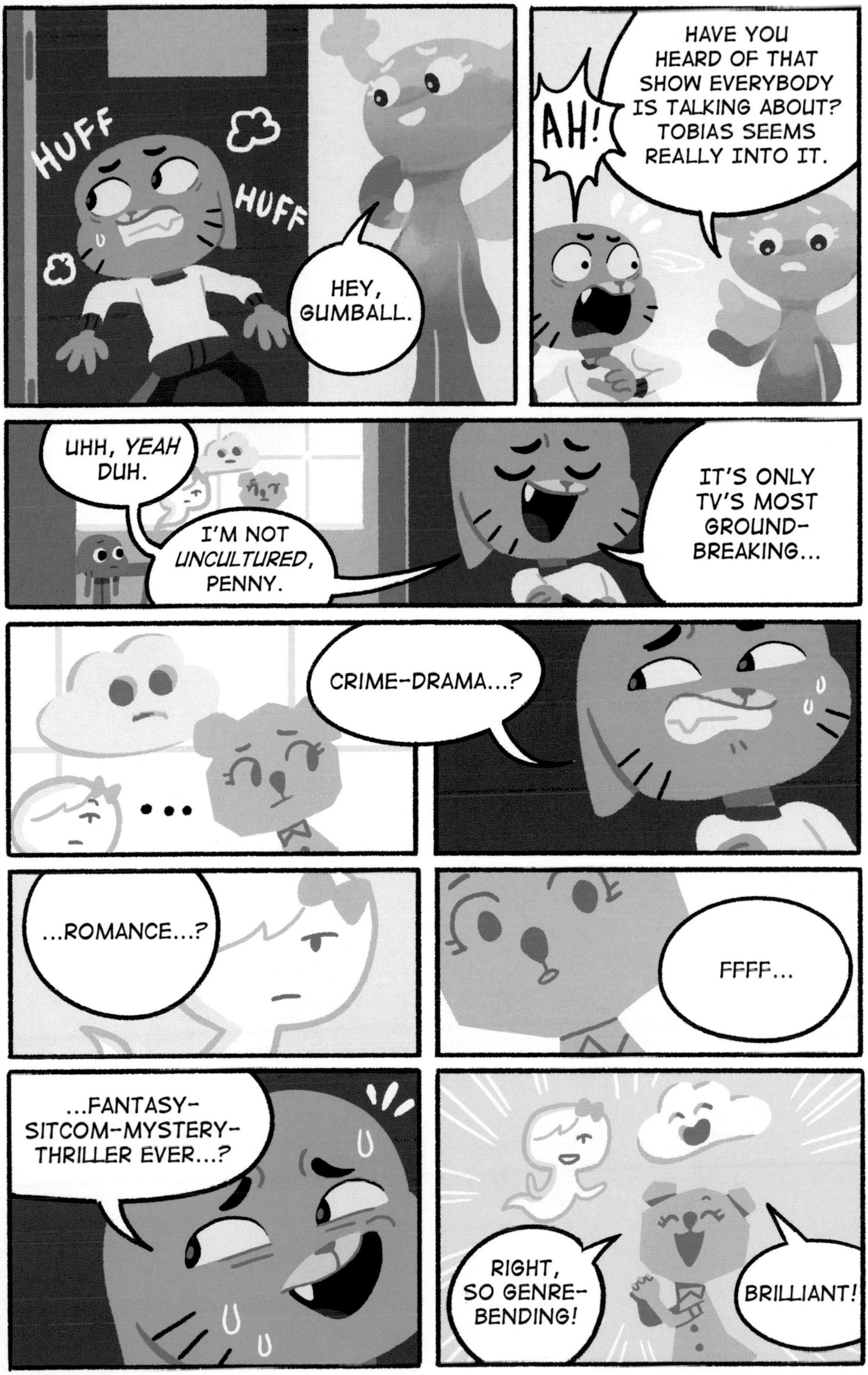
HUFF
HUFF
HEY, GUMBALL.
AH!
HAVE YOU HEARD OF THAT SHOW EVERYBODY IS TALKING ABOUT? TOBIAS SEEMS REALLY INTO IT.
UHH, *YEAH* DUH.
I'M NOT *UNCULTURED*, PENNY.
IT'S ONLY TV'S MOST GROUND-BREAKING...
CRIME-DRAMA...?
...
...ROMANCE...?
FFFF...
...FANTASY-SITCOM-MYSTERY-THRILLER EVER...?
RIGHT, SO GENRE-BENDING!
BRILLIANT!

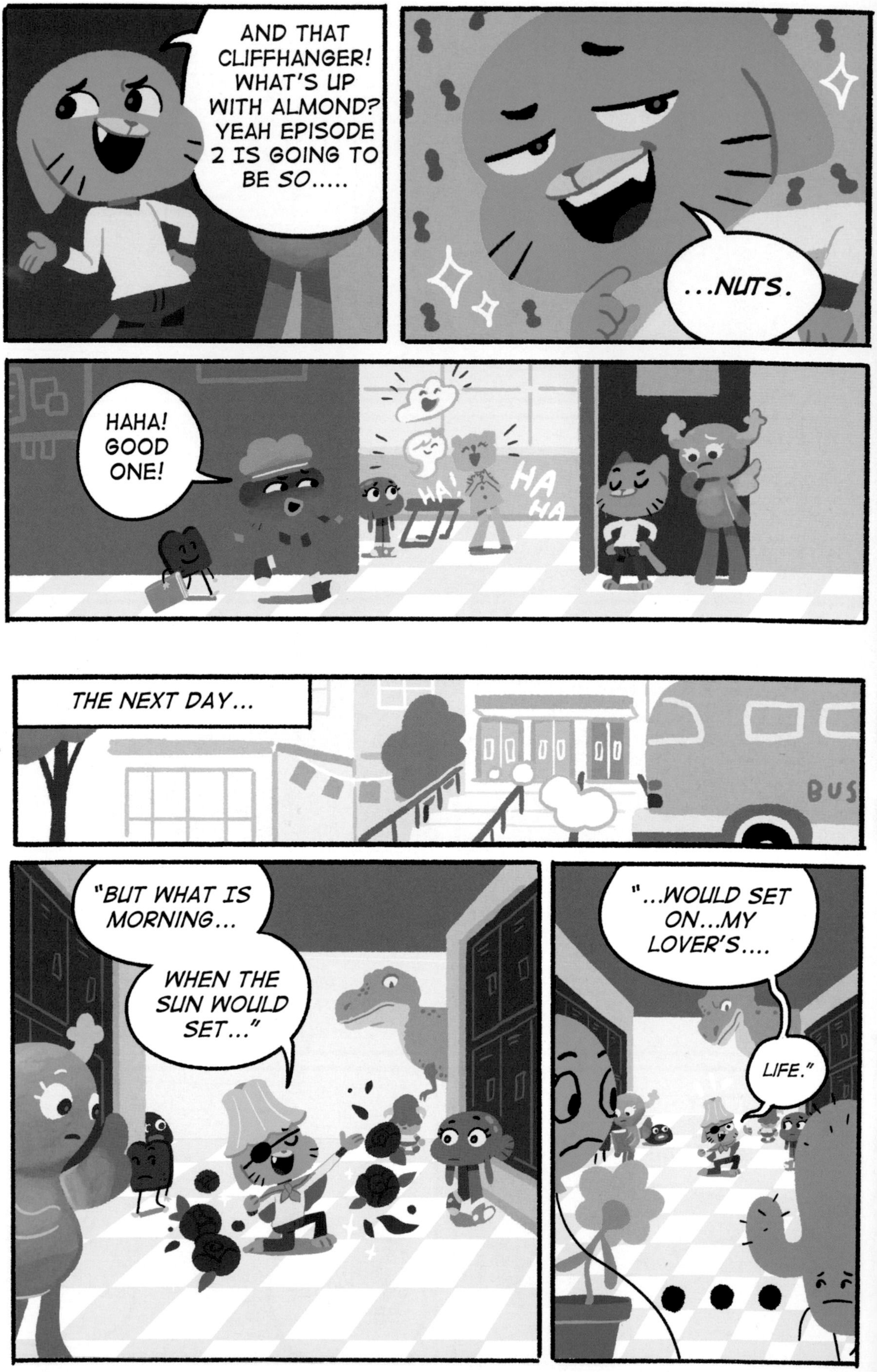
AND THAT CLIFFHANGER! WHAT'S UP WITH ALMOND? YEAH EPISODE 2 IS GOING TO BE SO.....
...NUTS.
HAHA! GOOD ONE!
HA!
HA HA
THE NEXT DAY...
BUS
"BUT WHAT IS MORNING...
WHEN THE SUN WOULD SET..."
"...WOULD SET ON...MY LOVER'S....
LIFE."

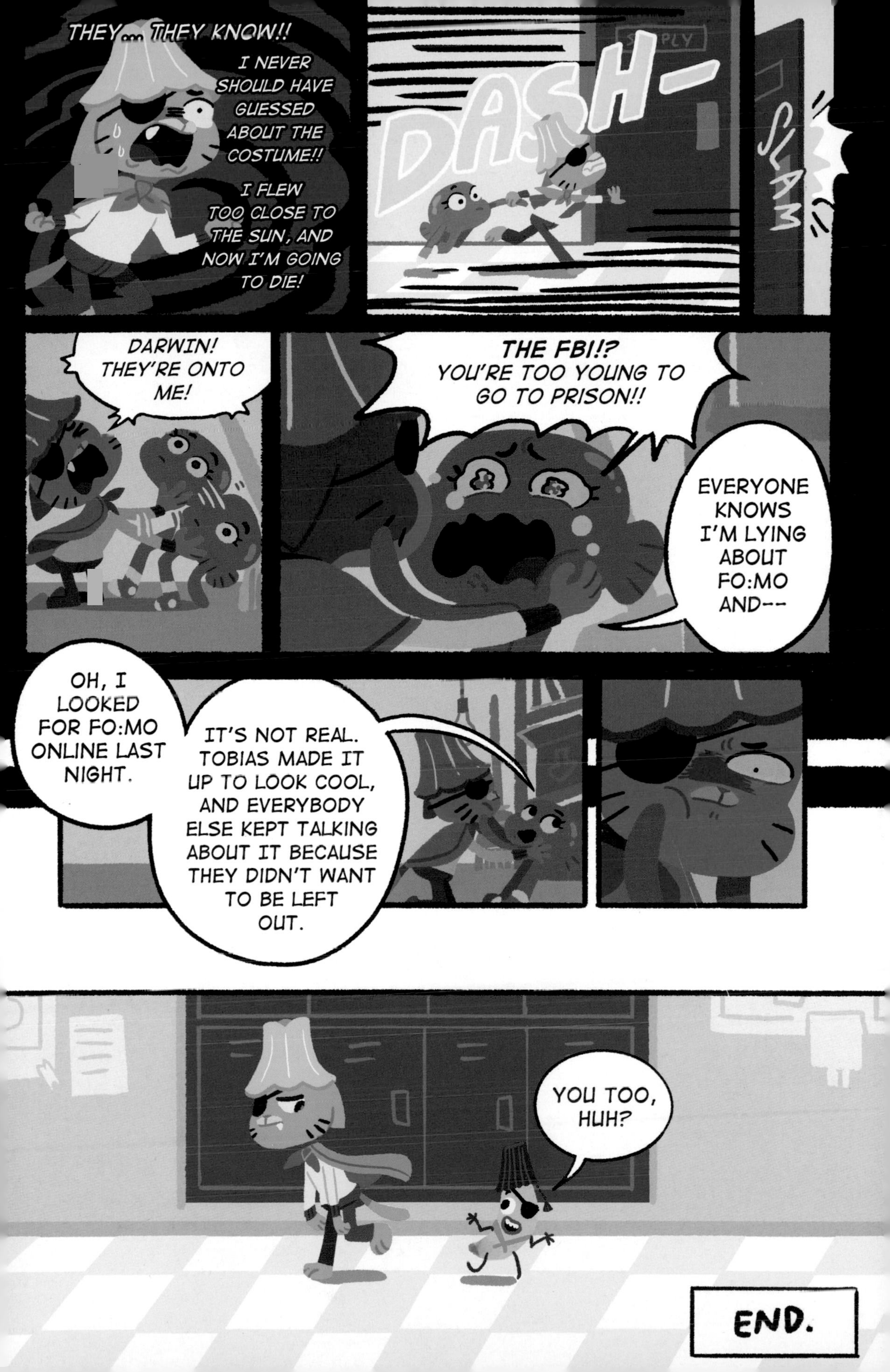
THEY... THEY KNOW!!
I NEVER SHOULD HAVE GUESSED ABOUT THE COSTUME!!
I FLEW TOO CLOSE TO THE SUN, AND NOW I'M GOING TO DIE!
DASH-
SLAM
DARWIN! THEY'RE ONTO ME!
THE FBI!? YOU'RE TOO YOUNG TO GO TO PRISON!!
EVERYONE KNOWS I'M LYING ABOUT FO:MO AND--
OH, I LOOKED FOR FO:MO ONLINE LAST NIGHT.
IT'S NOT REAL. TOBIAS MADE IT UP TO LOOK COOL, AND EVERYBODY ELSE KEPT TALKING ABOUT IT BECAUSE THEY DIDN'T WANT TO BE LEFT OUT.
YOU TOO, HUH?
END.

GRAND MUMMY'S CURSE

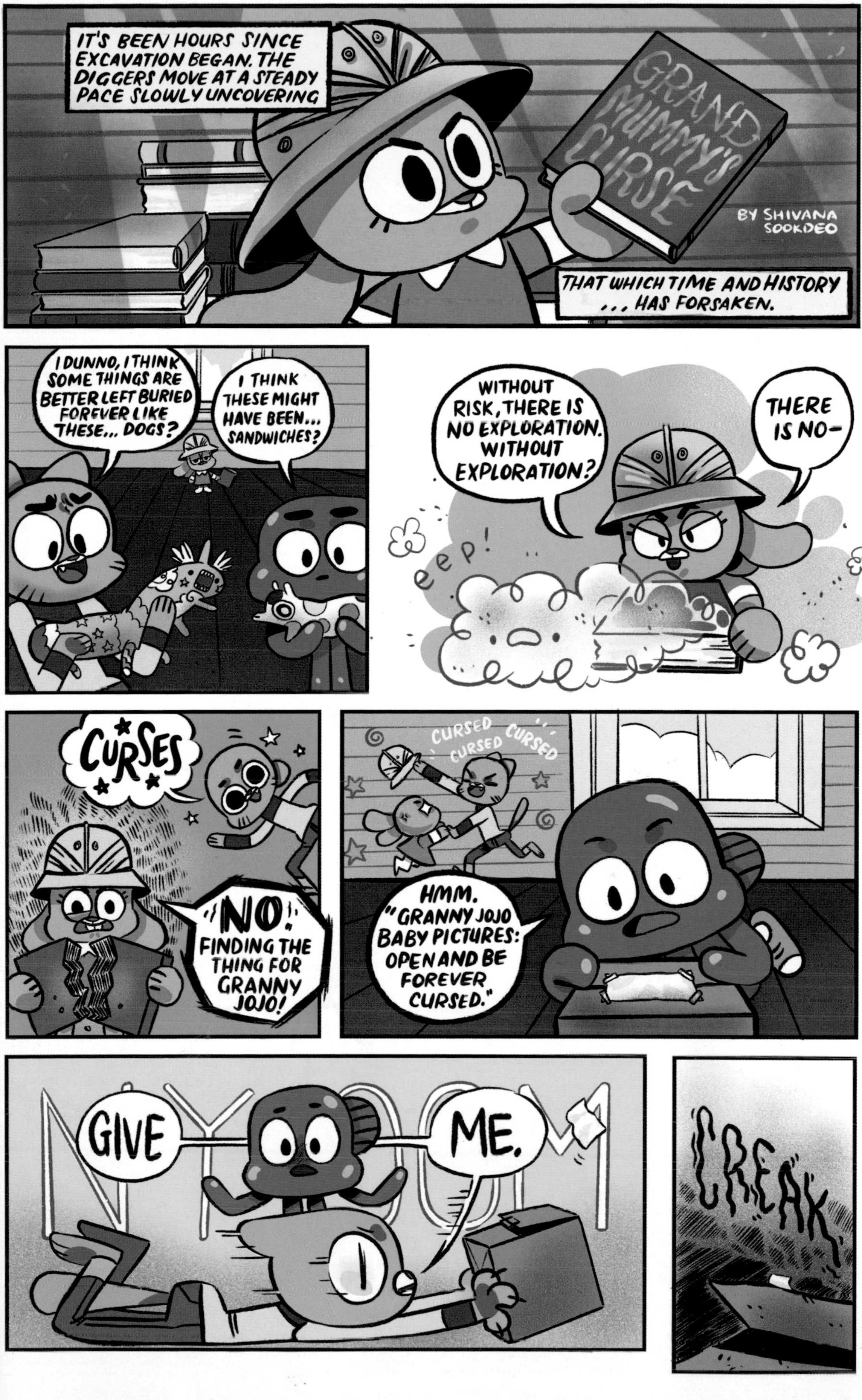
IT'S BEEN HOURS SINCE EXCAVATION BEGAN. THE DIGGERS MOVE AT A STEADY PACE SLOWLY UNCOVERING
GRAND MUMMY'S CURSE
BY SHIVANA SOOKDEO
THAT WHICH TIME AND HISTORY ... HAS FORSAKEN.
I DUNNO, I THINK SOME THINGS ARE BETTER LEFT BURIED FOREVER LIKE THESE... DOGS?
I THINK THESE MIGHT HAVE BEEN... SANDWICHES?
WITHOUT RISK, THERE IS NO EXPLORATION. WITHOUT EXPLORATION?
THERE IS NO-
EEP!
CURSES
NO! FINDING THE THING FOR GRANNY JOJO!
CURSED CURSED CURSED
HMM. "GRANNY JOJO BABY PICTURES: OPEN AND BE FOREVER CURSED."
GIVE
ME.
NYOOM
CREAK

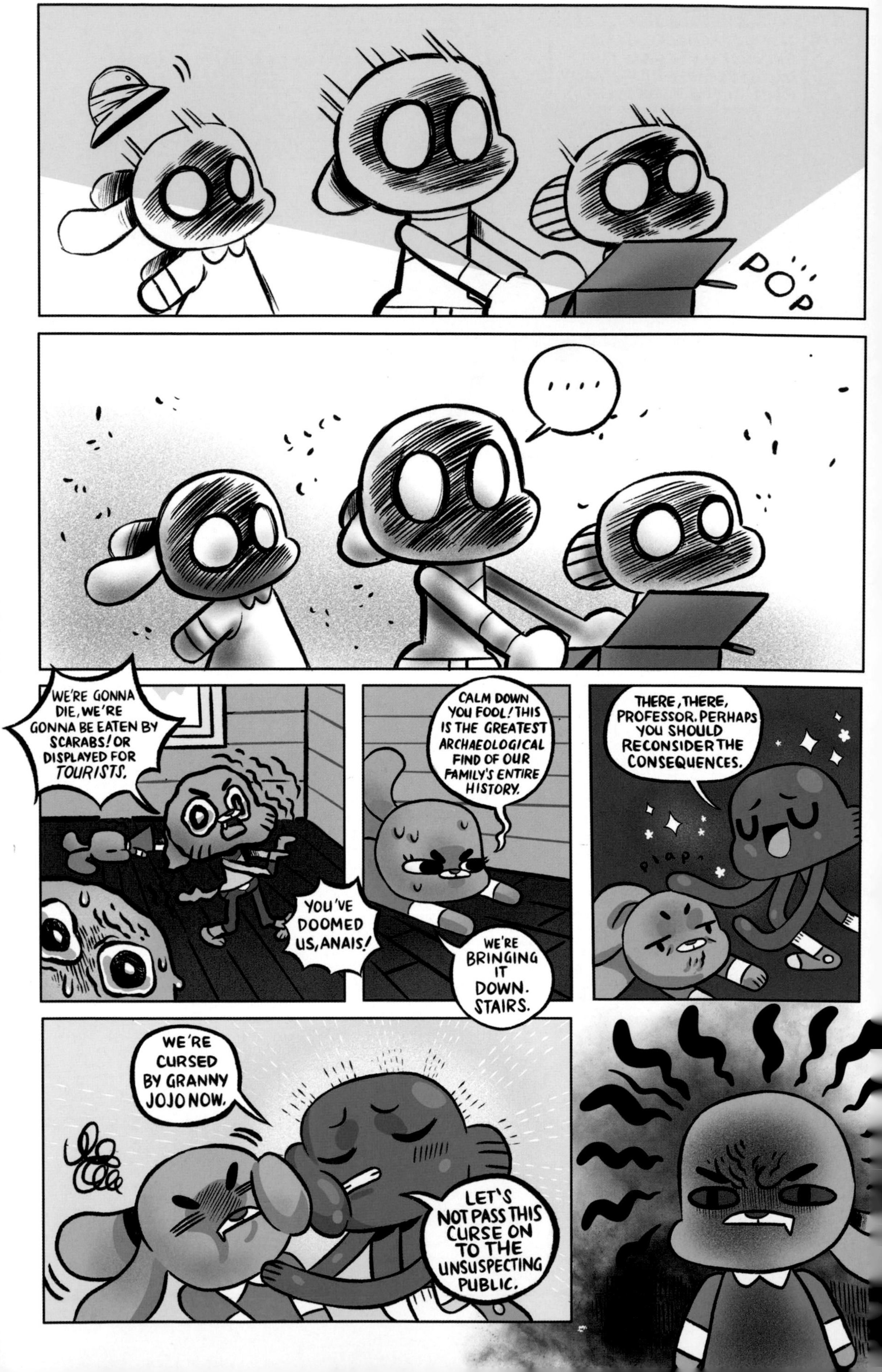
POP
....
WE'RE GONNA DIE, WE'RE GONNA BE EATEN BY SCARABS! OR DISPLAYED FOR TOURISTS.
YOU'VE DOOMED US, ANAIS!
CALM DOWN YOU FOOL! THIS IS THE GREATEST ARCHAEOLOGICAL FIND OF OUR FAMILY'S ENTIRE HISTORY.
WE'RE BRINGING IT DOWN. STAIRS.
THERE, THERE, PROFESSOR. PERHAPS YOU SHOULD RECONSIDER THE CONSEQUENCES.
plap
WE'RE CURSED BY GRANNY JOJO NOW.
LET'S NOT PASS THIS CURSE ON TO THE UNSUSPECTING PUBLIC.

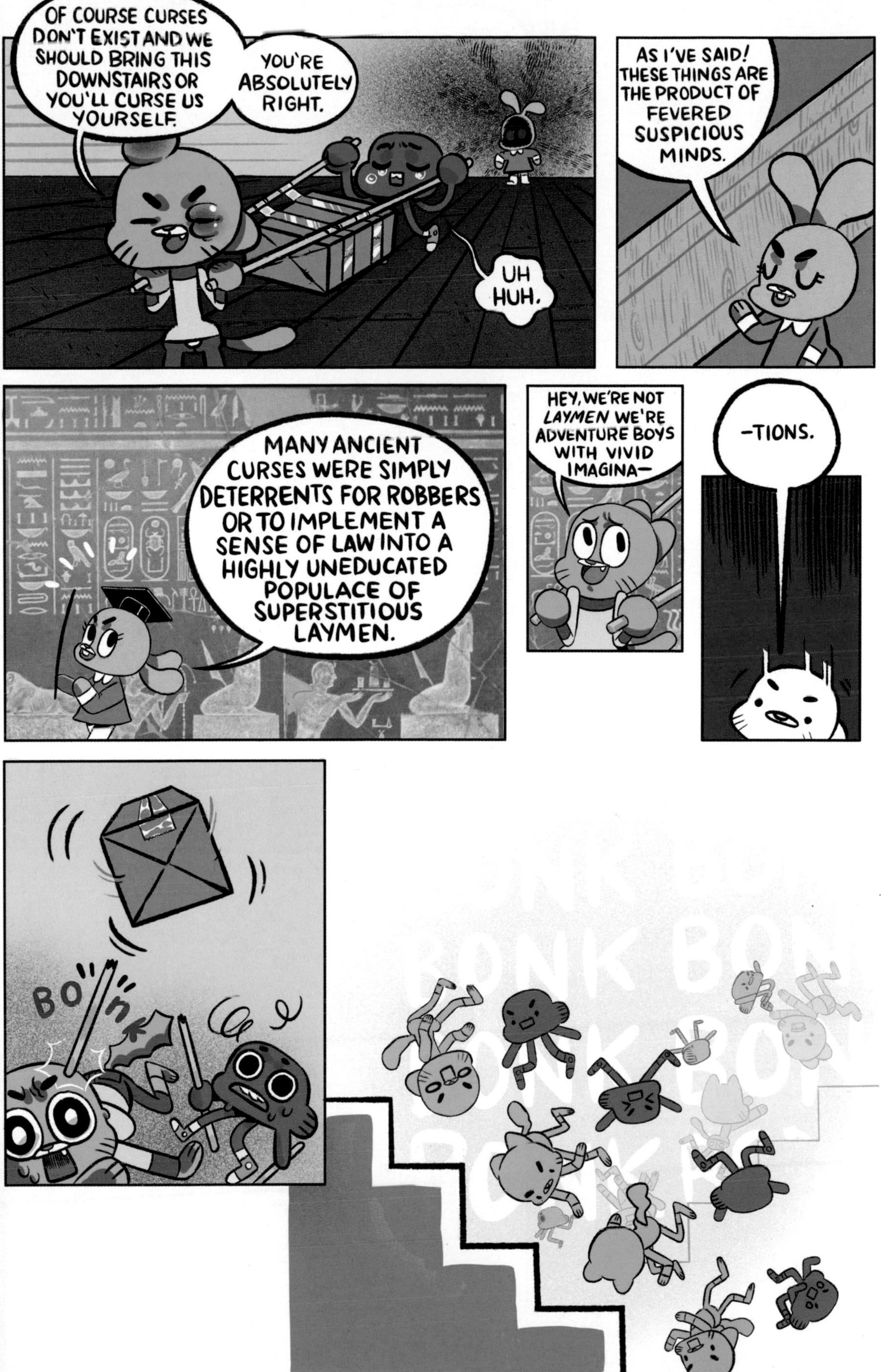
OF COURSE CURSES DON'T EXIST AND WE SHOULD BRING THIS DOWNSTAIRS OR YOU'LL CURSE US YOURSELF.
YOU'RE ABSOLUTELY RIGHT.
UH HUH.
AS I'VE SAID! THESE THINGS ARE THE PRODUCT OF FEVERED SUSPICIOUS MINDS.
MANY ANCIENT CURSES WERE SIMPLY DETERRENTS FOR ROBBERS OR TO IMPLEMENT A SENSE OF LAW INTO A HIGHLY UNEDUCATED POPULACE OF SUPERSTITIOUS LAYMEN.
HEY, WE'RE NOT *LAYMEN* WE'RE ADVENTURE BOYS WITH VIVID IMAGINA—
—TIONS.
BONK

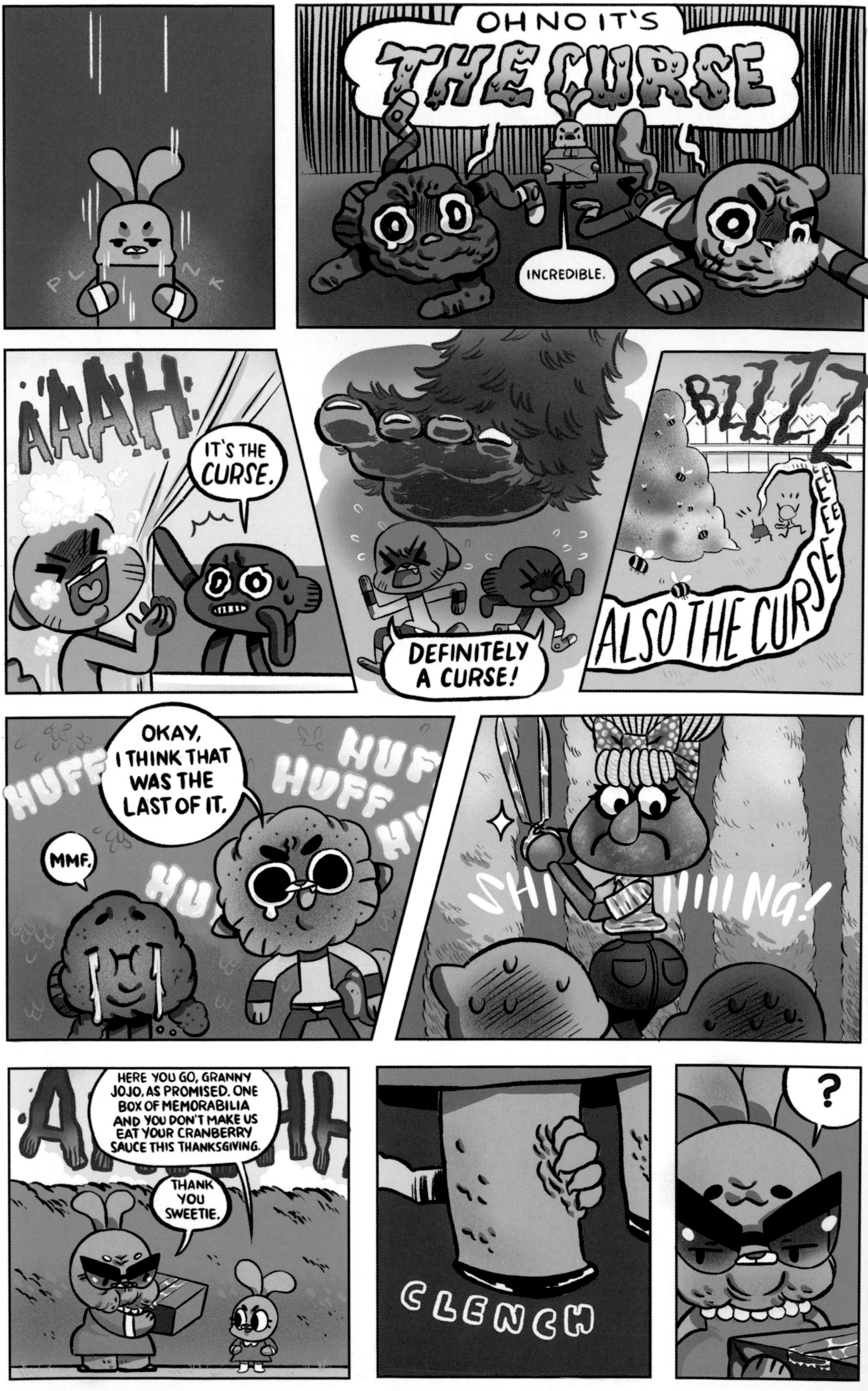
PLUNK
OH NO IT'S
THE CURSE
INCREDIBLE.
AAAH
IT'S THE CURSE.
DEFINITELY A CURSE!
BZZZZ
EEEE
ALSO THE CURSE
HUFF HUFF HUFF
OKAY, I THINK THAT WAS THE LAST OF IT.
MMF.
SHIIIIING!
HERE YOU GO, GRANNY JOJO, AS PROMISED. ONE BOX OF MEMORABILIA AND YOU DON'T MAKE US EAT YOUR CRANBERRY SAUCE THIS THANKSGIVING.
THANK YOU SWEETIE.
CLENCH
?

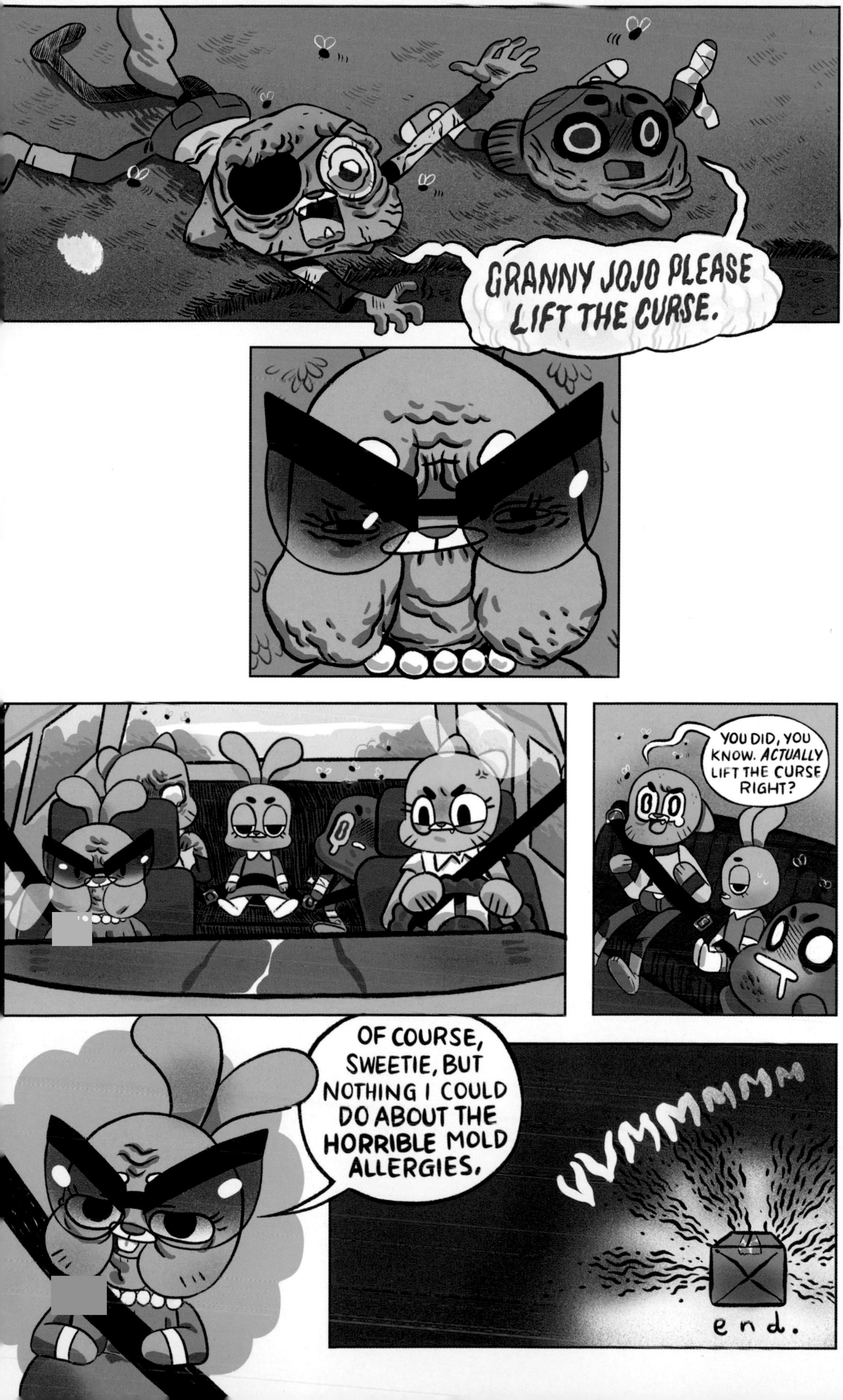
GRANNY JOJO PLEASE LIFT THE CURSE.
YOU DID, YOU KNOW. ACTUALLY LIFT THE CURSE RIGHT?
OF COURSE, SWEETIE, BUT NOTHING I COULD DO ABOUT THE HORRIBLE MOLD ALLERGIES.
end.

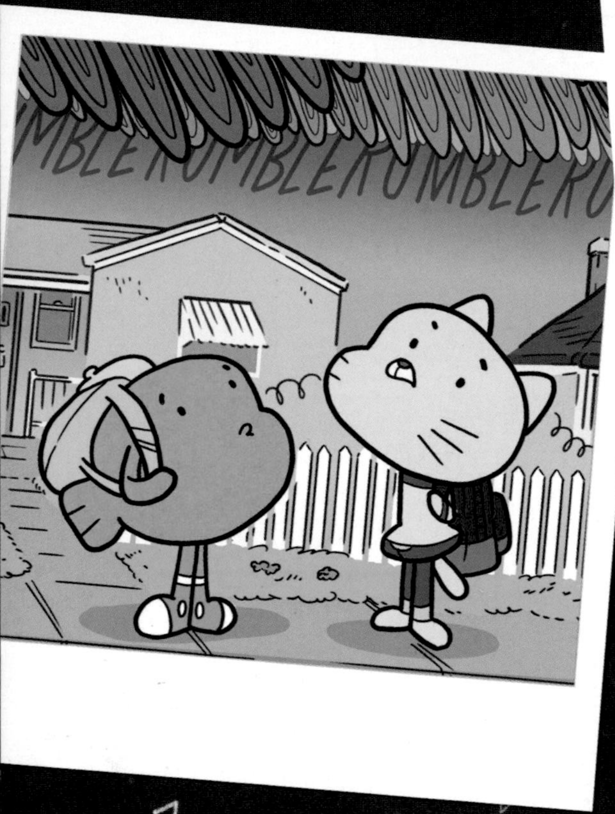
MBLERUMBLERUMBLERU

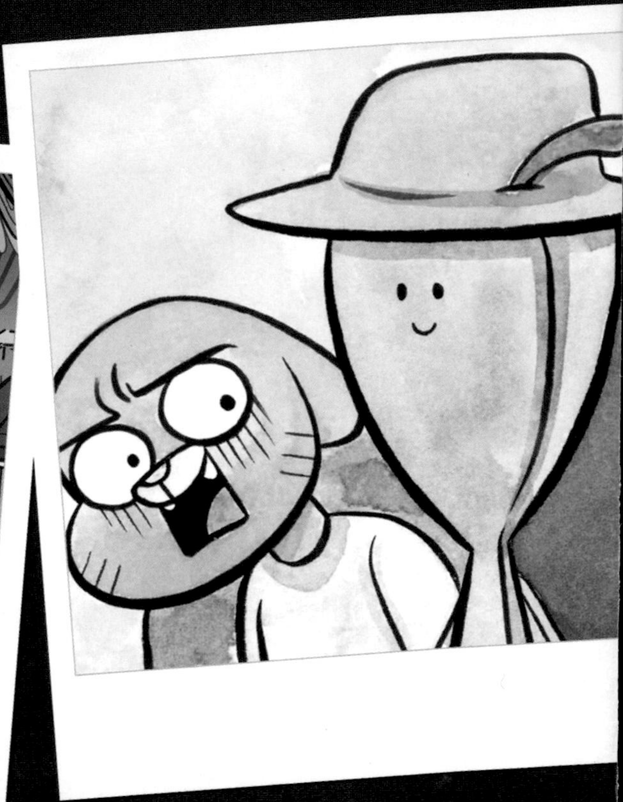

COVER GALLERY

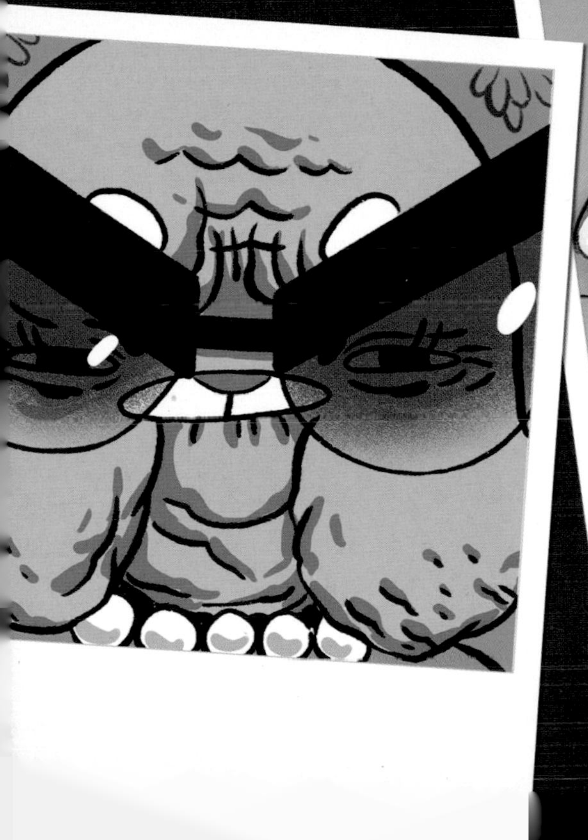

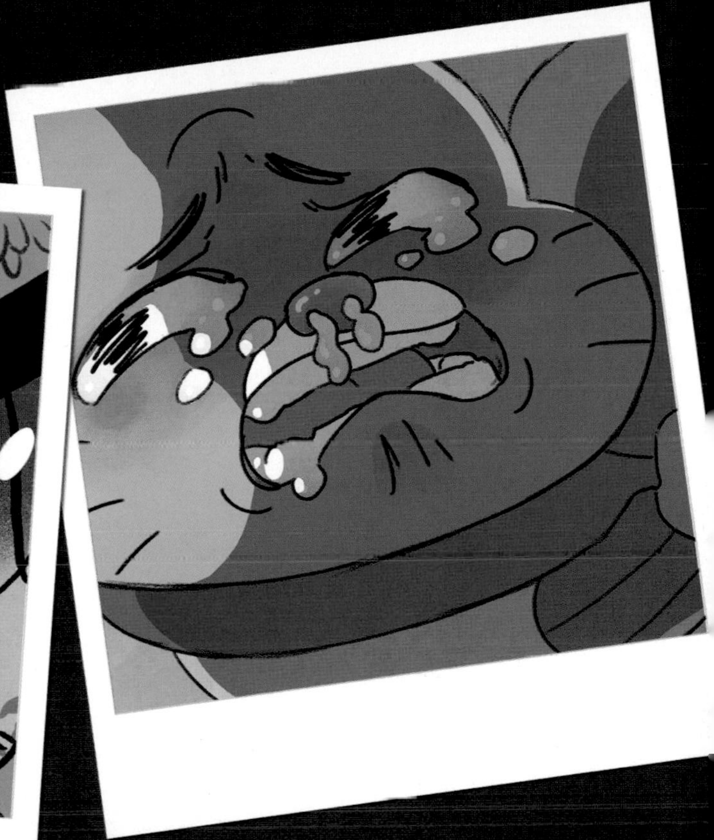

2018 GRAB BAG SPECIAL #1 MAIN COVER

CLAUDIA AGUIRRE

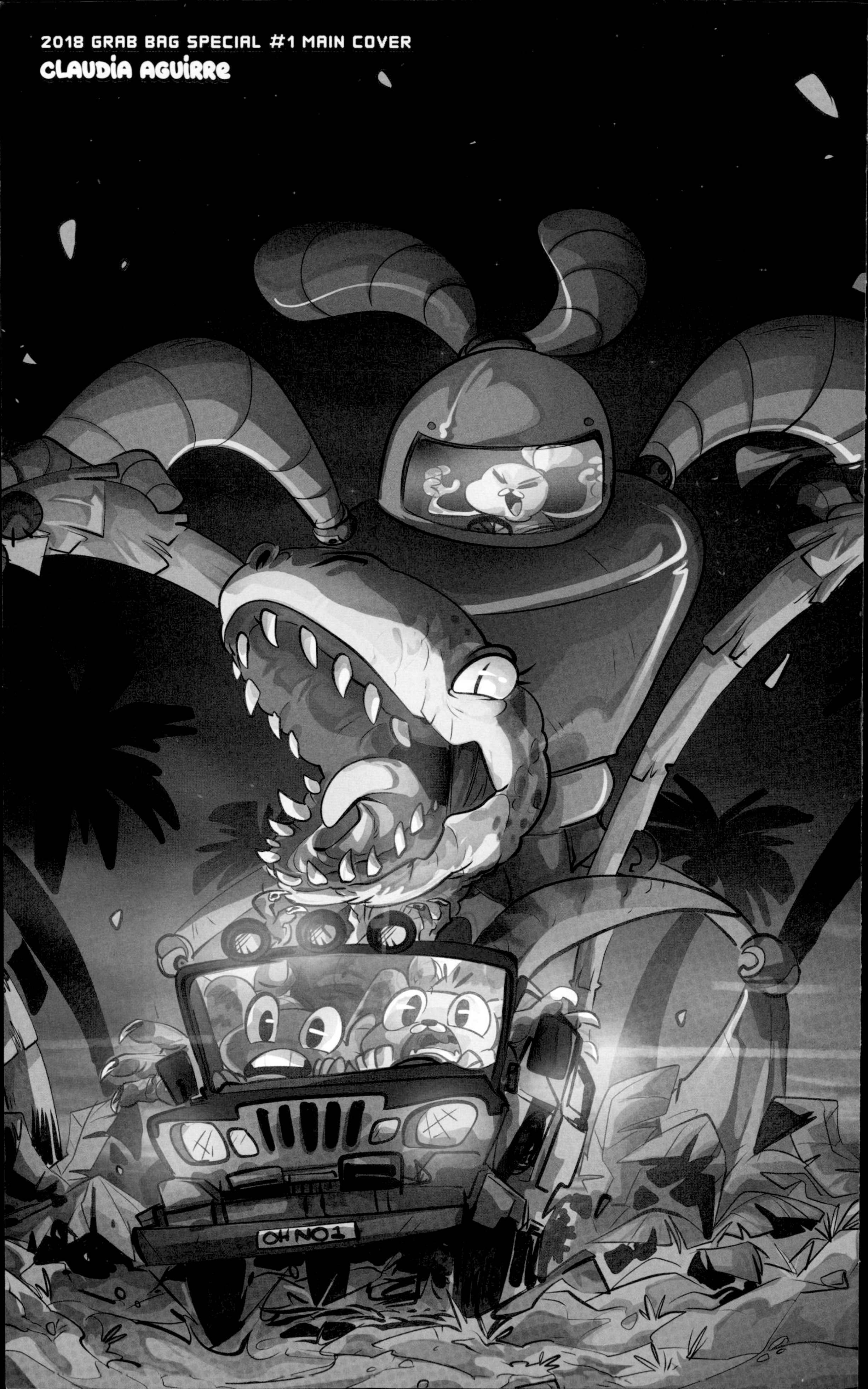
OH NO1

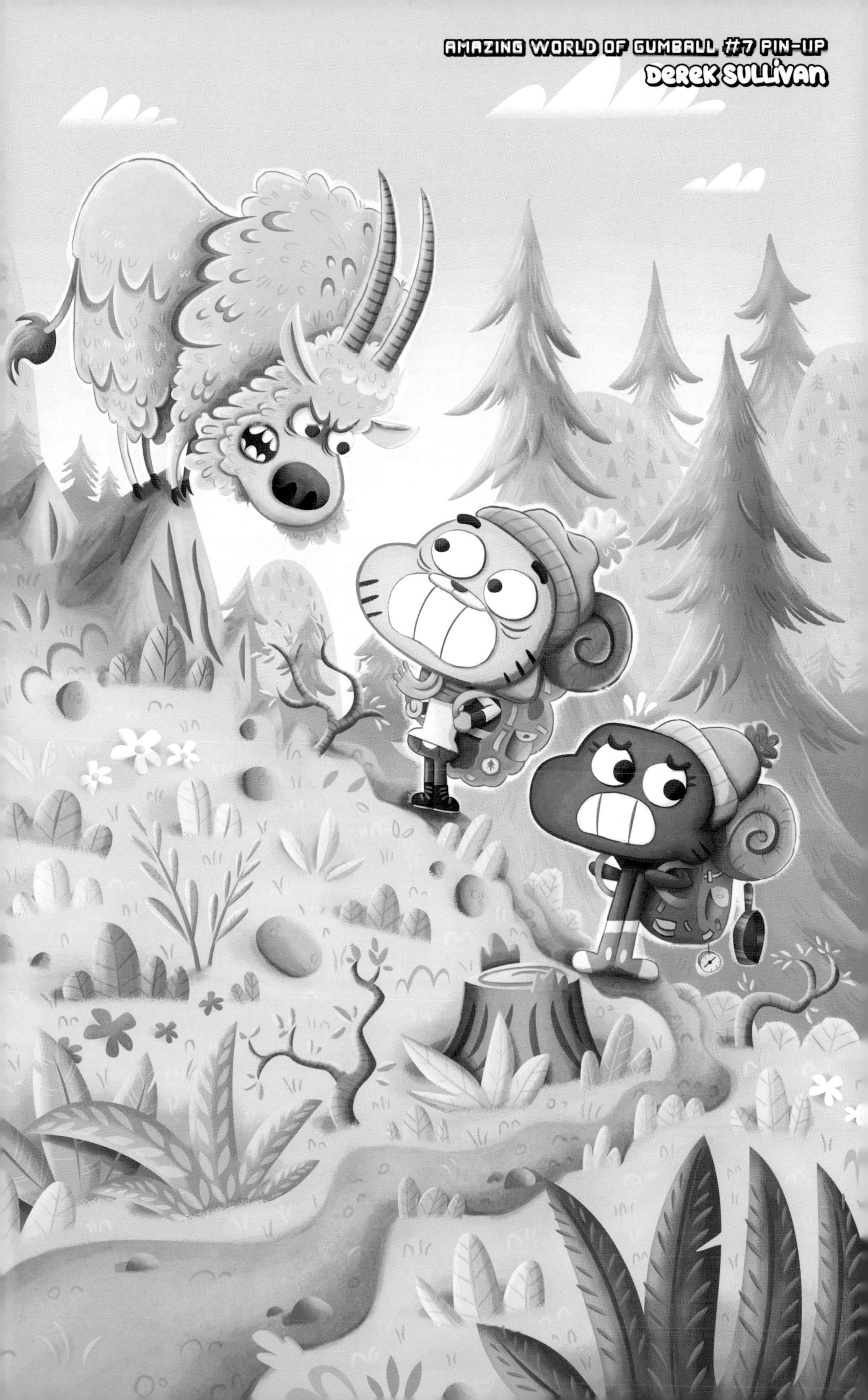

AMAZING WORLD OF GUMBALL #7 PIN-UP
DEREK SULLIVAN

2016 GRAB BAG SPECIAL #1 AD
PHILIP MURPHY

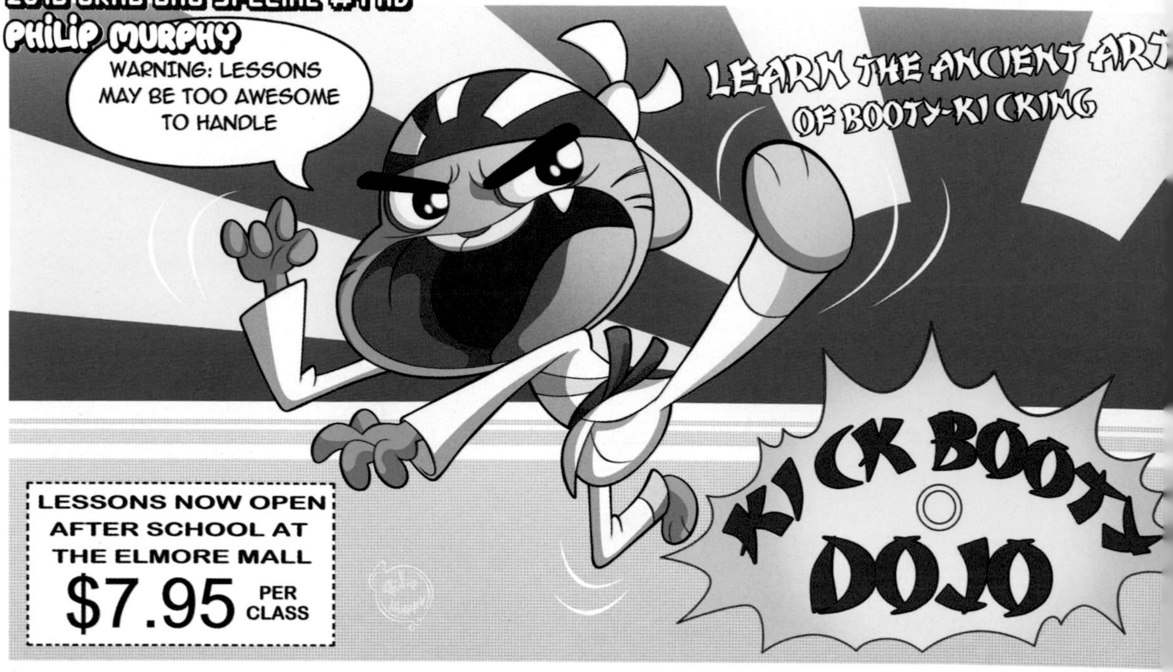
WARNING: LESSONS MAY BE TOO AWESOME TO HANDLE
LEARN THE ANCIENT ART
OF BOOTY-KICKING
LESSONS NOW OPEN AFTER SCHOOL AT THE ELMORE MALL
$7.95 PER CLASS
KICK BOOTY
DOJO

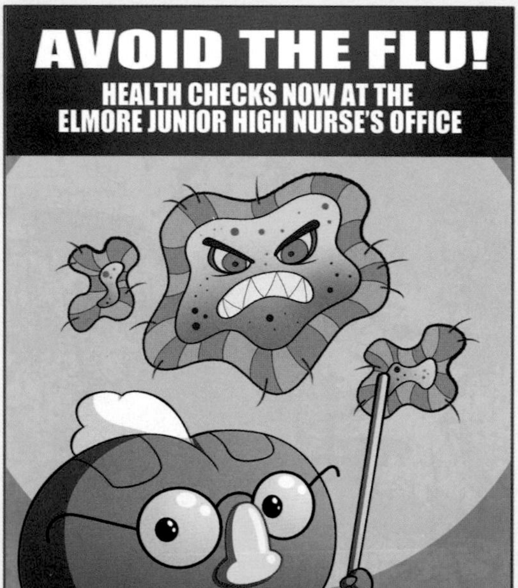
AVOID THE FLU!
HEALTH CHECKS NOW AT THE
ELMORE JUNIOR HIGH NURSE'S OFFICE
EH

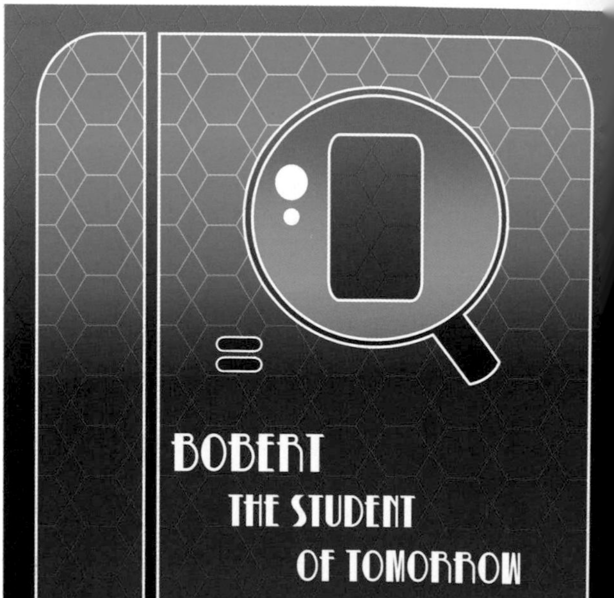
BOBERT
THE STUDENT
OF TOMORROW
...TODAY

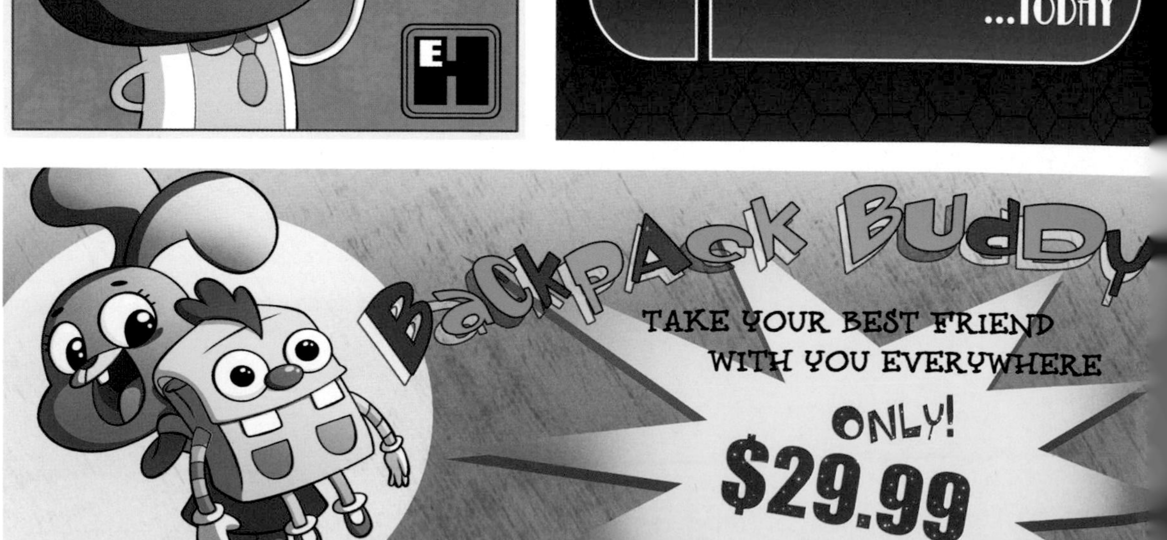
BACKPACK BUDDY
TAKE YOUR BEST FRIEND
WITH YOU EVERYWHERE
ONLY!
$29.99

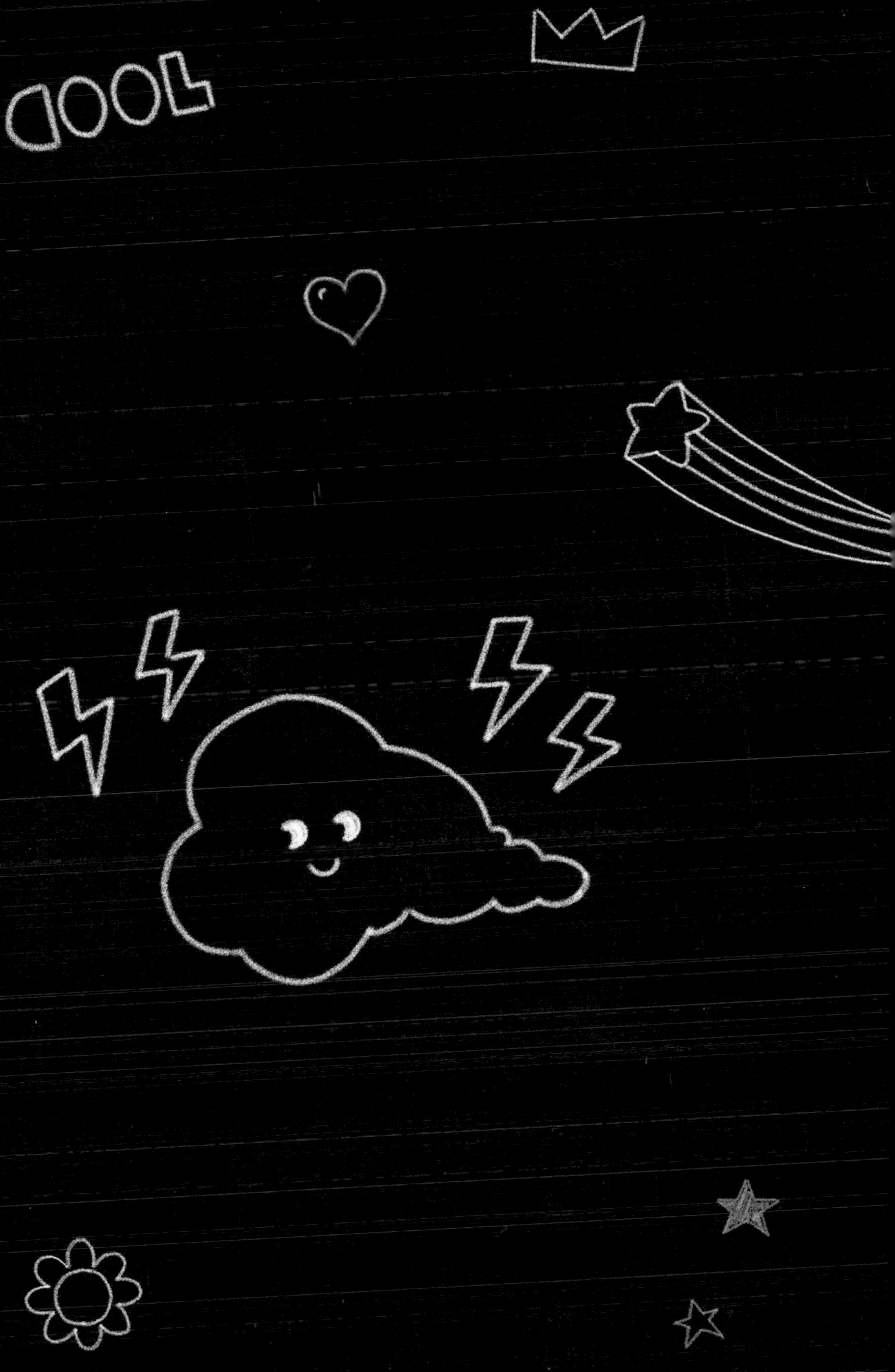
COOL

DISCOVER
EXPLOSIVE NEW WORLDS

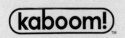

AVAILABLE AT YOUR LOCAL COMICS SHOP AND BOOKSTORE
To find a comics shop in your area, visit www.comicshoplocator.com
WWW.**BOOM-STUDIOS**.COM